CHAIN REACTION

JENESI ASH

HEAT

Heat

Published by New American Library, a division of
Penguin Group (USA) Inc., 375 Hudson Street,
New York, New York 10014, USA
Penguin Group (Canada), 90 Eglinton Avenue East, Suite 700, Toronto,
Ontario M4P 2Y3, Canada (a division of Pearson Penguin Canada Inc.)
Penguin Books Ltd., 80 Strand, London WC2R 0RL, England
Penguin Ireland, 25 St. Stephen's Green, Dublin 2,
Ireland (a division of Penguin Books Ltd.)
Penguin Group (Australia), 250 Camberwell Road, Camberwell, Victoria 3124,
Australia (a division of Pearson Australia Group Pty. Ltd.)
Penguin Books India Pvt. Ltd., 11 Community Centre, Panchsheel Park,
New Delhi—110 017, India
Penguin Group (NZ), 67 Apollo Drive, Rosedale, North Shore 0745,
Auckland, New Zealand (a division of Pearson New Zealand Ltd.)
Penguin Books (South Africa) (Pty.) Ltd., 24 Sturdee Avenue,
Rosebank, Johannesburg 2196, South Africa

Penguin Books Ltd., Registered Offices:
80 Strand, London WC2R 0RL, England

First published by Heat, an imprint of New American Library,
a division of Penguin Group (USA) Inc.

First Printing, August 2007
1 3 5 7 9 10 8 6 4 2

Copyright © Jasmine Communications, LLC, 2007

Heat is a trademark of Penguin Group (USA) Inc.

LIBRARY OF CONGRESS CATALOGING-IN-PUBLICATION DATA
Ash, Jenesi.
Chain reaction / Jenesi Ash.
p. cm.
ISBN: 978-0-451-22136-0
I. Scarves—Fiction. I. Title.
PS3601.S5226C48 2007
813'.6—dc22   2007004929

Set in Centaur MT
Designed by Ginger Legato

Printed in the United States of America

To Jenny and Anne, for making this book possible.

CHAPTER ONE

Lucas Carter was hell on her concentration. It was just a shame that she noticed that fact while she lay naked underneath him.

Amber Reed was all too aware of the bad timing. The fact that she was wet and writhing on her office floor during work hours didn't help. Her blouse was ripped open, her bra shoved to the side, and her pinstripe trousers were long gone. Lucas pinned her ankles against his shoulders, her black stiletto heels pointing at the ceiling.

The man seemed insistent on screwing her at work. Literally and figuratively. Had he fantasized taking her in every room of this building during the time he worked under her?

Now who was under whom?

A shiver of apprehension swept through her. Lucas was proving to be a worthy adversary. He was racing through the ranks of the company, closing the gap between his level and her hard-won position. Soon she might be working for him.

She gasped as her sex heated and creamed at the possibility. *No*, she didn't like that idea. Her status was one barrier he couldn't cross or destroy.

Amber remembered the moment he was promoted out of her department. She had felt the tension between them, fantasized about him for too long. Now she was rid of him and had breathed a sigh of relief and, she had to admit, regret.

That peace was short-lived. Lucas had set his box of belongings in his new office, strode back to hers, closed the door and taken her against her ego wall. The plaques and framed certificates banged with each stroke as he rutted her until she came apart. It had been raw and primitive, and she had loved every scandalizing minute of it.

That should have been her first clue that Lucas was going to be trouble. She had thought she could control him, but now she wasn't so sure. His arrogance wasn't a threat. She was used to supercilious men. Her response to his blatant masculinity was a concern, but it was his patience that she really needed to worry about. The man knew when to pounce.

He was built for sex and aggression, Amber decided as she watched him. His shirt hung open, revealing the sleek muscles of his chest. His pants were shoved to his knees, his thick cock aroused and ready as it slapped against his stomach.

Amber's stomach clenched as Lucas slid his hands under her ass. She shivered, although she didn't know why. After three months of having sex with him she should be used to his fingers spanning possessively against her buttocks.

Lucas reached to the side and grabbed a stack of binders that rested against the wall. He quickly tucked them under her ass.

"What are you doing?" The binders acted as a wedge, tilting her at an angle that promised deep penetration.

"Trust me." Lucas's fingers encircled her ankles, his hands making her lethal heels look frilly and delicate. Damn it.

He widened her legs apart and she felt the folds of her sex spread. She bet she was dark pink and glistening, if his growl of appreciation was anything to go by. Amber dug her fingers in the carpet, preparing for Lucas to shove into her.

Lucas surprised her by pressing the shiny head of his cock against her entrance. He slowly sank into her, slick, juicy sounds echoing between them. She was embarrassed by her body's eager welcome as her vaginal walls clamped down on his thick arousal.

He didn't fill her all the way, and started to retreat. Amber frowned as he gave another shallow thrust. She bucked against him to match his stroke, but Lucas held her immobile. She watched the muscles bunch in his jaw as he purposely gave another short thrust, and then a shorter one.

Amber gritted her teeth as he teased her. She wanted him to plow into her. Drive so hard that she screamed. He gave another short stroke. It was really beginning to piss her off. She should take control of the situation.

"Harder," she said in a growl. Her command sounded more like a plea, and Lucas smiled as he barely nudged her with his cock.

She could tease him right back. Amber cupped and fondled her breasts, preening as Lucas's eyes glittered with lust. She pinched her nipples, gasping as the bite traveled down to her clit. She squeezed harder, twisting her nipples, causing the sensations to fork through her body. Amber arched and moaned as the line between pleasure and pain blurred.

"Come on, baby," Lucas whispered. "Go with it."

She had a love/hate opinion about being called baby. If he ever said that endearment in front of anyone else, she'd kill him without hesitating. But right now it felt good. His husky voice wafted over her heated skin. She rubbed her palms against the tips of her breasts before she reached down to play with her clit. She caressed the swollen, slippery pearl, grunting as pleasure rippled through her.

Lucas shuddered and Amber tossed her head back, hiding her sly, victorious smile. Several strands of her hair swept across her face as she dipped her head to watch his expression. She liked how the ruddy color stained his high cheekbones. His chest rose and fell as he fought the need to thrust deep and long.

She knew he couldn't hold back for much longer, and then he was going to go wild. He would surrender to his lusty appetite and pound into her. But he would want her to come first.

Amber preferred being first in everything, and it was usually no different with sex. But not with Lucas. She wanted *him* to lose control first. And then—and only then—would she follow.

Lucas's muscles shook as his restraint slipped. His groan of surrender was her only warning before he slammed his cock into her. The binders under her ass squeaked in protest. She swung her hands out to hold onto something, her nails raking the carpet.

Her breath caught in her throat as his cock filled her. She swiveled her hips as the hot, sparkling ache intensified. Lucas thrust again, deep and hard, hitting a sweet spot that sent her reeling.

Lucas's strokes became faster. Harder. Amber rolled her head from side to side as the ache swirled inside her, gaining strength. Her hips vaulted off the binders as his thrusting grew rough.

He pushed her legs open as wide as they would go. She wanted to complain, disliking being on display for him, but she didn't refuse because she wanted him closer. She longed to have his cock burrow deep inside her. Amber held her breath, her vagina clenching with anticipation for a rough ride.

His pelvis hit her clit as he drove into her. Amber thought her eyes were going to roll back. A low moan dragged from her throat. That felt too good. One more stroke and she would come. She knew it, and she bet he knew it, too.

She caught the feral glitter in Lucas's hooded gaze. He was on the brink of control as he gave one powerful thrust. Amber squeezed her eyes shut as the pleasure bloomed and rolled inside her. She tried to muffle her cries as she came.

Lucas's restraint snapped. He set a furious tempo, pumping into her. Amber dragged her eyes open, wanting to watch him. His strokes were coarse and desperate before he found his release. He reared his head back, the veins bulging from his neck, as he came hard.

And for one infinitesimal moment Amber found peace. It wrapped around her tightly, cradling her like a warm cocoon. She exhaled slowly as her muscles relaxed.

She closed her eyes, wanting to capture the feeling and hold on to it, but it fluttered away. The thudding of her heartbeats came in a rush. The phone shrilled outside her door as the hum of machines filtered into her clouded mind.

She didn't move, almost hoping the peace would return, when she heard people walking by her office. She opened her eyes, realizing it wouldn't take long before someone needed her and tried the door.

Amber rose to her elbows and tried to remove her legs from Lucas's grasp. "I need to get up."

His fingers tightened around her ankles. Amber made a sharp move with her foot, aiming for his head. Lucas must have predicted her move because he held her legs wide.

Uneasiness coiled in her chest. She didn't like being at a disadvantage. And he knew she wouldn't struggle or request him to let go. She had only one defense. Amber squeezed her vaginal walls around his cock.

Lucas winced, the lines deepening around his eyes. Amber couldn't tell if she was tormenting him or giving him pleasure. Whatever she was doing, she hoped it prompted him to relinquish his hold.

He opened his eyes, and the devilish glimmer in them worried her. Her heart skipped a beat as she waited before he slowly released her ankles.

She immediately scooted away from Lucas, ignoring his hiss as she withdrew, and sat up. She caught sight of her panties under the desk. Amber didn't have to inspect the ivory silk to know it was torn. She glared at Lucas. "Do you know how many pairs I've gone through because of you?"

He offered no apology as he stood. "You should stop wearing them."

Ha. That would be unprofessional. Not to mention a concession to him. Why should she make herself more accessible to Lucas? If he wanted her anytime, anywhere, then he was going to have to work for it.

She awkwardly got to her feet, ignoring his offer of assistance. She looked around the room except for where Lucas stood. Her pinstripe trousers were bunched next to her overturned chair. She grabbed the pants and thrust her legs in one at a time, her moves shaky as she wobbled on her high heels. "You have to stop doing this," she muttered.

"Doing what?"

"Having sex in the office." She zipped up her pants and stuffed her underwear in the front pocket. "Like you can't wait until we get home?"

"Can you?"

She looked up at him in surprise. What kind of question was that? Of course she could wait until after hours. That's the main reason she had allowed him to move in with her; so he'd stop trying to put her in these situations at work. A lot of good that did.

At least *she* was in control of her libido, Amber thought as she buttoned her wrinkled blouse. She wielded self-discipline in every aspect of her life. Well, she used to, until she had sex with Lucas. These days she felt out of control, and it was beginning to show.

One only had to look at her office to mark the changes. Every file used to have its place. At one time, every paperclip could have been accounted for. Now stacks of papers littered her office. Files and binders were strewn across the floor. She hadn't seen the top of her desk in months. Not since the day Lucas kissed her.

If there was ever a sign that Lucas was not good for her, the state of her office said it all. Loud and clear.

She pulled on her jacket, buttoned it smartly, and hoped it hid the telltale creases in her blouse. Amber smoothed her hair back, noticing that the curls she had straightened this morning were beginning to spring out. She reached down and opened the bottom drawer of her desk, grabbing her purse. "If you will excuse me, I need to clean up."

"You don't have to." Lucas blocked her path. "I like the smell of me on your skin."

Amber's mouth dropped open as her face flushed red. She shouldered her way around him and almost gave a sigh of relief when he didn't stop her.

She could swear Lucas said those things just to rattle her. It started from the first day, when he showed up at the company, and it was only getting worse. Lucas Carter was getting too confident. Someone needed to take him down a peg or two.

And the only person who seemed to be capable of that was her. She didn't think she was up for the job. She was too busy trying to catch her breath from every move Lucas made.

Amber swung her office door open and marched toward the women's restroom. She kept her gaze straight, determined not to catch anyone's eye. She had worked hard for her ice princess reputation, and she wasn't about to let anyone think her icy reserve had cracked and melted.

When she stepped into the restroom, her poise didn't waver. She headed straight for the first available stall, closed the door and shoved the bolt home. Amber rested her head against the chrome door. The metal felt cool against her flushed skin.

What was she doing? Sure, she had longed for some fun and excitement. Okay, for some wild sex, too, but this craziness was invading her life. She had to focus. Acquire the tunnel vision that had helped her so much in the past. That meant regaining control. Over herself first, and then over Lucas.

By the time she left the restroom, Amber felt slightly better. Her strawberry blonde hair was ruthlessly pulled into its customary twist. She repaired her makeup and no longer had a flushed face or smeared lipstick on her swollen mouth.

Now if only her breasts didn't feel tight and heavy. She didn't like how her nipples ached as they grazed the bra when she moved. She definitely didn't appreciate how satisfaction rippled through her tired muscles.

She strode back to the office and took her letters and packages from the mailroom boy passing by. His leer disintegrated under her legendary frosty glare. Some men were still easy to handle, she noted as she stepped into her office, her stride breaking when she saw that Lucas sat in front of her desk.

He looked comfortable there. Rumpled, sated, with his legs sprawled in front of him. He was lucky he hadn't put his feet up on her desk. Or worse, sat in her chair. That would have been going too far.

Amber opened her desk drawer and tossed her purse inside. She closed the drawer with a bang. "What are you still doing here, Lucas?"

His mouth slanted with a smile. "Trying to get rid of me?"

"Yes," she said as she opened an interoffice envelope. "I have a lot of work to do." She reached in and frowned when she felt something soft inside. She tipped the envelope and saw purple silk cascade onto her desk.

Lucas whistled. "Nice."

That was an understatement. Try gorgeous, decadent and totally inappropriate. Which begged the question: Why would anyone send it to her?

She slid her hands under the silk and realized it was a long scarf. It seemed to go on forever, but she knew that she could toss it over her shoulders and it would probably dangle to her knees. Gold threads were woven into the silk, gleaming under the fluorescent lights, but the deep, luxurious purple made it impossible to look away.

The gift made her think of the exotic and the forbidden. It made her think of passion. Of sex.

"Who gave that to you?" Lucas sounded gruff and, for the first time, a little uncertain.

"Hold on, there's a letter." She picked up a laminated note. The paper, brown with age, was tattered and creased. She squinted at the faded ink.

"'Dear Friend.'" She read the words out loud. "'I am offering you the chance of a lifetime. You can live out your ultimate fantasy within one week of receiving this gift, provided you pass it on. All that is required from you is this: You must use the scarf during a sexual encounter in the next seven days.

"'Mail the scarf and this letter to a female acquaintance within one week of receiving this package. Do not tell or discuss it with the woman. Those who follow these instructions will continue a fulfilling sensual odyssey. Those who don't will never find satisfaction for as long as they live.'"

Amber looked up and frowned at Lucas. "It's signed Kali. I don't know anyone by that name."

Lucas shrugged as the amusement twinkled from his brown eyes. "Who would use their real name if they were sending a chain letter to *you?*"

She looked at him, then at the scarf and finally at the note. "It *is* a chain letter." The scarf had distracted her from the true reason of the gift. "Who the hell would send me a chain letter?"

"Obviously someone who doesn't know you very well."

Suspicion jabbed at Amber and she glared at him. "You didn't send this to me, did you?"

He held his hands up. "I had nothing to do with it. But I am more than happy to help."

"Help?"

Lucas gave a nod at the note on her desk. "You have to use the scarf in seven days."

She absently twisted the silk around her fingers. "Oh, please. I don't believe in that kind of crap. Chain letters. A *fantasy* chain letter." She scoffed and shook her head.

"You're not tempted?" Lucas asked, propping his chin against his fist. "Not even a little?"

A vision darted in front of her eyes. Her pulse skipped a beat as she imagined the silk bound tightly against her skin. She frowned and quickly pushed the image from her mind.

"Not even one bit," Amber declared, although the idea left her shaken. "I feel sorry for the poor souls who felt obligated to use the scarf."

She looked at the purple silk and wondered how many women had used it, believing it would give them the pleasure they sought. Those women didn't understand that they were the mistresses of their own destinies. No ancient promise was going to get them what they wanted.

She needed to remember that herself. The fun and games had to end. Starting now. Amber balled up the silk and tossed it in the direction of her trash can.

"You're throwing it away?"

"I don't have time for silliness." She glanced at her watch and rose from her chair. "I have a meeting to attend. I'm sure you can find your way out."

CHAPTER TWO

It was late by the time Lucas arrived home. He opened the door to Amber's apartment and found it dark. She hadn't left a light on or waited up. He had expected nothing less, but tonight it bothered him.

Lucas flipped the switch and set down his briefcase. The soft lights glowed in the elegant apartment, and once more he was struck by how the place reflected Amber. The muted colors, the sparse decor, and the straightforward lines of the furniture gave a glimpse of what she was really like.

He walked through the apartment to the bedroom, noticing that there were only a few items signaling that he now resided there. He had been careful about leaving his mark, but his patience was beginning to chafe. When it came to Amber Reed, he didn't want to hold back. Not anymore.

But playing it cool had gotten him far. He hadn't expected her offer to move into her place, and Lucas had agreed for two reasons. He wanted to be with her, and he wanted to get a better sense of the woman. He also knew that Amber would never have moved in with him. The loss of territory would be too much for her.

Lucas stepped into the bedroom and stopped at the threshold when he saw Amber asleep. The faint light from the other room barely reached her. His chest tightened at the sight of her sprawled in total abandon on the large bed, her long hair tumbling over the pillows. The sheets twisted around her slender body as the delicate straps of her nightgown slid down her shoulders. Her mouth parted in a soft smile, as if she enjoyed having the bed to herself.

Nice to know that he was being missed. He looked at his watch and grimaced. Once again he had stayed at work too late. He had a lot to get done, especially if he wanted to succeed on his timetable. He didn't know why he felt a flare of guilt. Amber didn't seem to mind his long hours.

That kind of got to him. He wanted her to miss him, or worry. He wanted her to call at night to show that she was thinking of him. He wanted her to care.

Most of all, he wanted her trust. Yet every time he showed her that she could rely on him, she found his act of strength a threat. And he sure as hell wouldn't show any weakness around her. She'd take that moment and run, and it would take forever to wrestle it back from her.

Which he would, he thought with a smile. He had no doubt on that score.

The woman got her way too much as it was. Whatever she wanted, she got. He understood that, admired it, but he didn't like how focused she was on attaining her career goals. Her path to success was straight and narrow. Everything else was getting shoved to the side. Meals on the go. Sex on the run.

He was gradually breaking her of that habit. Slowly and methodically wearing her down like water rubbing away stone. But he still had a long way to go.

Their relationship remained strictly sexual and based on stolen moments. He wanted to make it a priority and let it filter into every part of their lives, but that wasn't going to happen until she started to trust him. And he had just the thing to test her. The question was, would it break her?

He dipped his hand in his pocket and pulled out the silky purple scarf he had retrieved from her office. The gold thread caught the weak light. He looked at the scarf, wondering if it was worth the risk.

He didn't believe in chain letters, but the scarf gave him an idea. Lucas could easily see tying Amber's wrists to her bed. His cock swelled as he imagined her caught underneath him. She would try to break free, but each undulating move would turn her on. Every pull and tug would bring her closer to the inevitable. She would surrender to him.

Lucas walked to the dresser, opened the drawer Amber deigned to give him and stuffed the scarf in the corner. He wouldn't use it tonight. He would have to slowly prep Amber, kind of like how he had slowly placed his mark in her apartment. She didn't notice that he was quietly, systematically encroaching on her territory. And once she did realize, it would be too late to do anything about it.

He quickly stripped and headed for the shower as he considered his strategy. Visions of Amber tied up and twisting underneath him did little to cool his blood. He never realized how much he wanted her surrender until he saw that scarf. Even when he worked for her, he had imagined her under him, naked and willing, but he never thought of the word surrender.

His cock ached, eager to slide into Amber's slick heat. He stepped out of the shower and toweled off, determined to wake Amber up by any means necessary. It really bothered him that she never waited up. By the end of tonight, she'd learn from that mistake.

Lucas returned to the shadowy bedroom and slipped into the bed, the warm sheets dragging against his damp skin. He curled his arm around Amber, inhaling her scent, as he pulled her against him. Her spine rested against his chest and her pert ass cushioned his cock.

He spanned his hand against her stomach, the silk sliding under his palm. He didn't like her nightgown acting as a barrier. He wanted her to wear nothing at all, and made his preference known, but she ignored his wishes.

She stirred against him and he locked his jaw as her sensuous moves triggered something hot and elemental in his veins.

"Lucas?"

Did she have to ask? Of course it was him. The woman wasn't sleeping with anyone else. She wasn't like that.

He reached down and cupped her mound. The flirty hem barely concealed her, but he could feel her heat. "Yeah, baby?" he whispered in her ear.

"Not your baby," she muttered.

He could hear the pout in her voice, and wanted to smile in spite of her protest. She was his. He didn't need to put a brand on her, but he needed to do something to get the point across that she was his. How could he prove it? Make it stick so she wouldn't deny it, even in the hazy moment between sleep and wakefulness.

Lucas slowly stroked her slit, listening to her hum of pleasure. When her vulva lips gradually swallowed his finger, he began to caress and press down harder. Her throaty growl made his cock leap, and he tried to ignore the aching need growing inside him.

She grew damp against his hand as he rubbed her clit. He liked how the sound of her breathing changed. The quickening matched the erratic beat of his pulse. Amber tilted back, her spine on top of his chest. Lucas slid his arm under her and cupped the soft underside of her breast.

Amber curled her leg over him, which gave him better access to pleasure her. She rocked against the heel of his hand and he dipped his finger into her wet sex. Her sleepy moans pulled at his cock, but the scent of her arousal was like an aphrodisiac.

He nuzzled against her ear. "Miss me?" he teased.

She didn't answer. He hadn't expected her to. She never did when she knew she couldn't win the argument.

He nipped her earlobe as he pinched her nipple. She gasped and wiggled closer, but when he caught her clit between his fingers, she jerked and convulsed as she came, her grunts echoing in the bedroom as her release rippled through her body.

Before giving her a chance to catch her breath, Lucas slid out from under Amber and laid her on the bed. He moved above her, pausing at the sight of her, bare and flushed against the rumpled sheets. Her body still trembled from the aftershocks as he settled between her legs. Threading his fingers with hers, Lucas held her hands over her head.

He kissed her hard, probing his tongue into her mouth. His kisses weren't refined or seductive. They were hungry and merciless as he struggled to contain the fiery emotions slamming in his chest. To his surprise, Amber didn't fight back; she offered no resistance. Instead, she welcomed him, drawing him closer. He explored her hot mouth until he felt her pull against his hands.

Lucas barely refrained from an instinct to tighten his hold. He didn't want her to be too aware of his strategy, but he also didn't want to let go the moment she made the silent request. His best alternative was to distract her.

He trailed open-mouthed, wet kisses down the length of her neck, enjoying the salty taste of her skin. He stopped at her pulse and suck-led the tender spot until she tensed and arched underneath him. Her fingernails scraped his knuckles as she clenched her hands against his.

Lucas stopped as his mouth brushed against the spaghetti strap of her slip. His fingers flexed as indecision flickered through his mind. He wanted her naked so he could press his skin against hers, but it meant releasing her hands.

He wanted to hold her down.

He really wanted her naked.

But he wasn't ready to give up his advantage. Damn, he could use that scarf right about now.

Amber wrapped her legs around his waist. Her wet core pressed against his cock. A tremor swept down his legs, his knees buckling as he fought for control.

He reluctantly released her hands but didn't realize it until his fingers were skimming down her sides. "Take off your slip," he told her, his voice rough and low, as he grasped her hips.

She didn't question or bristle against the order. She grabbed the silk at her hips, clenching it in her hands, her movements fierce and clumsy as she struggled out of the slip.

Amber wiggled against Lucas as she rolled the silk up to her rib cage. The move made him wonder how much she would writhe with her hands bound. Lucas clenched his jaw, the muscle twitching in his cheek as his control went over the edge.

She shimmied and arched her back as the slip slid over her breasts. Her dusky nipples were crinkled. Lucas swallowed hard as he longed to taste and suck them. He easily imagined sweeping the tip of his tongue around the hard crests before nipping them with the edge of his teeth.

Lucas felt a tingling at the base of his spine. He couldn't wait any longer. He rubbed the shiny crown of his cock against Amber's slit. She swiveled against him as she fought with her slip, the silk tangling her arms.

Her struggles and frustrated groan clawed at him. He liked seeing her caught. He didn't want to help her get free. The dark revelation ripped through him like a jagged gash. The tingling in his body suddenly hit him like a hard kick. He sank into her with one slow, possessive thrust. Amber groaned as he stretched and filled her.

Her sex gripped him tightly, and he pumped harder. He couldn't stop watching Amber as she pulled the silk free from her arms. His strokes grew choppy and deep, the sound of skin slapping skin mingling with her small grunts and hitched gasps.

He came hard and fast, unable to hold back the inevitable. He hissed between his clenched teeth as the sensations pounded his body, overwhelming him.

Lucas tumbled against her warm curves. He sighed as he rested against her hot, sweat-slicked skin. He knew he was too heavy for her to support, and that he should roll over and hold her.

That plan disintegrated as Amber speared her fingers into his hair. As much as he wanted to tie her up, he liked the feel of her hands on him.

Next time, he promised as sleep pulled at him. Next time he would find a way to restrain Amber.

CHAPTER THREE

Amber was not in a good mood. She was never much of a morning person, whether she had eight hours of sleep or pulled an all-nighter, but today it seemed worse. Nothing she did could hold back her temper.

Sienna, the receptionist, stood before her desk doing her best not to cry. That seemed to annoy Amber more than anything. Why did her employees always feel the need to cry in her presence?

She watched Sienna slowly back away to the door, as if the receptionist were alone in a room with a viper ready to strike. Amber had noticed that she always had that effect on her coworkers, even when she was in a good mood. Usually she called them right back into the room, but it looked like Sienna was about ready to cry buckets.

"Sorry," Sienna said, her constant smile dimming as her voice wobbled. "I am so sorry, Amber. Next time I will follow up with the carrier. It won't happen again."

"See that it doesn't." She turned to her computer screen and heard the scuffle of shoes as the receptionist fled.

The issue was resolved, yet her bad mood was simmering under the surface. She had a feeling she knew it wasn't because of the morning, or an employee's mistake, but she didn't want to poke at the reason and reveal what was underneath.

"What's wrong with Amber?" she heard one of her employees mutter outside. "She just chewed off Sienna's head."

"Sweet Sienna? Awww . . . How is she taking it?"

Sweet Sienna? Amber wanted to snort at that nickname. Sienna Bailey might appear sweet and wholesome, from her friendly nature to her floral dresses, but she was apt to make mistakes just like everyone else.

"Amber is such a bitch. Someone ought to teach her a lesson."

Helloooo? She was right here, with her office door open. She had obviously hired a bunch of idiots who still subscribed to the belief if she wasn't looking at them then that meant she couldn't hear them. Amber was tempted to turn and glare at her employees, simply to watch them scatter like frightened birds.

"Maybe Amber isn't getting any," one daring employee said as he walked by.

Ha. Amber rolled her eyes at that theory while she heard the others murmur their agreement. Little did they know! She was getting plenty. Just not the way she had thought.

She looked down at the keyboard and stared at her hands. They looked the same. No rings. Manicured but unvarnished nails. A thick, expensive watch at her wrist.

Her hands looked strong and feminine, but they had failed her last night. She turned her hands over and stared at the palms. The criss-crossing lines looked the same.

The night before she had tried to move her hands, but Lucas held her down. And he didn't want to bring it to her attention. That was what really worried her.

She could have struggled harder. Or she could have told him to let go. He would have. Amber frowned at her assumption. Wouldn't he?

Maybe that's why she hadn't told him to. Because she didn't know if he would have let go. Lucas wasn't one to obey.

And if he refused to listen, what power did she have over him?

She shivered at the idea. Why was she with this guy? He was ruthless, powerful and could destroy her if he felt the need.

She was with him because he was the mirror image of her. She had the same ruthless streak, the same craving for power. Could she destroy him? Probably. Did she want to? No. She didn't have that killer edge when it came to Lucas. And she needed that.

Amber stretched her fingers out and positioned them on her keyboard, and paused. Had it all come down to a fight for absolute power? She first had sex with Lucas because she wanted to. She wanted to know she had power over him once he left her department. So what if the power was sexual? She never flexed those muscles and it was a heady experience to see someone so powerful and dangerous become weak and needy because of her.

But somehow she lost control of every situation. Of every move. She wasn't acting—she was reacting. That was unlike her. And she had to wonder if she was cornered and simply hadn't realized it yet.

Now that she thought about it, the one time she put her foot down was when he wanted her to move in with him. She made her apartment the deal breaker. She wanted it to be on her turf. Now she wondered if that was a really bad idea.

"Amber?"

Amber looked up with a start and saw Lucas standing at her door. From the look in his eye, it hadn't been the first time he had called her name.

"Yes?" she asked coolly as her pulse skipped a beat. She hated how her body reacted to the mere sight of Lucas Carter.

He raised one eyebrow. "Are you ready?"

"For what?" Sex? Always, apparently. Had she ever said no to him?

"Our meeting."

Meeting? They had a meeting? Her gaze flew to her calendar. Sure enough, they did. She was seriously losing it. She didn't forget things like this. At least, she hadn't until the moment Lucas took her against the wall and ripped the blinders off of her, showing all that she had been missing.

"Remind me," she said, hoping her voice sounded haughty instead of husky. "What is this meeting about?"

"It can wait," Lucas decided as he closed the door behind him. She heard the snick of the lock and her sex creamed. She was like Pavlov's dog. It was so humiliating.

Amber glared at him. "Why are you locking that door?"

His knowing smile set her on edge.

She tilted her chin up. "What makes you think that I want to have sex right here and now?"

"Because you do."

He seemed too confident. How did he know? Could he smell her wet scent? She watched him stride to her desk, the pulse at her neck beating erratically under her skin. Amber knew of one way to stop him in his tracks. "Why were you holding me down last night?"

Lucas paused, but quickly masked his surprise. "I didn't hold you down."

Amber leaned back in her chair and looked directly in his eyes. If he lied, she'd know. "You wanted to."

"But I didn't."

His admission startled her. "You didn't because I didn't let you," she corrected him.

Lucas smiled, but said nothing. It was as if he was humoring her, and that pissed her off.

"What?" she asked in a sharp tone.

Lucas sat on the corner of her desk. "If I really wanted to hold you down, I could."

He was in for a rude awakening. "I'm stronger than you think."

Amusement danced in his dark eyes. "No, I know exactly how strong you are."

"And I fight dirty," Amber felt compelled to add.

"I'm familiar with how your mind works."

"Really?" She folded her arms across her chest. "Guess what I'm thinking right now."

One corner of his mouth hitched up higher. "You're wondering why you're getting turned on by the idea of my dominating you."

"I am not!" She jumped up from her chair. "You wish!"

"You wish I wasn't so close to the truth."

She placed her hands on her hips. "Just try."

Lucas frowned. His gaze drifted from her face down her body. Amber's skin tingled, but she remained silent until he looked in her eyes.

"You want me to wrestle you to the ground?" he finally asked.

"Try and pin me down," she clarified.

Lucas gave a shrug and stood up. "If you insist."

Oh. My. God. Amber's eyes went wide. He was really going to do this. She couldn't believe it. She had thought he would refuse, but that didn't make a lot of sense. She had poked at his competitive edge.

She took a good look at Lucas. He was taller than her, but not by much. The crisp white shirt and blue tie made him appear more intimidating. True, his lean body was packed with solid muscle, but she worked out just as much as he did. They were equals. She could take him.

He stepped behind her and Amber braced herself. Her heart was beating fast as she felt him brush against her back. She flinched as he scooped his hand against her jacket collar.

"What are you doing?" She tried to turn around but Lucas prevented her from moving.

"You don't want to get this ruined," he answered as he drew the jacket down her arms.

He was probably right. The last thing she needed was to walk out of the office with torn clothes. "Fine."

"Or your heels," he suggested as he tossed her jacket to the side.

Amber made a face. She wasn't falling for that ploy. "Trying to declaw me?"

"Have you seen the marks you made on my back?" Lucas pressed his mouth against her ear, his warm breath tickling her skin. "Not that I'm complaining."

"Enough stalling." She frantically tried to remember her self-defense class. She was going to flip this guy over her desk. Make the biggest crash ever. And then when everyone was crowded around her door asking if she was okay, she would unlock it and—

Amber jumped as Lucas slipped his fingers in the collar of her blouse and cupped her breast. She grabbed his wrist, all too aware of the strength under her hand.

"You can't fight me off yet," Lucas said before giving a playful nip to her earlobe. "I'm not trying to pin you down."

"You're touching me," she said through her teeth. Her entire body felt clenched.

He pressed a kiss behind her ear. "The question is whether I can pin you down."

"Get on with it." She was getting jumpier by the minute.

"Sorry, I was distracted," he said as he glided his mouth down the curve of her throat.

Yeah, right. The point was to distract her.

He fondled her breast and Amber tried to ignore the sparkling sensations flooding her chest. She stared straight ahead at the bookshelf in front of her. But no matter how hard she tried to ignore Lucas's touch, her nipple tightened.

She felt him go for the clasp of her bra. "Try to get me naked and I will pin *you* down," she warned him.

His fingers stilled. "Why are you mad at me?"

She kept her gaze firmly on the bookshelf. "You tried to hold me down while we were having sex."

"And this is bad because . . . ?" His other hand skimmed down to her waist.

"You can't stand it when I have the advantage."

"And when was the last time that happened?"

Amber tried to remember. It couldn't have been *that* long ago. Her mind was feeling fuzzy, and she kept her attention on his long fingers on her waist.

He dipped his hand under her waistband and sought the heat of her sex. Amber slanted her hips up to meet his touch until she remembered she should be warding him off.

"Is this how you wrestle?" she asked hoarsely as he slid his hand inside her panties.

"Only with you."

Yeah, it had better be that way. She gasped as he rubbed his finger along her wet slit. When he dipped his finger inside her, Amber's legs trembled and buckled. She swallowed back a cry as he pinched her nipple with his other hand.

Maybe she should move. But no, that would require her to lose her advantageous position.

Anyway if she turned . . . oh! He slid another finger inside her, and she shimmied her hips to accommodate him. Uh . . . why couldn't she turn? Oh, yeah, his mouth. She might kiss him and that would be that.

Amber licked her lips. She really wanted to kiss him. . . .

No, it wasn't about kissing. She needed to flip him over her shoulder. Her knees sagged as his finger went deeper. Sparks burst under her skin.

Okay, it was now or never. She would—

Boom. She blinked rapidly as her world went topsy-turvy. One minute she was staring at the bookshelf in front of her, the next she was face-first on her desk. The stacks of papers were underneath her and Lucas's large body pinned her from on top. His heat enveloped her as his hard cock pressed against her buttocks.

Damn it! Amber wanted to scream with frustration and stomp her feet. She should have known better. She shouldn't have let him touch her to begin with.

"Okay, you win," she said reluctantly, sure her voice was muffled in the papers. "You can pin me down if you want to."

Her womb twitched as she said it. Too bad his fingers were still inside her, feeling her flesh respond. "You can get off of me now," she continued in a rush.

"No, I don't think so."

"You've proven your point."

"True," he said as he removed his hand from her breast and slid it down her bottom. "But now I'm going for my prize."

CHAPTER FOUR

Amber scrunched up her eyes. Not because she was worried, but because his threat got her excited. Lucas could take her now and there was nothing she could do about it. She had felt this particular potent mix of excitement and fear before. It was when Lucas had held her down the night before.

But it wasn't quite fear. It was something foreign and complex. She felt helpless. Defenseless. Out of control.

No. Horror streaked through her chest. She didn't feel that. She would *never* feel that. Ever.

She kicked out at Lucas but her heel didn't connect. Her violent move aided him, though, as he wrenched her skirt above her hips. The excitement was swirling deep in her belly. Damn, she didn't want this. Correction: She didn't *want* to want this.

"Well, come on," she said and puffed at a loose strand of hair that dangled against her eye. "Get it over and done with."

"You are a poor sport." He patted her head. His condescending manner really made her mad.

"Oh, I'm sorry," she responded with deep sarcasm. "Is this where I'm supposed to scream and beg you to stop? Does that feed into your fantasies?"

"No, but maybe it will feed into yours."

She scoffed at his suggestion. Her fantasies? She didn't have any. A vision of a purple scarf bound tight—round and round—pressing into her skin, invaded her thoughts. Her sex flooded at the vision. She bit her lip as Lucas pulled her panties down her legs.

She jumped as the phone rang. Real life invaded at the shrill sound. Amber made a grab for the phone, but didn't get anywhere near it.

"Leave it," Lucas ordered.

Hell, no. She strained for the phone, the insistent peals screeching in her head. Lucas's large hand suddenly covered hers.

"Amber"—his mouth was against her ear—"I told you to leave it."

Did he really think she was going to listen? The phone suddenly stopped ringing and Amber began to struggle in earnest. He could bend her over her desk and rut her like an animal. He could do it during her workday. But he was *not* going to interfere with her work.

Lucas held her arms against her desk, his body covering hers, his legs parting hers. She wasn't going anywhere and she knew it.

"Why did you want to answer the phone?" he asked as he traced the shape of her ear with the tip of his tongue.

She shivered as he hit a sensitive spot. "Because it's my job!"

"Can't be anyone important," he decided. "I'm already here."

"You are so egotistical." She gasped as she felt his cock bump against her slit.

"I have reason to be, don't you think?"

She wasn't going to dignify that remark with a response. When the phone rang again, Amber lunged for it. Her fingertips brushed against the black, sleek handset before Lucas pulled her back.

"Stop it, Lucas," she growled out. She wanted to scream the words, but that would have brought her employees running. The last thing she wanted was for them to see her in this position.

She was angry for starting this, for getting into this position. Amber swung out, hoping to catch Lucas unaware, but she only managed to cast papers onto the floor.

"Stop what?" he taunted, sliding his cock along her slit.

Her knees shook as she imagined how good it would feel when he drove inside her. "You keep doing this. You're always getting in the way of me doing my job." The moment the complaint came out of her mouth she winced, regretting it.

"Is that what you think?" He glided his hand along the curve of her bare ass. Her skin tingled with warning. If he so much as spanked her, he was going to pay for it.

The phone stopped ringing, and Amber glared at the handset. She didn't know whether to scream or cry with frustration.

"You are the only person in your way," Lucas said.

"What's *that* supposed to mean?"

"Take it any way you want." He pressed the tip of his cock against her wet core. "Take *me* any way you want."

She was about to give a scathing reply when he pushed into her. She gasped for her next breath as her whole world zeroed in on his cock. The edge of the desk bit into her legs, but the pain was dull compared to the pleasure Lucas gave her, slowly filling and stretching her.

And the most horrifying, humiliating aspect was that she liked this. She liked struggling under Lucas, and matching her strength and wit against him. She liked the way he challenged her. Deep down, she liked that he won.

How could she like that? That wasn't her! Amber struggled against him as he held her down. She refused to let him have the easy victory. She kicked, she twisted and she tried to buck him off, but nothing stopped him from dominating her.

Her chest and stomach were pressed hard against her desk, the piles of papers sliding out from under her and falling to the floor with every thrust. Lucas lay heavily against her back and she found it a struggle to breathe.

He kept pumping into her with sure, slow strokes, as if he were dragging out his victory. He lowered his head and kissed the corner of her mouth. Amber turned her head, but his mouth was already there, waiting for her. She kept dodging his lips, but she knew she couldn't escape.

As much as she hated to admit it to herself, she didn't want to escape, yet she also wanted to get the best of him. Push him to the edge. Make him work for every small victory. Amber turned her head, resting her forehead against the desktop and avoiding his lips. The submissive position rankled, but she got the final say.

Amber tensed when she felt Lucas's hand span along the back of her head. He firmly held her in place, her nose pressed to the desk as his thrust increased, his other hand holding her hip still.

She tried to turn her head, but he wouldn't allow it. She wanted to tell him to let go, to get off. She wanted to tell him that he'd had his fun, but his masterful touch made her sex cream. She had never felt her body pulse and shake like this before. The insistent throb in her sex promised an intense, white-hot pleasure that would leave scorch marks on her soul.

Lucas turned her head and covered her face with rough, open-mouthed, wet kisses. He stabbed his tongue in her ear. She gasped and jerked from his hold, trying to get away, but once again Lucas had the upper hand.

That sense of helplessness unleashed something dark and hot inside her. She closed her eyes as the wave of pleasure crashed through her. It pulled her under, dragging her into a place she'd never known. She was floating, her skin on fire, her mind numb. She pulled back, scared, not sure what was going on, her body still pulsing as Lucas came violently on top of her.

Later that night Amber walked to her apartment with heavy, reluctant footsteps. How was she going to face Lucas after he took her so easily against her desk? How could she stand toe-to-toe with him as his equal when they both knew he could flip her over and take her at a moment's notice? And that she would enjoy it and want more?

Okay, enough already. Amber pressed her hand against her forehead. She had time to retreat and regroup.

She opened the door to her apartment, and discovered that he had beaten her home. Her shoulders sagged. He seemed to be beating her in everything! She dropped her purse and briefcase by the door before tossing her keys in the bowl on the table.

If only she had come up with a strategy to regain control. Over Lucas. Over her life. Over herself.

But first she needed to act on the information she had gotten from her coworkers, shared during a cocktail party. It was amazing what people would divulge after a few drinks, and it was a good thing she listened to the gossip. She had had no idea that Lucas Carter was in the clear running for promotion over their division.

Lucas had no intention of sharing that tidbit of information with her, and with good reason. That promotion had been hers for the taking. Amber closed her eyes and sighed.

But it wasn't over yet. She had to stay focused and keep an eye on Lucas. She was a firm believer in the old saying about keeping your friends close and your enemies even closer.

She heard Lucas moving around in the kitchen. It sounded so . . . right. She didn't want that! She wanted him to feel off balance and in foreign territory.

Amber opened her eyes and really looked at her apartment for the first time. With one sweeping gaze she saw Lucas's possessions in every corner. When had that happened? How could she not have seen this before?

She hurried across the living room, needing to get away. Amber passed the kitchen and propped her arm against the door frame to watch Lucas. She hoped she looked serene and in control as her worries and emotions slammed inside her.

Resting against the kitchen sink, barefoot, with one leg crossed over the other, Lucas looked very much at home eating leftovers from a Chinese take-out box. Yet, while she was dressed in a cocktail dress and heels, she felt as if she was at a disadvantage. In her own place!

"I didn't know you were home." She wished she hadn't said that word. *Home.* A tactical error on her part.

Lucas put the carton on the counter. "Did you have fun?"

She shrugged. "It was nice to catch up and get the latest office gossip." She watched his eyes, which were usually a good indicator if he was hiding something. Lucas didn't seem overly concerned. Either the gossip was highly exaggerated or he didn't seem that worried about her reaction.

The problem was—she did care! It was one thing to be dominated in the bedroom, but to have the same man be her boss at work? What's next? Would he be head of the household? The household that was hers to begin with?

Dread shuddered through her. She couldn't handle that. She needed to believe that she had the same power over him. At least, in one aspect of her life. Which one would she choose? She wished she had the time to decide, but she felt like she was being railroaded into a corner.

Amber couldn't let that happen. She still held power in everything she did. It was time to enforce it.

She strode across the kitchen floor, her heels clacking on the linoleum. When she stood before Lucas, she reached up on her tiptoes and kissed him, tasting the spices on his tongue. "Did you miss me?" she asked against his mouth.

If he was suspicious of her sweet greeting, he didn't let on. Lucas accepted the kiss, and another, following her lead as she set the pace. She deepened the kiss, dragging it out until she felt his erection pressing against her. She smiled against his mouth. No matter how much control he had, he couldn't hide his responses.

Amber reluctantly pulled away and took a step back. As she idly told him who she saw at the party, she shrugged out of her fitted, cropped jacket. Once it slid from her arms, revealing the strapless dress hidden underneath, she tossed the jacket on the counter before she turned away from him.

"Could you do me a favor?" She gestured to the zip at the middle of her back. "Unzip this for me, please?"

He didn't say anything, and she wondered if he knew she could handle the zip perfectly fine without him. Would he call her on it? She tensed when she finally felt his hands brush against her spine before he slowly drew down the zipper.

Amber dipped her head and hid her smile. She couldn't believe acting so helpless would work to her advantage. When he had unzipped the dress and spanned his hands against her hips, Amber turned around. "Thanks."

She felt a bit triumphant when Lucas reached up and cupped her breast. She didn't say anything. She only looked into his eyes and shivered when he grazed his thumb against her nipple. She leaned into his hand and kissed his mouth again. Slowly, as if she had all the time in the world to draw out the pleasure.

Lucas gently tugged at her cocktail dress, slowly revealing her breasts. It was as if he was being cautious, unable to figure out her mood. Smart move on his part, Amber decided as she let her dress fall to her waist. Considering how he had taken her against her desk, he needed to treat her with kid gloves.

He bent his head and slid his mouth against her throat and collarbone, finding the pulse points with unerring accuracy. Did he feel her pulse fluttering nervously? He didn't comment on it before he trailed kisses down her cleavage. He fondled her curves before he took one nipple in his mouth.

Amber gripped the back of his head as he suckled the tip of her breast. The fierce tug echoed deep inside her. She bunched his hair between her fingers and pushed him closer, wanting him to take more of her breast in his mouth.

Lucas felt the need to do the opposite. Amber couldn't stop a disappointed sigh as he let go of her breast and moved his mouth down her stomach. He curled his fingers around the fabric at her waist and drew it down her hips.

Amber's legs trembled as he peeled her dress, nylons and panties from her. His whiskered jaw swept against her hip and he brushed kisses against the protruding bone. She knew he was inhaling her aroused scent. He could tell how wet she was by just one look. She wanted him on his knees in front of her, but why did she feel like the vulnerable one?

He pushed the clothes on top of her feet and helped her step out of them, but he didn't make a move to remove her shoes. The spindly heels suddenly felt wobbly.

Lucas held her hips, his fingers digging into her skin, and burrowed his face in her pubes. Amber gasped at the audacious move, her knees buckling when she felt the curl of his tongue against her clit.

The man knew exactly what she liked. The quick flicks of his tongue tapped insistently on her clitoris, creating a ripple of sensations. Amber swayed and grabbed for the sink in front of her. Her hands slipped on the chrome and she cried out when Lucas captured her stiff bud between his teeth.

Her knees sagged when he sucked on her clitoris. A moan dragged out of her throat as her skin flushed. She didn't think she could stand up for much longer, even if Lucas was holding her hips. Each encouraging murmur he made, each lash of his tongue, made her want to collapse into a heap at his feet.

She couldn't let that happen. The whole point was to show him that she was in charge. She could take him any way she wanted, when she wanted to, and he needed to know that. But she wasn't quite ready to sacrifice the delicious sensations he was giving her.

"Lie down," she ordered in a raspy voice. Her chest rose and fell, aching with every breath she took.

Lucas tipped his head up and looked at her. "What?"

"I want to ride your mouth," she confessed. "Lie down."

She saw a wicked glow in his dark eyes before he lay down on the kitchen floor facing her. Amber stood by his head, her stiletto heels outrageously sexy as they bracketed his face. She squatted down, the senses of vulnerability and power colliding in her chest.

She held onto the sink before Lucas guided her to his mouth. A shudder swept through her at the first long stroke of his tongue. She bore down on his mouth, gasping for breath as he darted into her core.

Amber rocked and tilted against Lucas's mouth. Tingles swept through her body at every knowing curl and flick of his tongue. She felt it from the crown of her head to the soles of her feet.

She delicately rode his tongue. One touch set a lightning bolt of pleasure through her system. As he drove in deeper, she started to ride him harder. Faster. Soon she rode his mouth at a fierce pace, desperate for more, unable to grab that moment of pure pleasure, when suddenly it caught her.

Amber froze as the ecstasy gripped her. It pressed against her, pushing and straining inside her until she shattered. She cried out as the sensations swirled and rushed out of her.

She was dimly aware of Lucas rolling her onto the kitchen floor. Amber flinched when her spine made contact with the cold linoleum floor. Before she knew it, Lucas had stripped off his jeans and entered her with one sure thrust.

Amber held her arms against the crown of her head, using them as a buffer between her and the sink. Each thrust had her bumping against the cabinetry. She didn't ask him to move. She wasn't going to say anything, just watch the savage beauty of his face as he drove into her, igniting a new level of pleasure.

She was surprised he didn't try to get his way until now. Had she caught him by surprise, or did he let her have her way? She would never know unless she tied him down and made him as defenseless and helpless as she felt.

Although there was one way she could find out. What would she use? She gasped as the idea occurred to her. Hey, that purple scarf in the chain letter. It must be specially made for that. Did she still have it or did she throw it away? She couldn't remember.

She would go to her office tomorrow and look for it. Amber smiled as she rocked her hips against Lucas, the hot, thick pleasure zipping through her veins. She'd tie him down with that scarf and she'd truly have her way with him.

And this time, there would be nothing he could do about it.

CHAPTER FIVE

It was the next afternoon when Lucas finally found Amber in her office. He was kicking himself for not thinking of this location sooner. So what if it was a Saturday? Amber lived and breathed her work. Where else would she go when she needed some peace and solitude?

He stood at the threshold and watched her organize her bookshelf. She looked different wearing a sweatshirt and jeans. She seemed more approachable. Touchable.

Amber was always about elegance, but she wore her dresses and designer suits as armor. The stiletto heels were definitely weapons, he thought with a wry smile. She always wore the most feminine clothes, even when she tried to give them a more masculine approach. Nothing she wore would ever make him forget she was all woman.

She reached up to the highest shelf, her whole body stretching to meet her goal. He liked how the soft, faded denim stretched along the curve of her pert ass. The jeans emphasized her long, slender legs and tiny waist.

Her old college sweatshirt hitched up, revealing a swath of pale skin. Lucas pursed his lips, remembering how she tasted. Her skin was always smooth and lightly scented with an expensive perfume that went straight to his head. His mouth watered for more.

But she didn't want more of him. At least it felt that way. She had risen early while he had still been asleep. She left some vague note about running an errand. Her cell phone immediately kicked over to voice mail when he tried to call. She didn't need to make the message more clear: He managed to scare her when he let her take control of their sex.

He thought that it had been the right tactic after taking her on her desk. That had spooked him. He'd like to think he was more civilized.

But, he had to admit, she tested his dominance and his right to display it. The lust still burned in his gut at the way she had struggled. He even got off from watching her act tough when she was melting for him.

Maybe he liked it too much and Amber sensed that. There was no way she could tame that side of him, and he wouldn't let her if she tried. He wanted to go further and test his restraint as well as hers. Lucas dipped his hand in the pocket of his leather jacket and touched the purple scarf. It was time to throw this down between them like a gauntlet and see how she would handle the challenge.

He knew she wouldn't handle it well at first, but he was willing to show some patience. Amber needed to know that he wouldn't take unfair advantage of her. He would never hurt her, and she had to take that at face value without constantly testing him. She needed to take a leap of faith and trust him.

Yeah, right. He shook his head. That won't happen in a billion years.

He watched Amber tense as if she scented danger. It was obvious that she had just now realized that someone else was there, watching her. She whirled around and flinched with surprise when she saw him standing by the door.

"Lucas!" She held her hand over her heart. "You startled me."

He didn't apologize. He didn't feel like it. "I thought you were running an errand this morning."

"I was," she said as she continued to rearrange the books on the shelf. "But I got distracted and started straightening up my office. It needed it."

Understatement of the year. Lucas slid his hands deeper in his pockets and fondled the scarf as he silently surveyed her office. There was a lot more than straightening up going on.

Wastebaskets and garbage bags were overflowing with junk and stood outside her office like battered soldiers. Her office was now in pristine condition. The stacks of papers were gone and the binders were put away, probably arranged by color, knowing Amber. The woman was cleaning house and he had a nasty suspicion that he was next on the recycle list.

He spied a laminated paper on her otherwise empty desk. Hope shot through him and settled in his chest. It was the chain letter that came with the scarf. She didn't throw it away. Why not? He was really interested to discover the answer.

"It looks like you've done enough for today," he announced, leaning his hip against her desk. "You should come home now."

"I have one or two more areas to go through." She didn't look at him as she straightened a small crystal trophy on the bottom shelf.

"It can wait." He let an edge creep into his voice.

She slanted a look at him. "Not really," she replied, and continued shelving the books.

"Did you finish your errand?" he asked casually.

Amber froze. "My errand? Oh, uh . . . no. I thought I left something here, but I can't find it."

"Maybe I can help," Lucas offered, folding his arms across his chest. "What are you looking for?"

"You don't need to help," she said as she brushed her hands off on her jeans. "It wasn't that important."

He raised one eyebrow. "It must have been if it got you out of bed early and you're still looking for it."

She hesitated and changed directions in her argument. "What I mean is, you wouldn't understand."

"Try me."

She shook her head, ignoring the harsh tone of his voice. "It doesn't matter."

"I bet I can find it." He stepped away from the desk and approached her.

Amber rolled her eyes. "Lucas, not everything has to be a competition."

"And I bet I know what you're looking for."

"No, you—" Her voice drifted off when he reached in his jacket pocket and slowly took out the purple silk scarf.

Amber felt her mouth sag open. Her eyes stung as she widened them. She shook her head, trying to clear the fuzziness, but Lucas was still standing in front of her holding it.

As much as she wanted to deny it, the irrefutable fact was dangling in front of her face: Lucas Carter was always one step ahead of her.

She flexed her fingers and curled them tightly against her palms. The temptation to snatch the scarf from Lucas was far too great. "What are you doing with that?" Her words came out in a stunned whisper.

"I thought it might come in handy."

He allowed the scarf to slip through his fingers and he grabbed it with his other hand. It slithered and danced for him. The sight of the undulating silk in his hands had a mesmerizing effect on Amber.

"Is this what you were looking for?" he asked.

She gave a sharp nod and slid her bottom jaw to the side. "I thought I threw it away."

"You did," he said as he wrapped the length of silk around his hand, "but I retrieved it."

And he held on to it for at least five days without saying a word. That spelled trouble. She wasn't sure how she knew that. Call it instinct. "Why?"

"Why do you think?" Lucas asked as he slid the scarf back into his pocket.

"Planning to follow the chain letter?" She tightly crossed her arms against her chest. "I had no idea you enjoy those things."

"I'm not following the orders of an anonymous letter."

"The scarf wasn't sent to you," Amber felt obligated to point out.

His expression indicated that he hardly cared. "I won't let that detail stop me in the pursuit of my fantasy."

"Fantasy?" The word twisted deep inside her. She felt like she had stumbled on something dark and exotic. She was afraid to explore this any further, but she knew Lucas wouldn't let her tiptoe around it anymore. "You never told me about a fantasy of yours."

His gaze ensnared hers. "I didn't know about it until I saw you open the chain letter."

Amber ducked her head and took a deep breath as searing-hot emotions roiled inside her. She was going to hunt down whoever gave her the letter, and destroy her! The nameless woman had no idea what havoc she had caused.

She had to face this head-on. She couldn't afford any misunderstanding or lingering beliefs. She didn't know what Lucas wanted to do with the scarf, but if he had any thoughts of using it to make her immobile, he was out of luck.

"What's your fantasy?" she asked, hating how her voice sounded tight and uncertain. Why couldn't she ask in a smoky, seductive tone to mask the turmoil going on inside her?

"Nothing out of the ordinary," Lucas said, shrugging a shoulder. "I'm a man of simple tastes."

Amber gave a snort at that. Lucas was probably the most complex man she knew. She usually liked that about him, but not at this very moment.

"I want to tie you up," he said, watching her intently. "Bind your wrists to the headboard of our bed."

Oh, is that all? He said it as if he was suggesting vacation plans. Well, he was in for a surprise if he thought she would meekly follow his idea.

"No, thanks." She skirted around him fast before he could catch her. She headed for her desk. While he had the scarf in his possession, she felt the need to have a large, heavy piece of furniture between them.

"Why not?" he asked.

"I'm not into bondage," she answered lightly.

"Is that right?"

Why was he so set on questioning that? Amber put her hands on her hips and faced him. "That's right."

Lucas strolled toward the desk, as if he was thinking about something. "Amber, why were you looking for the scarf?"

She paused, not sure how to answer that without getting caught in her own hypocrisy.

His eyes lit up as he stumbled onto the truth. Lucas pointed an accusing finger at her. "You wanted to tie me up."

She was really tempted to swat his hand away, but she wasn't getting near him. "I didn't say that."

"You don't have to," he said dryly. "Why the secrecy? No shame in having a sexual fantasy."

"It's not my fantasy." She pushed each word through clenched teeth.

"If it's not you— Ah." His eyes gleamed. "I get it. You weren't going to ask my permission to tie me up." Lucas tilted his head and watched her squirm under his questioning. "Were you going to spring it on me while I slept?"

Amber felt a blush sizzle in her cheeks. The man really did know how her mind worked. "I didn't think that far ahead," she lied.

Lucas seemed more amused than angry about the possibility. "It doesn't matter what your plans were because I wouldn't have let you."

"Do you hear yourself?" Amber made a face and clucked her tongue. "You want to do something to me, but you won't let me return the favor."

"What's your point?" He seemed genuinely perplexed. "I never claimed to be fair."

"What's good for the goose is good for the gander."

Lucas's slanted smile made her melt a little in spite of it all. "If I allow you to tie me up, you will let me tie you up? Is that what you're saying?"

Amber rubbed her hand against her forehead. "I'm not saying that at all."

He flattened his hands on her desk and leaned closer. "Come on, baby. What are you scared of?"

She dropped her hand and glared at him. "Nothing!"

"I won't hurt you." The words came out rough, as if it pained him that he had to make that assurance.

Amber closed her eyes, trying to maintain her composure. "I know that."

"Then what is the problem?"

"I don't trust you!" She blurted out the words and instantly regretted it. Amber pressed her lips together, but it was too late. The damage was done.

She reluctantly opened her eyes and saw Lucas's face. The sexy gleam in his eyes was gone. She had snuffed it out with that statement, and she wanted to take it back. The problem was, it was true.

"I know you don't trust me," Lucas said, his voice rough and gravelly. "That's *why* this is my fantasy. I can't imagine anything sexier than you naked and tied up, willing and trusting to follow my lead."

That was his sexiest scenario? Try scariest! Her chest constricted so tightly that she felt like she was wheezing for air. "You want me to be your sex slave for one night and I should expect nothing out of it?"

"I'll make sure you'll enjoy it."

His arrogance made her want to scream. He was so confident that this would work. He truly believed that she'd love it and wouldn't be able to wait to do it again. After all, he wasn't sacrificing anything.

Amber paused as she considered that. What if he had to make a sacrifice? How much did he want this fantasy? How much longer would he push for it, if he had to risk something?

"What?" His gaze sharpened on her. "Come on, Amber. I know that look. What's up?"

"I'll make a deal with you," she said slowly, her stomach flipping like crazy. Her heart pounded so hard against her chest that she thought it was going to burst.

He raised an eyebrow. "Seriously?"

"I will let you tie me up tonight . . ." Oh, God, she couldn't believe she was saying this. She should think this through, try to plug up any loopholes and make it to her advantage.

His expression was so primal that it took her breath away.

". . . if"—she paused, trying to think straight—"if you let me act out my fantasy with the scarf tomorrow night."

Lucas pushed away from the desk as he thought about it. He slid his hands in his pockets and braced his legs apart. It was his classic negotiation pose. "What's your fantasy?"

She had no idea, but she'd come up with something that would make it worth her while. "You'll find out tomorrow."

"No, forget that." Lucas saw right through her plan. "You're going to try to break me. Humiliate me or something. I just know it." His expression darkened as he thought of all she could do to him.

"Lucas, I'm hurt." She playfully put her hand against her heart. "Do you really think I'm capable of something like that?"

"Yes," he said with no hesitation.

She clucked her tongue. "Okay, how about this." She held up her hand as a pledge. "I solemnly vow that I won't do anything that would cause permanent injury or mental anguish."

His eyes narrowed into slits. "Yeah, right."

"That's the deal, Lucas." She tapped her finger against the desk. "I'll be your sex slave tonight, but you have to be mine tomorrow."

Lucas didn't like the terms and he wasn't going to hide his true feelings. "You don't have a bondage fantasy," he argued. "You just want to hedge your bets. If I do anything you don't like tonight, then I will suffer the consequences tomorrow."

And it was a brilliant insurance plan if she said so herself. "Lucas," she said with a pout, "don't you trust me?"

He studied her with a penetrating stare. It felt like he was stripping away layer upon layer until he saw her very heart. Suddenly the wicked gleam in his eye reappeared.

"I do trust you," he finally said, "and I'll take you up on your offer."

Amber's eyes widened as her stomach did a free fall. Lucas had called her bluff? Oh, *damn*.

CHAPTER SIX

t's showtime.

Amber stared at her reflection in the bathroom mirror. She had been in there longer than necessary, but this was an important night. She'd bathed, plucked, tweezed, waxed and pumiced to within an inch of her life. If she could have thought of a way to buff and varnish her skin, she'd have done it to waste time.

Her nail polish now matched her lavender negligee. Her hair had been up, twisted, and then braided before she decided to let it down. She had flossed her teeth three times.

She was a nervous wreck before she took off her nightgown. Before she saw Lucas. Even before she stepped into the bedroom. It wasn't a good omen for what lay ahead.

You don't have to do this, she reminded herself for the umpteenth time. She didn't have to follow any rule Lucas or that stupid chain letter made. She didn't have to accept the challenge.

But, in a way, she did. Amber flattened her hand against her stomach and tried to take a deep, calming breath. If she didn't completely trust Lucas—if she didn't at least try—what was she doing with him? Without trust, the relationship would falter and stall. It would wither away before she could fix it.

She had to give it a chance now. Even if it scared her witless. If she couldn't learn to develop a smidgen of trust in Lucas Carter after tonight, then he was out. No use wasting time over a doomed relationship.

You could always skip the challenge part and kick him out now.

She raised her eyebrow at her reflection. Hmm ... The idea had merit. Amber immediately frowned at her reflection. No, it didn't. That would be the worst choice to take. It was the coward's way out.

Which didn't quite explain why she was still hiding in the bathroom.

Amber closed her eyes and exhaled slowly. She rolled her head and shrugged her shoulders. She was going to do this. It was now or never.

She grabbed the door handle and wrenched it open before she talked herself out of it. Amber stepped into the shadowy bedroom and shivered at the drop in temperature. She squinted at the bed. In the stream of light from the bathroom she could tell he wasn't there. "Lucas?"

"Over here."

Said the spider to the ... No, no. She straightened her shoulders. She wasn't going to take that attitude. It would only make the night longer.

Lucas's voice came from the direction of the overstuffed chair in the corner. What was he doing there? Was she supposed to go over there? Lie on the bed? Wait for his instructions?

She hated not knowing the rules of the game. The indecision was unlike her. She'd rather charge in, get what she wanted, and find out what she had done wrong later. But even she knew that if she tried that tonight, it would bring more trouble upon her.

"Come here."

She immediately bristled over his order. *Shake it off,* she told herself fiercely. *Just shake it off. And he'll get his just deserts tomorrow, with a big second helping.* She made her legs move, each step awkward as she quietly approached him.

She knew he never told her to be silent, but she didn't trust herself to speak. There was a running commentary in her head calling Lucas and the chain letter all sorts of creative names. The last thing she needed to do was say them out loud. She wasn't going to give Lucas an excuse to punish her.

Punish. Her stomach clenched at the thought.

Lucas sat before her like a king on a throne, she decided uncharitably. His legs were sprawled out, and his hand was propping his jaw. She realized he wore black silk pajama bottoms and nothing else.

It was the first time she'd seen him wear those. He looked good, damn it. She had given the pajamas as a gift, but the man preferred to sleep in the nude. Seeing him wear her gift—tonight of all nights—made her breathe a little easier.

The relief was short-lived. Her heart stuttered in her chest when he grabbed the scarf off the side table and unfurled it in front of her. The gold threads winked at her as Lucas tossed it from one hand to the other, as if he was taunting her.

"Amber," his voice rumbled, and it made her skin prickle in warning. "You know I don't like it when you wear something to bed."

She gestured at his legs. "You're wearing something."

"That's not the point."

"I'm also not in bed yet." She clamped her mouth shut. She shouldn't say anything. Amber knew her body vibrated with attitude, and she had to think of a way to stay quiet and still.

But what did Lucas expect? Did he really think she was going to roll over and play dead? She may have agreed to have her wrists bound to the bed, but she never agreed to stay there. She would tear the fabric off before he could live out his fantasy as her lord and master.

"Take off your nightgown."

She shifted her bare feet as her nipples tightened and poked against the lavender silk. "Don't you like it?" she asked, stalling for time.

"It's beautiful," he admitted, "but I want you naked."

She tightened her tummy as her sex heated. "What if I say no?"

He tilted his head slightly, his eyes never leaving hers. "Your nightgown is coming off of you with or without your cooperation."

Amber hesitated.

Lucas tsked with regret. "It would be a shame to see your favorite nightgown ruined."

She got the message. Amber grabbed the silk at her hips and started bunching it up. She felt him watch her hemline pass her knee, move up her thigh and over her hips. Her skin flushed and tingled as she grabbed the material by her waist and pulled it up over her head.

Amber fought the temptation to shield her naked body with the silk negligee in her hands. She had nothing to be ashamed of. Nothing to worry about. Lucas Carter was her live-in lover and had been for months.

But something was different about this time. Lucas looked her over with more than a hint of possession. He knew he owned her for one night.

"Go lie down on the bed."

Her knees went weak with relief. Finally. She could get this night over and done with. Amber tossed her discarded negligee in Lucas's direction before turning toward the bed. She half hoped the silk hit him in the face, but she wasn't going to hang around to find out.

She strutted with way more confidence than she felt. Amber looked at the bed, wishing she didn't have a headboard that made it so easy to tie her wrists to it. She used to love the simple beauty of the Mission-style wooden slats. Now the design felt like her prison bars.

Amber gingerly lay down and stretched out on the bed, which tonight felt cold and unyielding. She left her hands by her sides. If Lucas wanted her hands up, he was going to have to ask for it. He was not in for an easy night.

Lucas knelt down on the bed and straddled her hips. Uncertainty tripped down Amber's spine. She was going to be well and truly caught. She felt his erection heavy against her stomach, straining against the black silk.

He reached for her wrists and held them above her head. No requests, no playing games. He knew what he wanted and wasn't going to dance around it.

She didn't look up at her hands as he tied her wrists to the headboard. She was almost afraid to look, to see those complicated knots and know that any attempt to escape was futile. Instead she watched Lucas's face, her nerves shredding and unraveling at his intensity.

He tied the last knot and viewed it with grim satisfaction. Amber automatically tugged at it. She couldn't help herself. She needed to test the bindings. They were snug, but not tight.

Lucas dropped his hands down her arms and along her collarbone. He traced the features of her face as if he was memorizing every line and angle. The tender caress was at odds to the dark sensuality lurking in his eyes.

When his fingers skimmed her mouth she nipped his fingertips with her teeth.

Lucas drew back in surprise. He narrowed his eyes but she saw the gleam of reluctant respect. She smirked back at him, wanting to tell him there was more where that came from.

He tucked his fingers under her chin, forcibly closing her mouth. "Don't try that again."

She turned her head away, but with a firm, insistent hand, Lucas guided her gaze back to meet his. "Did you hear me?"

"Yes," she answered, gritting her teeth. That one word just about killed her. If he made her say "sir," she was going to blow a blood vessel.

He lowered his head and brushed his mouth against hers. He tasted like male heat and temptation. "Don't fight it," he urged her. "Follow my lead."

Easier said than done! But she kissed him again, letting the familiar, exciting sensations curl around her. His kisses almost made her want to sigh and melt. Kissing was safe territory, even when he did that thing with his tongue that made her head spin. She could kiss him forever.

Lucas had other plans. His hands skimmed her breasts with a

possessiveness that stunned her. When he pinched her nipples, Amber yelped and tried to turn as the sting invaded her senses. The scarf didn't let her get far.

Lucas seemed to like her reaction a little too much. He pinched her nipple again, this time harder. Amber let out a guttural groan and twisted to the side. The fire streamed to her clit, but she couldn't move her arms. She gritted her teeth as the scarf bit into her wrist.

"Okay, I'm done," she announced, blinking rapidly as her tears stung the back of her eyelids. "You can untie me now."

Lucas hushed her and placed his warm palms over her reddened, tight nipples. "I haven't started."

"Hey!" She tried to dislodge his hands with no success. "I fulfilled my promise. You got to tie me to the bed tonight. Guess what? You did. Now untie me."

He rubbed his palms in small circles over the tips of her breasts, his attention riveted on the design he was creating. "No."

She jerked her head back. "No?" He couldn't say no.

He didn't say anything at first as he gently stroked her breasts with his long, lean fingers. "Give it a chance," he encouraged her.

The bed frame rattled as she pulled on the scarf. "I did," she reminded him coldly. "Now move on."

Lucas shook his head. "I didn't pinch you any harder than I usually do."

Was he saying she was lying? "That is not the point."

"Do you want your fantasy tomorrow?" he asked, looking away from her breasts and into her eyes. "If you do, then you need to follow through."

She glared at him and pursed her lips. "That's blackmail."

He didn't seem concerned about her accusation. "I don't even know what you have in store for me, but I agreed to the deal. I trust you more than you trust me."

"Well, I guess you're the better person," she said, her voice dripping with sarcasm. "Good to know. Now untie me." She tugged at the scarf, causing the headboard to bump against the wall.

"When I'm ready."

"Lucas! You—ooh!" Her eyes bulged when he took her nipple in his mouth and curled his tongue around it. She could feel herself melting under his ministrations. Just when Amber lowered her guard, Lucas captured the nipple between his teeth and sucked it hard.

Amber's eyes rolled back as her sex flooded. She felt alive and tingly as the sparks danced just under her skin. Lucas moved his hands all over her body, his touch light and teasing.

She wasn't sure what was going on. Why couldn't she predict his next move? And why did a flirty, almost soft touch feel like a sting to her?

What Lucas said must be true. He wasn't doing anything different, but her body felt everything with more intensity. The simplest touch could bring almost unbearable pleasure.

Lucas settled between her legs and continued stroking and licking and kissing her. She twisted and turned, flexed her hips, and tried to prod him with her knee, but she couldn't hide from his mouth. Every time she pulled at her bindings, the silk scratched her wrist. The abrasion didn't distract her from Lucas's mouth. It added to the sensations.

Amber couldn't stand it any longer. She wanted to grab him by the hair and position his mouth against her sex. She wanted to buck against his tongue and set the pace.

It wasn't going to happen tonight. Nothing she could say or do would change anything. Amber stopped pulling on the scarf and stopped wishing it would miraculously give way. She sighed in defeat and let her arms sag.

Lucas showed no signs of victory. He didn't swoop in for the kill or become more aggressive. His light, feathery kisses and teasing strokes were torture enough.

"Lower," she ordered, and winced when she realized she had said it out loud.

Lucas lifted his head. "What was that?"

"Lower . . ." He was going to pay for this. "Please."

She knew he was smiling over that concession. Lucas lowered his mouth and slowly, leisurely licked the wet folds of her sex until she was twisting from side to side uncontrollably. The headboard banged against the wall, but Lucas didn't stop.

"Come on," Amber bit out, giving the scarf a good hard tug, but her movements made the knots tighter. "Enough already! Untie me!"

"Not yet." He rested his hand against her stomach. If it was supposed to be a gentling touch, it failed miserably. The span of Lucas's hand made her more aware of his strength and power.

"Now," she ordered.

"Give it up, baby," Lucas said in a raspy voice. "There is nothing you can do about it."

There wasn't. She closed her eyes as he continued to stroke her with his tongue. This was so much different than what she had anticipated. It wasn't anything like the time he took her against her desk. Then she still had a chance to get the upper hand and even the score. She had no chance now.

Lucas dipped his finger in her core. She gasped as sensations flickered through her. She wanted to quench them, to grab his hand and sink all of his fingers inside her, but she couldn't. She had to take what she could get.

He pumped his finger inside her as he played with her clit with his tongue. His moans of satisfaction and enjoyment hummed against her. She rocked against his hand, but she couldn't control his touch. Worse, she couldn't control her responses.

The roll of her hips deepened. Each breath she took felt strained and thready in her throat. The sensations rippling through her were powerful and Lucas hadn't entered her yet.

Amber tried to rein in her emotions, but she was quickly losing control, and that scared her. Hiding her reactions was her strongest weapon, but now she couldn't conceal every thought and emotion racing through her mind. The more she tried to hide, the harder her heart would pound, and the more she felt out of control. It was swirling into a vicious circle.

Lucas knelt between her legs and pressed his hard, thick cock against her entrance. Amber bucked and rolled her hips wildly. She couldn't help it. She wasn't fighting Lucas, or the inevitable. She was fighting to maintain her last internal restraint.

He slid his cock into her wet opening, and the last restraint dissolved. Every wild, hungry need came clawing out of Amber and there was nothing she could do to stop them.

Lucas fed off of this primitive side of her. He held Amber's hips down and thrust deeply, meeting each of her moves with a mastery that sent her in an emotional tailspin. He let her twist and struggle, but he wouldn't stop whispering soft, gentle encouragements that didn't reach her ear.

The heat climbed higher and higher inside her. She felt like she was going to disintegrate. And, just when she thought she couldn't stand the hunger anymore, the intense heat flashed through her. The pleasure was so acute, so pure, that it stopped her cold.

This was not the blissful cocoon she'd reached for in the past, Amber dimly realized as Lucas climaxed ferociously against her. It wasn't quiet and peaceful. This was the gateway to a new world.

It promised to be beautiful. Sensuous and exotic. She wanted to explore, but it was still unknown. It scared her, knowing this territory lay deep inside her.

Amber pushed the realization away with all her might. She wanted to avoid that place. She couldn't reign supreme over what she didn't know or understand.

Could she?

CHAPTER SEVEN

A lazy Sunday at home had never been so stressful.

Lucas was acutely aware of Amber as she rose from the couch and walked to the bedroom. Her purposeful stride caught his attention. She was getting ready for her turn to tie him up.

He was dreading it, and had watched Amber all day, gauging her mood. Far too often he saw Amber staring off into space. It didn't matter if she was reading the paper from beginning to end or watching a television program. Her brow would crease like it always did when she was deep in thought, or she would bite her lower lip. He knew that on these occasions she wasn't thinking of work. She was plotting her revenge.

And if that wasn't enough, every time she caught him watching, she would rub her hands together like an evil mastermind and cackle gleefully.

Payback was hell.

Amber peeked out from the bedroom door. "Lucas?"

It was the sweetness in her voice that set off the alarm bells in his head. The moment he'd been worried about all day had arrived, but he was going to take it on the chin. Lucas looked up from the file he was reading. "Yeah, baby?"

Amber narrowed her eyes at the endearment like she always did. "Where did you put the scarf?"

"In my drawer," he informed her. For one brief moment he wished he could truthfully say he'd lost the scarf. "I'll get it."

She held her hand up, gesturing for him to wait where he was. "Don't worry, I'll get it. Give me five minutes and then come in."

Lucas watched her disappear. He closed the file and tossed it on the end table, exhaling slowly, but the tension didn't seep from his body. He was in for it.

He knew it was going to be bad when he made the deal with Amber, but he wasn't going to renege. He wanted her to trust him and he was willing to go the distance to gain that trust.

The night before was worth anything Amber tried to do to him. Watching her untamed responses was amazing, but knowing that she submitted to him—and had submitted like that only to him—made him hard and ready every time he thought about it.

But he didn't think he could submit to her. He didn't want to try. It made his skin crawl. This was going to be a night to endure, and knowing Amber, she was going to put him through his paces.

At least there was one good thing about tonight: He knew she would bind him with the scarf. He was stronger than the silk. If it got too bad he could always tear his way to freedom.

His confidence took a dip when he remembered how hard Amber had tugged on the scarf. It never frayed, even when the bed shook. Okay, he *might* be able to get free, Lucas decided. He had a fifty-fifty chance.

What was he thinking? Lucas rubbed the heels of his hands against his eyes. He was screwed.

"Lucas," Amber called from the bedroom. "I'm ready."

I'm not. "I'll be right there." He rose from his chair and turned off the lights. He could do this. He *would* do this. If Amber felt any affection or tenderness for him, she would not humiliate or hurt him.

It was the possibility of humiliation that worried him the most. He could handle pain, and he might be able to endure a humble moment or two. As long as no pictures were taken.

He froze in midstep. *Crap!* He had forgotten to make that rule. It was too late to amend the agreement. More importantly, he didn't want to bring it up now and give Amber any ideas.

Lucas opened the bedroom door and stepped inside. It was brightly lit and, with one sweeping gaze, he noticed nothing out of place or added. The room looked like it always did, but tonight he felt as if he was stepping into a trap.

Amber stood by the bed. He blinked slowly, struck by how beautiful she looked. Tonight she wore an ivory satin chemise and wrap he had never seen before. Her choice of sleepwear surprised him. He had expected pinstripe flannel pajamas, or boxers and a tank top. Something to give her the masculine edge she usually strove for.

But the chemise and robe emphasized her sexy elegance. Her regal beauty was in full force. He drank in the sight of her from her tousled strawberry blonde hair to her bare feet. He froze when she casually pulled the scarf from her robe pocket.

His gut twisted as the purple silk unwound from its hiding place. He bunched his hands at his sides and slowly stretched out his fingers. He could do this. He gave his word.

"I've been giving tonight a lot of thought," Amber said as she tossed the silk from one hand to the other. Lucas wondered if she was going to copy every move he had made last night. "There were so many choices . . . so many positions . . ."

Lucas folded his arms across his chest. He was going to be generous and let her have this moment. If she strayed too far, he would snap her back into reality so fast her head would spin.

"I thought up all sorts of scenarios," she continued, reaching up and tossing the scarf onto his shoulder. Lucas was proud that he didn't flinch at the first touch of silk. He didn't move when she dragged the scarf down his chest. "But I finally decided what I wanted for my night. *My* fantasy."

Amber swept the silk around his waist, looping it around his back and holding the ends tight. She gave the scarf a jerk, propelling Lucas forward. Amber smiled, obviously enjoying her moment of power. She tried to do it again, but he had grabbed the silk at his sides and held them in his fists. "What did you decide?"

Amber looked at him from beneath her long eyelashes. "Once I tell you, I don't want to hear a word out of you."

"I can't promise that."

She tilted her jaw so she could look directly in his eyes. "Then you can suffer the consequences."

Lucas's nostrils flared as he inhaled deeply. He had to take a leap of faith. He knew that, but there was a stronger possibility that Amber would pull the rug out from under him.

So what if she does? He'd be disappointed, a little battered and bruised, but he would also know where he stood with her. He was ready to take the risk, and if he fell flat on his face, he was strong enough to get back up. At least, he liked to think so.

"Okay," he said tersely. "You won't hear a word out of me."

Amber looped the scarf around the back of his neck and pulled him closer. "Promise?" she asked, her face next to his.

"Yeah, I promise." Irritation crept into his voice, but how many times did he have to give his word? "What is it?"

Amber took a step back and allowed the scarf to slither off him. She broke eye contact and Lucas knew that wasn't a good sign. His stomach twisted so sharply that he wanted to double over with pain.

"I want you to tie my hands behind my back."

Lucas stared at her. He barely heard her soft, hesitant request. She wanted to be tied up? Again? She didn't want to tie him up?

There had to be some trick. Something really devious that for the life of him he couldn't see. That would be classic Amber. "Say what?" he asked, his mind whirling.

Amber glared at him. She planted her hands on her hips, the movement causing the satin to strain against her curves. "You promised you wouldn't say anything."

"I—" He closed his mouth abruptly. Why was Amber giving this moment up? She had him by the balls. She could have made him grovel and bend over backward, but she was giving him the control again. It didn't make sense.

He stared at Amber. She stood before him, proud and defiant. The truth hit him, knocking him sideways. He was almost staggered back by what this all meant.

Lucas lowered his eyelids, hooding the stark emotion that he knew shone from his eyes. Amber wanted to be bound and she didn't want him to judge her. That was her fantasy. No judgment. No control. No consequences.

He could give that to her. Hope and pride poured through his chest. Amber trusted him a hell of a lot. He wasn't going to mess this up.

He was humbled by this gift, if not more than a little relieved. He would never judge her for her sexual fantasies, but she would figure that out someday. Tonight he would lay the foundation for that.

He silently reached out for the scarf. Amber hesitated for one moment before she relinquished her hold. The silk felt cool and liquid-smooth against his hand.

Lucas watched as Amber shrugged off her satin wrap. His chest tightened with anticipation. He wanted to say something. Some words of assurance or that what happened in this room remained between them. But he could feel the words stick in his throat. Whatever he said would probably cause problems.

He covered up his uncertainty by walking over to Amber and gripping her upper arms, turning her to stand with her back facing him. Sliding his hands down the length of her arms, he drew her wrists together.

He felt the natural resistance of her arms, and maybe there was a last, instinctive struggle from Amber. The position didn't look comfortable, but Amber didn't show any sign of pain. He doubled up the long scarf and quickly tied her wrists together.

Lucas let go and her hands swung against the curve of her ass. She arched her back to accommodate the change of weight, and her posture made her breasts appear fuller and more prominent.

"Kneel on the bed," Lucas instructed.

Amber raised her leg to climb onto the bed and teetered. She put her leg back down abruptly.

He saw her look of frustration. "Do you need help?" he asked, ready to assist her.

She shook her head and tried again. This time she crawled onto the mattress. Her movements lacked her usual grace, but she managed to kneel at the center of the bed.

The struggle to do a simple task brought it home for him. Amber was defenseless. Kneeling and bound at the wrists, she would have to follow his every command.

Lust ripped through him. He felt guilty for finding dark pleasure in her predicament. But if Amber had a hint of this, she didn't judge him. He should feel free to show his true reaction, but he didn't want to scare her.

Lucas stripped, his skin hot and flushed. It was a relief to get rid of the clothes that contained his body heat. He knelt on the bed behind Amber and watched her shoulders stiffen. He realized this was a deviation from her fantasy.

He didn't want to ask exactly what she'd hoped for, step by step. He was supposed to take control, and one way of doing that was to keep her guessing.

Lucas wrapped one arm around her waist and cupped his other hand over her breast. He nuzzled her throat, licking and kissing the erratic pulse beating under her skin. Her taste was like an aphrodisiac to him and he couldn't get enough.

He plucked her nipple with his fingers, enjoying how quickly it tightened under his touch. He lingered and teased the tips of her breasts until they became stiff crests. When he sucked the pulse point at her neck, Amber moaned and her nipples pinched into tight buds.

He allowed his other hand to drift down her pelvic bone and graze against the wet curls concealing her clit. Amber's moans hitched in her throat when he caressed her clitoris with light, almost flirtatious touches.

The need rumbled deep inside him. He wanted to sink into her, claim her, and dominate Amber completely. Lucas trailed kisses from her throat to the base of her neck. He felt her tense as he licked and kissed his way down her spine.

He withdrew his hand from her clit. Amber bucked against him, her murmur of protest echoing in the room, only to be replaced by a sigh as he slid his hand from behind her and stroked the folds of her sex. He saw the muscles in her legs tighten and shake as her desire took hold. When he dipped his finger in her sex, her flesh gripped him tight.

Lucas pulled away and reached around for the pillows. He piled them in front of her knees. "Bend over."

Amber went rigid. "What?" The word cracked through the air like the lash of a whip.

He placed a comforting kiss on her brow and whispered in her ear, "Trust me."

Amber didn't move at first. She guardedly bent down until her stomach rested on the pillows and her forehead touched the mattress. Her ass was tilted high in the air.

"Comfortable?" he asked, caressing her buttocks.

She turned her head to the side. "Not really."

He stopped teasing as he watched her grimace. "Are you in pain?"

"No," she admitted.

He stroked the slick folds of her sex with his fingers. She was wet, and his cock was so ready that it slapped against his stomach. Lucas drove his hard, eager cock into her. He felt the sense of triumph swell in his chest when Amber reared her head back and moaned as pleasure crashed through her. The sound of her voice triggered something primitive inside Lucas.

Lucas pounded fiercely into her with short, quick strokes. Amber's moans grew deeper and longer as one small climax pulsed into another, gaining power. Her hot, wet core pulled and squeezed his cock. He lingered after each thrust, unwilling to retreat from the tight flesh.

Raw need slammed into him, rattling him to his bones. He gave one final thrust, a harsh growl tearing from his throat as he came.

Dark spots danced before his eyes and he fought for his next breath. His body ached and his muscles shook in the aftermath. There was nothing he would like better than to collapse on top of Amber. But he knew that she had been bound long enough.

Lucas gradually withdrew from her hot, tight core, which still pulsed like a heartbeat. He struggled to untie the scarf from her wrists. His fingers fumbled against the knots.

"I'll get you out of this," he promised, his voice sounding sluggish. He half expected a sarcastic comeback, but Amber didn't say anything. Her silence made him work faster.

Just when he was considering going into the kitchen to get a knife to slice the silk, he finally loosened a knot. Lucas worked fast and quickly unbound her wrists. He paused when he saw the crisscrossing red marks on her wrists. He felt incredibly proud of her.

Lucas gently rolled Amber onto her back. "Did that fulfill your fantasy?" he asked with a slanted, tired smile as he briskly rubbed her arms.

She frowned, the skin pleating between her eyebrows. "Hey," she said with her eyes closed. "I don't want to hear a word about this from you."

"I'm supposed to keep quiet the rest of the night?" he teased. "Good luck on that."

"I mean no comments about this. Ever."

Forever? His hands stilled on her wrists as he stared at her, but Amber didn't open her eyes. He wasn't supposed to talk about the most amazing night of his life with the woman he shared it with?

No, Lucas thought as he narrowed his eyes. He had not agreed to that. Somehow he would make Amber break her own rule. If he didn't manage that, how was he going to get a repeat?

When Amber saw Lucas walking toward her office Monday afternoon, she knew her reprieve was over. It hadn't been easy to avoid Lucas in the morning, and she had been surprised that she'd managed to some degree. But obviously Lucas had decided her time-out was over.

Her first instinct was to run to the door and slam it before locking him out. Not that a locked door would stop Lucas from what he wanted, but it would stall him, and she needed some time to compose herself.

She knew that look on Lucas's face. He was ready for a showdown. She had two options: She could either distract him or meet him head-on. Whatever she chose, she would handle him with grace and cool manners.

But if he made one reference to her penchant for getting tied up, she would throw her chair at him.

Lucas stepped into her office, but unlike every other time, he didn't close the door. He didn't even touch it. Amber looked at the door, then back at him, before she looked at the door again. What was going on?

"What brings you here today, Lucas?" Amber asked as she made a show of glancing at her calendar. "We didn't have a meeting scheduled."

His slanted smile was arrogant. "Have I ever needed an appointment?"

She automatically looked at the doorway, but no one was in earshot of their conversation. "Maybe you should," she said. Amber leaned back in her chair and studied him. "You have been taking far too many liberties and that's going to stop. Effective immediately."

"Is that so?" He sat down across from her desk and stretched his legs out. His tone and stance showed how little he was concerned about her proclamation.

"We have to stop having sex in the office," she whispered fiercely, giving another quick glance at the open door. "It wreaks havoc on my schedule, with my level of productivity . . ."

"And someone might find out," he added smoothly.

She slapped her hand on her desk. "Exactly. When that happens, you'll get a pat on the back from the good old boys and my reputation will be ruined."

"That's true."

"Then we are agreed. Good." She tossed her hands in the air. "No more sex during work hours."

"I didn't agree to that."

She tilted her head back. "Lucas."

He rubbed his hand along his jaw. "I kind of like the idea of tying you up against that office chair and—"

Amber rose from that very chair. She grabbed the armrests and had lifted it from the floor when she saw someone walk by. Amber froze and waited until the person disappeared from her sight before she dropped the chair back onto the floor.

"You are not tying me up ever again," she informed Lucas. "And you aren't going to discuss it. From this moment on, it's purged from your memory."

"Why? You liked it. I liked it. We're consenting adults. Don't tell me to forget last night."

His dark expression warned her to tread delicately around the subject. "That's beside the point. I am not a submissive person."

Lucas rolled his eyes. "No kidding."

She poked her fingers against her breastbone. "I am your equal in every sense of the word. I don't want you to tie me up, here or in my bedroom, and have you see me as subservient to you."

He looked like he was giving her words some thought before he shrugged. "Fair enough."

She saw something move in the next room. Amber saw an employee curiously peer in as he walked by before abruptly turning his face. "Good," Amber said, and sat back down.

"But what if we played out that fantasy in a place that wasn't a part of our real life?"

"What?" She looked away from the open door. "I don't understand?"

"If I reserve a hotel room during the odd afternoon," Lucas said, his casual tone at odds with the intent look in his eyes, "we could be away from work and home, and indulge in a little bondage."

Amber squinted at him. "Why would we want to do that? We already live together. We don't need to rent a room. Renting rooms is for people who can't find a place to be alone."

"But this hotel room would be different. Think of it as a neutral playing field. Once we step into it, we drop our everyday roles and we have the freedom to explore our fantasies."

"You mean"—she gave another glance at the door before she lowered her voice—"you will only tie me up when we are in this hotel room?"

"That's right."

Lucas's offer was seductive. She might be able to handle his compromise. She wanted to explore her boundaries without it invading her real life. It was like having the best of both worlds.

Amber licked her lips and took the risk. "Okay, it's a deal," she said in a rush. "Do you have a hotel in mind? We'll need something close by in—"

Lucas pulled a hotel key card from his jacket pocket and tossed it onto her desk. It skittered across the polished mahogany and bumped against her fingers.

Amber picked up the key card and noted the swanky hotel's emblem. Lucas was going all out for this fantasy. "You're always one step ahead of me, aren't you."

"I try."

She pressed her lips together at Lucas's attempt to be humble. "What are you going to tie me up with?"

Lucas's smoky look sizzled her nerve endings. "The purple scarf, of course."

"No, you can't." Amber sat up straight and snapped her fingers. "Which reminds me."

She reached for her bottom desk drawer and pulled out a plastic shopping bag. "I have to get rid of this."

Lucas's eyes widened when she pulled out the scarf. "What? No, you aren't getting rid of that."

She tapped her fingertip against the laminated letter. "The rules specifically said seven days."

He looked at her as if she had said something crazy. "You're following the chain letter? You don't believe in that crap."

"So what?" Amber stuffed the letter and scarf into the interoffice envelope.

"But this scarf is special."

She tied the envelope closed. "Don't get all sentimental on me, Lucas."

Lucas gave her a dark look. "Who are you sending it to?"

She shrugged. She hadn't thought that far. The letter had said to give it to a woman, but that was the only rule. She looked up and saw the receptionist skirt around the door, as if she were trying not to catch Amber's eye.

"Sienna Bailey," Amber said as Sienna disappeared around the corner.

"Sienna?" Lucas gave a bark of laughter. "Sweet Sienna?"

"Why does everyone say that? She's not all that sweet," Amber said as she wrote Sienna's name in block letters. She hoped the change in her penmanship would mask her identity.

He gestured at the envelope. "Sienna Bailey wouldn't know what to do with that scarf. She's probably still a virgin."

Sienna did have the wholesome look going for her, but that didn't mean she couldn't use a fantasy chain letter. "Then her luck would change a week from now."

Lucas shook his head mournfully. "I can't believe you're giving it away."

"Oh, cheer up, Lucas," she said as she reached in the drawer and grabbed her clutch purse. "Think of this as an opportunity."

"How?" he asked as he rose from his seat and Amber got up from her chair.

"You're no longer limited in what you can tie me up with," she said as she walked around her desk.

Lucas perked up considerably at the endless possibilities. "We might have to make a stop before we get to the hotel."

"It's a good thing this hotel doesn't charge by the hour," she muttered.

"An hour? Please." He made a face. "What kind of lover do you think I am? Prepare yourself for a long, mind-blowing afternoon."

Hot desire coiled tight in her belly. "Maybe I should cancel my appointments for the rest of the day."

"Don't worry, baby," he said as he escorted her through the door. "I already did that for you."

"Lucas!" She glared at him.

"You can thank me later. In fact"—he reached for her hand and pressed his mouth against the faded red marks on her wrist—"I know just how you can show your appreciation."

CHAPTER EIGHT

"**P**atty, you can take my seat," Sienna Bailey told the elderly woman on the express bus home.

"No, I can't do that," Patty said, but she was already making her way to Sienna's spot, her pursuit fast even though the bus swayed and lurched.

"Sure you can." Sienna rose from her seat and gestured for the woman to take her place. "I've been sitting all day and it feels good to stretch my legs."

"Thanks, Sienna. You are such a sweet girl," Patty said. She sat down and gave a great sigh of relief.

Sienna smiled in response and held on to the metal bar above her. Why did everyone think she was sweet? Or worse, a girl. She was a twenty-five-year-old *woman*, for crying out loud.

But she didn't correct Patty, or anyone else. They wouldn't believe her even if she showed hard, cold evidence to prove her point. Not that she would show anyone in town, but if she did, no one would accuse her of being so nice anymore.

Sienna felt the corners of her mouth twist slyly. She kind of liked having the saucy part of herself hidden. After growing up in a small town where everyone had known her since forever, having a secret was a luxury.

She looked out of the bus window and watched the trees and houses go by. Sienna liked being from here, where her family and lifelong friends belonged. She enjoyed small-town living and had no plans to leave, but there were times when she wanted a little spice in her life. Something to look forward to after a predictable week. Something that gave her a zing—gave the world more color.

Something like Adam Taylor. Sienna sighed as she remembered the last time she saw him. His long, black hair fell down in waves, framing the angular, aggressive lines of his face. His dark blue eyes could pin her to the spot. Adam had a dangerous edge that he kept firmly in check, but every once in a while she caught a glimpse. Those moments held her spellbound.

"Ooh," Patty said next to her, her voice rising with interest. "What's that look?"

Sienna was pulled out of her hazy daydream with a jolt. "Excuse me?" she asked.

"I know that look. Who's the guy?" Patty leaned forward, as if trying to catch a secret. "He can't be anyone from around here."

Sienna pursed her lips, catching her immediate reply and holding it back. If she wasn't careful, Patty would find out the full story. "How can you be so sure?" Sienna hedged.

The older woman made a face. "None of those guys know how to make a girl smile like that."

Sienna felt her cheeks warm, wondering how ridiculous she had looked standing there smiling off into the distance. "You might be surprised."

Patty scoffed at the suggestion. "I doubt it. So, tell me. Who's the guy?"

"Oh, here's my stop," Sienna told her. And not a moment too soon! She didn't think she could have held off Patty for a couple of more blocks. "See you tomorrow."

She got off the bus and gave a quick thanks to the driver, fully aware that her face was still hot pink. She had to work on her blushing. Being single and in a small town meant a lot of questions about who she was dating. She had to come up with some general answers or she would be facing a firing squad of the town's best gossips.

Sienna looked at her watch and muffled a shriek. She was much later than usual. She had to hurry or she'd miss out on her night with Adam.

Adam was such a stickler when it came to punctuality. *Her* punctuality, Sienna admitted as she rushed down the old, cracked sidewalk. He could be as late as he pleased, but if she was a second behind schedule, she suffered the consequences.

Sienna ran home, not stopping to check the mail. The moment she entered her tiny one-bedroom apartment, she kicked off her shoes and ran to her closet. Stripping off her work clothes, she grabbed a pair of brown cargo pants and an old beige concert T-shirt. She couldn't remember which concert it was for since the design had cracked with age.

She looked in the mirror next to the closet and ruffled her hair. There was only so much she could do with her blunt cut, and the mussed look was as good as it was going to get. She studied her reflection, wanting to add layers of eyeliner and lipstick. Maybe go wild and add a fake tattoo.

That wouldn't make her look rough and sexy. It would make her look ridiculous. She would look like she was playing dress-up. And if anyone saw her . . .

Oh, who was going to see her? Sienna thought as she turned away from the mirror. Only Adam, and he liked her bare. She didn't have to wear anything seductive or go heavy on the makeup. She didn't need to pretend to be a bad girl. He already knew how bad she could be.

Sienna glanced at the clock again and hurried back to the door. Stuffing her feet in slouchy boots, she stepped out into the hall, locked her door and slid the key in her cargo pants' pocket before racing outside.

Slow down, she warned herself as she hustled along the sidewalk. She had to be prompt, but she didn't want to look overeager. And she definitely didn't want to draw attention. The neighbors speculated enough already.

Why was she like this every time she planned on seeing Adam? Or, for that matter, any time she thought about him? She knew she was showing more than a goofy smile. Sienna felt the glow inside her ready to burst out.

After all these months the excitement should have died down. If anything, the sneaking around and living a double life should have gotten old. She should have found her limit by now and said: That's it. I'm done.

But instead she couldn't wait for her Tuesday evenings. She lived for Tuesday. Sienna wished she could see Adam more frequently. Every day, every minute, but that was impossible. Being with Adam was a secret adventure away from her life, not a part of it.

Adam was becoming like an addiction. She had thought it would have been a one-time deal, maybe even a wild weekend. She was long past that. It was no one but Adam for her. She dropped her Tuesday night bowling league, declined dates, made excuses to her family, and did everything in her power to make herself completely available for this guy.

Was he worth it? Her footsteps faltered as the question snuck into her thoughts. He was for the moment. *Just live for the moment,* Sienna decided as she walked on. *Don't think about the future.*

She arrived at the pool hall just in time. Sienna went around back, her feet kicking the gravel from the parking lot until she reached the back door. She opened it as if she had every reason to be there and quickly entered. Climbing up the rickety steps to the second floor, Sienna suddenly faced the door to Adam's apartment.

Her pulse gave a sharp kick like it always did. Sienna knocked briskly on the door and took a deep, calming breath. *Please be there. . . . Please be there. . . .* She didn't want to wait another minute to see him again.

Her heart lurched when she heard the scrape of the door lock. So much for the calming breathing technique. Her blood roared in her ears when the door opened and revealed Adam.

Sienna struggled not to drop her jaw. Adam Taylor wore nothing but a pair of faded jeans. Her eyes went from his long bare feet up the soft, torn denim to the rippled muscles of his abdomen.

Her breath caught in her throat when she saw the whitened scars puckering his hard chest and the fierce dragon tattoo coiled on his large shoulder. She knew each mark on his body had a fascinating story behind it, but Adam never talked about his past.

Sienna looked in his face and, as always, her heart squeezed and turned over.

She wasn't sure why she always reacted that way. Adam was not a handsome man. There were too many lines, too many sharp angles. But it was his eyes that always ensnared her. Dark blue and weary, they held a wealth of secrets and pain.

"You were almost late," Adam said as he let her into his apartment.

"I'm sorry. I—" Her words trickled off when she saw a leather hammock suspended by metal chains hanging from the ceiling of his sparse apartment. "What is that?"

"That is a sling."

A *sling*? Adam said it so casually, as if he'd said "a chair" or "the coffee table." He acted like there was nothing unusual about having a sexual apparatus in the middle of a studio apartment.

Sienna couldn't take her eyes off of it. She didn't remember mentioning anything about a *sling* in her list of fantasies. Getting tied up, yes. She looked at the cuffs on the sling for the arms and legs and decided that didn't count. She wanted to be bound or strapped down, not flying in midair.

Sienna chewed on her bottom lip. Trust Adam to spring this on her. He always kept her off balance and second-guessing. That was usually part of the fun.

"Take off your shoes."

Her body jerked as Adam's smoky voice curled around her. Those words were the signal that their scene was beginning. Her sex immediately heated as her nipples tightened. After so many months, her senses were conditioned and primed for their next sensual encounter.

She slowly shucked off her boots, taking another long look at the sling. When her feet were bare, she stood to her full height. Adam stepped behind her, his chest pressing against her spine.

Sienna turned to him, gladly taking her eyes off of the sling. She stood on her tiptoes and kissed him, sighing with pleasure as his lips claimed hers. His mouth slowly, thoroughly tasted hers until she was clinging to him.

Adam reached the hem of her shirt and bunched the cotton in his hands. Her stomach clenched with anticipation. Sienna took a step back and raised her arms, allowing Adam to whisk off her shirt. She wore nothing underneath and her nipples puckered under his hot gaze.

He curled his fingers around the waistband of her cargo pants. She loved the intense look on his face when he dragged her clothes down to her feet. She kicked them aside and stood before him naked.

"Are you ready for the sling?" His voice was a low, soft growl.

She looked at it over her shoulder. It appeared cold and foreign. Sienna suddenly felt sick with nerves. She swallowed back the metallic taste of panic. "I thought we were working toward the dress."

She couldn't wait to be bound in an oriental rope dress, and Adam knew it. She wanted the ropes and knots crisscrossing her body. It was the most beautiful, erotic image she had ever seen, and Adam was her only chance to achieve it for herself.

Sienna had first seen it in an adult magazine an ex-boyfriend tried to hide from her. He had been turned off by the sight, but she had been secretly aroused. Unfortunately her ex-boyfriend had not been interested in a little bondage. In fact, he had been horrified, and it had been the turning point of their relationship. He accused her of not being the sweet girl he thought she was.

When she met Adam, he saw that "Sweet Sienna" was a guise. It was as if they shared an instant connection. They were kindred spirits, but when she discovered he knew all about ropes and knots, she knew they were destined to be together. She would finally have her rope dress.

Or so she thought. She had been bound, cuffed and clamped down, but he had yet to rope her breasts or hips.

"You need to work up to it," Adam said as he gestured toward the sling.

She tried not to glare at him. Adam always said that, but never gave her the opportunity to work toward her goal. "But I thought—"

Adam placed his finger against her lips. "Do I need to gag you?"

She shook her head. Sienna knew Adam was teasing her, but she didn't want to push her luck. She gave up trying to change his mind and cautiously lay down on the leather sling. Sienna grabbed for the chain as the sling careened.

Adam uncurled her fingers from the metal. "I got you," he promised before he cuffed her arms to the sling.

The metal-and-leather contraption rocked like a pendulum as Adam cuffed her feet. When he was done she was outstretched for his perusal. Sienna felt the moisture dripping from her core and couldn't hide her building excitement. She was open and supine, suspended in the air.

Sienna shifted her hips and the sling lurched. She cried out, but she had nothing to grab on to. Her world spun as she tried to keep the sling still.

"Relax." Adam held the chain until the sling stopped moving.

She nodded, but thought his order was impossible. Not that she could tell him that. She didn't want to fail. Half the fun was testing her boundaries, pushing further than she expected and redefining what she could and couldn't do.

Adam caressed her body, his hands large, warm and calloused. They were male hands, gentle and protective, but they could be playful or domineering. His touch teased her senses and, little by little, the tension seeped away from her muscles.

He stroked her breasts and tweaked her nipples until she was tossing her head from side to side. Adam leaned over and sucked her reddened nipples. Sienna arched up and the sling weaved in the air like a flying magic carpet.

She jerked in surprise and slammed her body back down on the leather, which caused the sling to pitch and ripple.

"You can't control the sling," Adam said gently as he skimmed his hands down her stomach.

Her muscles bunched under his fingertips. "I know," she said breathlessly.

"Give up and go with the motion."

She was trying. She really was. Sienna closed her eyes and tried again. The movement of the sling gradually slowed down. The creaking of the chains quieted. When Adam reached down and caressed her clit, the sling was the last thing on her mind.

Her breath hitched in her throat as he drew small, lazy circles along the folds of her sex. Sienna couldn't help but buck against his hands. The sling rocked, and she fought her instincts to struggle against the waving motions.

Adam dipped his finger and pumped into her wet, tight core. Her hips bucked and jerked as the sling moved side to side. The sling moved counterclockwise to Adam's hand. And then, without even realizing it, she started to move with the sling.

Sienna forgot about the chains holding her up. The leather at her back no longer existed. She came suddenly, like a flash of lightning. She arched her back, her fingers wide out, her eyes squeezed shut. She felt like she was free-falling and nothing was there to catch her. A bright white energy swept through her. She was floating.

She had done it. Sienna felt her mouth tug into a tired, satisfied smile. Only when she was with Adam did she feel like she could do anything. Be anyone.

But it was just pretend.

Sienna's smile dipped. Or was everything outside Adam's door the pretense?

CHAPTER NINE

"**S**ienna." Lizzie, Sienna's coworker, glided up to the reception desk Wednesday morning and rested her elbows on the high counter. "I know this nice man who would be perfect for you."

"I don't do nice," Sienna said with a smile.

"Yeah, right." Lizzie rolled her eyes. "Seriously, David is a friend of my brother's and I thought you guys would be perfect together."

"No, I couldn't. I'm—" She stopped herself just in time before she mentioned Adam's name. The man was always in her thoughts and she sometimes forgot that no one else knew of her double life. "I'm not interested."

"Come on," Lizzie pleaded as she leaned over the edge of the reception desk. "You need to go out just once in a while."

"I do," Sienna protested, but she knew she'd curtailed her social life in the past few months.

"Really?" Her friend's tone was dubious. "What did you do last week?"

Sienna thought about it. It hadn't been a particularly busy week. "I went to my grandmother's birthday, and my cousin needed help—"

"Let me rephrase the question," Lizzie interrupted. "Did you do anything that wasn't a family event?"

"Sure, one of my friends took me to her knitting club."

"Knitting club?" An expression of horror floated over Lizzie's face. "You need to go out places where you can meet a man."

"No, that's not necessary." She had found her man, and met him every Tuesday. Adam had never been to her place, which was just as well. If he saw the country casual look, the embroidery project, or even the collection of family photos, he would make a run for it.

And with Adam, she really didn't want to go anywhere. She was with him for just one reason: so he would help her explore her sensual boundaries with bondage. If she went out somewhere, that would be like a date, and she might see him more as a boyfriend than a sex partner.

"You should really go out with David," Lizzie insisted. "I'll give him your number."

"No, you won't." Sienna's voice sharpened.

"Your e-mail address?"

"No."

"Why not?" Lizzie asked with a hint of exasperation. "You don't date."

"I—" She stopped, unsure how to explain her feelings. She didn't want to date, but no one in her small world would understand it. She wasn't looking for a man to settle down with. Right now she wanted to have sex. A particular type of mind-blowing sex, and lots of it. She'd take that over working on a relationship. At least, for now.

"Exactly what I thought." Lizzie tapped her hand on the desk. "That's why you need to go out with David."

"Why aren't *you* going out with him?"

"Me? No way." She shook her head and her large hoop earrings jingled. "I'm a free spirit, and David is not the type to have a fling with. He's one of those you marry and have kids with. He would rather spend the weekend fixing up a house than go to the club."

Sienna stared at Lizzie. "You think I'm attracted to that kind of guy?"

"You are like two peas in a pod," Lizzie exclaimed. "Give me one good reason why you won't go out with him this Friday."

Because he probably isn't into bondage? Because he doesn't want to see the naughty side of me? Because he doesn't have dark blue eyes that glow—

"Uh-oh." Lizzie stood up straight. "Here comes Amber. Look busy. Act like we're talking about something business-y."

Sienna automatically grabbed a sheaf of papers and tapped them into a straight pile. She couldn't remember a time when she was happier to see her tough-as-nails boss.

"So I'll have him confirm the time with you," Lizzie said in a brisk, professional voice before stepping away from the desk.

"Huh?" Sienna frowned at her friend until Lizzie mouthed the word David. Oh, now she understood. "I—uh . . ."

"Is there a problem, Sienna?" Amber asked. Her stiletto heels clacking on the floor sounded like a machine gun opening fire.

"No," Sienna responded brightly as Lizzie slipped away. She wished she could grab her friend by the collar and haul her back. She had never agreed to meet with David.

Amber gave Sienna a searching look but didn't say anything. The arch of her eyebrow pretty much said it all before she strode off.

Sienna kept her smile up until her boss turned the corner. Had she just agreed to go on a date? She couldn't go on one. It didn't feel right. It felt like cheating.

But was it cheating? She didn't have an agreement with Adam. They weren't a "couple." For all she knew, he could be banging other women on the other six nights.

Her stomach cramped at the thought, and Sienna hunched over. She had never thought of that before. Adam had always been *hers*. Her secret. Her fantasy. Her man.

Now that the possibility was in her head, she couldn't get it out. Damn, why did Lizzie have to start up with this? She picked up the department mail and started to go through it, needing to keep busy. She came across an interoffice envelope with her name on it. Opening it up, she peered inside and found a lush purple fabric.

Sienna reached in and felt silk. She pulled out the long fabric, her eyes getting wide as the purple unraveled before her eyes. What was this? Why was someone in the office sending her this scarf? She checked the interoffice envelope and her name really was on it.

She looked inside the envelope and saw some laminated paper. Sienna pulled it out, suddenly overcome with a sense of foreboding when she started to read it.

Dear Friend,

I am offering you the chance of a lifetime. You can live out your ultimate fantasy within one week of receiving this gift, provided you pass it on. All that is required from you is this: You must use the scarf during a sexual encounter in the next seven days.

Mail the scarf and this letter to a female acquaintance within one week of receiving this package. Do not tell or discuss it with the woman. Those who follow these instructions will continue a fulfilling sensual odyssey. Those who don't will never find satisfaction for as long as they live.

Kali

Oh, no. The letter fell from Sienna's hands and slid along her polished desktop. *Oh, nooo!* Sienna clapped a shaky hand over her mouth as her heart pounded in her chest. Someone knew about her secret. Someone in this office.

She peeked over her desk, almost too scared to look. Her coworkers were busy at work. No one was sneaking a look at her. No one was waiting to tell her it was all a joke.

Someone knew about her.

And they were letting her know it.

The knock startled Adam. He turned and looked at the door. It wasn't Tuesday, and Sienna was the only visitor he had.

He was tempted to ignore it. Nothing good ever came out of unannounced visitors, but curiosity won out. Adam strode across the room and answered the door. "Sienna?"

"Can I come in?" she asked, clearly agitated as she speared her hand through her thick black hair.

"Sure," he said, and stepped back to let her enter. Adam took in Sienna's appearance and slowly blinked. He hadn't seen her like this before, dressed in a bright blue floral dress and matching heels. She looked beautiful and wholesome. The effect was jarring compared to what he was used to, and he wasn't sure which version of Sienna he liked best.

She pivoted on her flirty kitten heels and faced him. "I'm sorry I didn't call first."

"Don't be." He frowned as she tightly folded her arms across her chest. It was as if she were holding herself together. "What's wrong?"

She pursed her lips as regret flashed in her eyes. "I came to tell you that we need to end this."

"End . . . this?" Was she talking about their meetings? Their scenes? He felt like someone punched him. "Why?"

"I got this at work today." She reached into her large purse, pulled out a purple scarf and held it out to him.

Jealousy pierced through him like a jagged fork of lightning. Who gave her a sensual gift like that? How well did this guy know her, and why was Sienna showing it to him?

He took the scarf from her and stared at the deep purple, wishing he could give something that luxurious to Sienna. All he could give her was a good time.

"It came with this letter." She reached in her purse again and revealed a laminated note. The paper was brown with age.

She wanted him to read it? Did she think he really wanted to know how another man felt about her?

He reluctantly took the note and scanned it. He stopped and glanced up when he realized he had it all wrong. This wasn't from some lovelorn guy. Adam read it again, and still wasn't sure if he understood what was going on.

Adam held up the note. "Someone sent you a chain letter, and you want to call it quits?"

"Not just any chain letter," Sienna insisted. "It's about *bondage*."

He skimmed through the letter again. The word "bondage" never came up, nor was there any mention about being bound or tied up. "They're not specific about that."

"They don't have to be. It's kind of obvious when the scarf comes with the letter."

Adam couldn't argue with that, but then he saw bondage situations and props where others didn't.

"Don't you see what this means? Someone knows!" She started to pace. "I don't know how, but someone found out that I'm into bondage." Her voice hitched on the last few words.

He didn't think it meant that at all. Sienna got a chain letter that also happened to be about something she was secretive about. She was being paranoid, and it was going to take some time convincing her otherwise.

"Someone is taunting me with this knowledge. They're going to blab all over town." She gasped and her face went pale. "My *grandmother* is going to hear about this!"

Adam shrugged his shoulders. "So what?"

"So what?" she screeched, and slapped her hands on her forehead. "If word got around that Sweet Sienna liked being tied up, I would be put through hell!"

He wanted to gather her in his arms and tell her everything was going to be okay, but Sienna looked like she would bolt if he touched her. "You and I are consenting adults," Adam reminded her. "What goes on between us is no one else's business."

Sienna scoffed. "That is so easy for you to say. No one dares get into your business."

She had a point. When he moved to town a few years back, the solid, upright citizens took one look at him and kept their distance.

"I deal with people every day," she said as she started to pace again. "There's my work, my family, my friends . . . I'm dealing with someone almost every minute of my life. And that's not a problem, as long as I fit the label of nice girl."

Okay, maybe he didn't understand the full ramifications if someone had this kind of gossip spread about them. Was bondage illegal in this town and he just didn't know it, or were all sex acts considered immoral? "Worst case scenario, what would happen if word got out?"

Sienna flipped her hair out of her eyes and put her hands on her hips. "You mean besides becoming a social outcast, getting disowned from my family and losing my job that I got in the first place because of my clean-cut image? I don't even know how others are going to react when they realize my nice-girl act is nothing but a sham."

"It's not a sham." Even when she was dressed to blend into the pool hall, she couldn't hide the taint of respectability. She was a nice girl with a deep wild streak that she hadn't begun to tap into.

"Sometimes it feels like it is," she said wearily and looked away. "I don't want to talk about it. I came by to tell you I have to end this."

He had to stop her, but he didn't know what to say that would change her mind. "You're giving up something because of what people might think?"

She hesitated. "No, but this is a wake-up call. I need to stop now before it's too difficult to stop."

Sienna was already at that point and she had no idea. "Do you think you can stop?"

"Sure." She plucked the letter from his hand.

"Then why did you come here?"

"To tell you, of course." She didn't look at him as she stuffed the letter back in her purse.

"You could have called. Or not showed up."

She glanced up in surprise. "I couldn't have done that."

"Sure you could." Then again, the woman had ingrained good manners and a code of conduct he sometimes found baffling. "But you know what I think?"

She stiffened as if his low voice alerted her of trouble. "What?"

He took a step closer. "I think you want me to convince you to keep doing it."

"No, I don't." She reached for the scarf, but he dodged her hand and held the silk out of reach.

"You don't want to give it up," he told her. "It's already a part of you."

Her eyes narrowed. "It is not."

Adam shook the scarf in front of her. "Think you can enjoy sex without bondage?"

She lifted her chin with defiance. "Yes."

"Without me?"

"Yes."

If he hadn't seen the expression on her face, he would have crumbled from the pain of the automatic rejection. "That's a shame," he said softly.

"I'll be going now. And I'll take that." Her hand was outstretched.

Adam looked at her hand and then back in her eyes. "Why? You aren't planning to use it."

She reared her head back. "Are you?"

"Maybe." He held the scarf up and inspected it. "The gold threads will give an extra bite to the skin, don't you think?"

"Give it back." She made an unsuccessful grab for it. "I need to find out who sent it to me."

"And do what? Your best option is to ignore the chain letter. Or . . ." He lowered his arm as another idea occurred to him.

"Or?"

He held the ends of the scarf with both hands and started to twist the silk into a tight rope. "Use it for its intended purpose."

She looked at him like he was crazy. "Haven't you been listening to me? I'm not doing any more scenes with you. I'm not visiting you anymore."

"You have seven days to use this," he reminded her. "Why not do it?"

She vehemently shook her head. "And give someone seven days to catch me in the act?"

"You're safe here." He had gone to great lengths to protect Sienna and their time together. It was a point of pride to him.

"I thought so, but obviously not." She glanced at the windows. The shades were drawn, but that seemed to bother Sienna more. It was as if she knew someone was out there and she couldn't see who it was.

"Come visit me every day this week," Adam suggested. He ignored her outright rejection. "At the end of the week, you can decide whether or not you want to continue."

"I've already made my decision."

"No, you're letting someone else make the decision for you." Adam's voice took on a hard edge and he didn't try to soften it. "You're letting your fears get the best of you."

Sienna made a face, but it couldn't hide that his words had found their mark. "And a week of getting tied up will cure me of my fears?"

"No, but then you'll know what you really want to do." He turned and walked to the door. "And I'll give you back the scarf after the seven days."

She frowned. "Why?"

"You will have earned it."

Sienna bit her bottom lip and stared at the scarf in his hands.

"So what's your decision?" he asked as he grabbed the handle to the front door.

"It's a deal," she said softly.

"Good." Satisfaction mingled with relief flooded his chest. "Take off your shoes."

She flinched at his change in attitude. "Now?"

"You only have seven days," Adam said as reached for the lock to his front door and shoved the bolt home. "We need to use every minute we can."

CHAPTER TEN

Sienna's mouth gaped open. "Are you serious?"

"Yeah." He gave her a strange look, as if he was surprised that she wasn't jumping at his offer. "Why are you asking?"

She had been so ready to forgo their scenes, and now she was given a seven-day reprieve. She was going to make the most of this time and fulfill the rest of her fantasies.

"You have nothing prepared." Her body was ready as awareness twanged through her muscles. His words gave a kick to her blood and her skin tingled. An ache of desire pooled low in her belly, and her breasts felt full and heavy. She felt alive and crackling with energy.

Adam shrugged. "I'll improvise."

"You can't do that." She didn't know why she was arguing. She wanted this, but at the same time she knew she shouldn't have agreed to an extra seven days. "You're the one who always says you can't be spontaneous if you want a safe and satisfying scene."

He leaned against the door and slid his hands into his jeans pockets. "You'll have to trust me on this."

Sienna realized she had an opportunity and wanted to seize on it. "If you have nothing planned, then I say we should do the rope dress."

Adam shook his head. "No."

"Why not? Why do you always refuse to give me the rope dress?"

"You're not ready for it," Adam said.

"You always say that." She wanted to stomp her foot. "I only have seven days."

Her argument didn't sway him. "I wasn't expecting you today and I have to be in the pool hall. A rope dress takes time that I don't have right now."

"Oh." Now she felt stupid for her outburst. "I'm sorry."

It was easy to forget that Adam had a life outside his apartment. She liked the illusion that he had no interest other than her. It was heady and seductive to think he was there simply for her pleasure.

"Take off your shoes," Adam said, his voice taking on a rough edge. "Don't make me repeat it."

She never had to make him say it twice, and she wouldn't dare make him say it a third time. She didn't want to contemplate the consequences. Sienna hurriedly slid her feet out of the blue heels and stood before Adam in her stocking feet.

He was silent for a moment. "Undress for me."

She looked at Adam just as he had trained her. Sienna watched him, but didn't give him eye contact. He preferred a demure stance, when she watched him from under her eyelashes.

She reached for the belt of her dress. Her fingers shook as she removed it from her waist. It didn't matter how many times she undressed for him; it always felt like a new experience because she didn't know what was going to happen next.

"Why are you looking at the door?"

She jumped and her gaze darted to his face. She didn't realize her attention had drifted. Now Adam looked annoyed, which was rare.

She ducked her head and whispered, "I'm sorry."

"That doesn't answer my question." His voice was gruff.

"I keep thinking that someone is going to walk through that door and see us."

His frown deepened, but Adam's voice was calm and reassuring. "I locked the door and no one is coming up here."

"I know." She knew that, but she couldn't shake off the feeling.

Adam crossed his arms. "Keep undressing."

She reached for the top of her dress and slowly unbuttoned it to the hem. She hesitated before she peeled the dress off her body. Sienna winced, knowing the moment of indecision was going to cost her.

"What is going on?" He pushed off the door and stood toe-to-toe with her. "Do we need to end this scene?"

"No!" Sienna's eyes widened with alarm. They hadn't had to abruptly end a scene for months. Adam had done it only when he sensed she wasn't ready, but that was when she was a novice. It was a matter of pride that she could do whatever he asked.

"Are you sure?"

"Adam"—her voice came out as a plea—"we only have seven more days. You don't want to waste them."

"I will if you can't focus."

"I can't help it. What if someone can see us?" She shuddered at the possibility and held her dress tight against her chest.

"It's your imagination. Look around us." He gestured at the windows. "The shades are drawn."

"Someone must have seen something," she insisted. "How else would they have known to send me a scarf?"

Adam speared his hand in his hair. "Sienna, stop thinking about what goes on outside that door."

It was too late. Someone had already invaded her sanctuary when they sent the chain letter. Her fantasy life was breaking up and, if she wasn't careful, it was going to turn into a nightmare when she stepped back into the real world.

"Don't think about anything but us," Adam suggested.

There wouldn't be any more "us" in seven days, but she didn't need to remind him. She wasn't ready for that moment, but she had to make the most out of the time she had left.

"Okay." She gave a sharp nod. "I'm ready to continue."

"We'll see about that."

Great. Now she had managed to aggravate him. She had to do better.

Sienna quickly removed her dress and let it fall to the floor. Now she only wore her bra, underwear and pantyhose.

She wished she hadn't worn the pantyhose. Sienna rolled the nylon past her hips and down her legs. It wasn't a very attractive look and there was a jagged run that she hadn't known about. She didn't want Adam to have any lasting memories of her looking like this.

She stripped off her bra and underwear and stood naked before Adam. She bowed her head in deference, and her hands were clasped in front of her.

I hope no one can see in. . . . The unbidden thought flashed in her mind before she could stop it. She tried not to react or take another peek at the door. She had to trust that Adam would keep her safe and hidden.

She stayed in the dutiful position, waiting for Adam's next command. The minutes stretched. Sienna tapped down the worry building inside her. The uncertainty and anticipation heated her blood as her pulse quickened.

Why was Adam making her wait? Was it punishment for hesitating? Did he know the thickening silence made her nipples hard? Or was he simply distracted? She took a sidelong glance but saw nothing.

Adam stepped forward and Sienna jumped in surprise at the sudden movement. She immediately went back into position. Her muscles tightened and locked. The pulse in her neck fluttered against her skin.

"Much better," Adam said. "Stay still. Don't move a muscle."

He cupped her face with his large hands. His touch was gentle and sure. She wanted to sigh, enjoying the moment of feeling cherished.

Adam lowered his head and kissed her. Long, wet kisses that she felt all the way to her toes. Sienna clenched her hands together, her fingers stinging from the exertion, when she really wanted to grab Adam by his shirt and pull him closer.

He lifted his head. "You aren't staying still. I want you to be motionless."

She thought she was, but sometimes she forgot her self-discipline when Adam touched her. Sienna planted her feet more firmly on the floor, bracing herself for whatever happened next.

Adam continued to kiss her as he drifted his hands down her back. His touch was so light that it almost tickled. She shivered with pleasure and ruthlessly stopped. She wasn't allowed to move.

The shiver echoed inside of her. She was vibrating with need and it was difficult to stand still when her knees were caving in. Her restraint was slipping and she didn't know any tricks to regain it.

Adam cupped her bare ass with his hands. She felt her knees wobble but she stood rigid. He roughly kneaded her buttocks, growling with admiration in the back of his throat. When he teased her puckered rosebud with his finger, Sienna couldn't help it. She arched against him.

"You moved," he said against her mouth.

He didn't have to sound so smug about it, Sienna decided. She couldn't help it. She bet he would have jumped had their roles been reversed.

"I need to bind you," he announced.

Her sex flooded at his words, but Sienna showed no expression. She didn't say a word as her body sang with expectancy. Her heart raced as he guided her to the simple bed.

"Lie down face-first," Adam told her softly.

Oooh, boy. Her stomach pinched at the request. He was already taking away one of her senses by limiting her vision. She wouldn't be able to predict Adam's moves.

She lay in the center of the bed. The mattress was firm and unyielding, much like its owner. Her nipples poked against the cool cotton sheets.

"Tuck your knees underneath you."

Sienna followed his orders. Adam reached for her ankles and spread her legs far apart. The position made her more vulnerable as her ass tilted high up in the air. It was disconcerting to fully expose her sex to him.

He bound her ankles with ropes at the bottom corners of the bed. Next, he took her wrists and drew them back beside her legs. He cuffed her wrists with more ropes tied to the bottom corners. She pulled at the ones holding her wrists and found that they rendered her motionless.

Adam stood at the foot of the bed right behind her. He trailed his hands along her legs and ass. "You're so ready for me," he said after he slid his fingers along her wet slit.

It was true. She was almost embarrassed by how easy it was for him to arouse her. It never took long for her to be wet and ready for Adam.

She heard the rustling of his clothes and her stomach gave an excited flip. She felt the tip of his cock pressing against the slick folds of her sex. Sienna groaned as he slowly, relentlessly, filled her to the hilt. She rocked against him and felt the sting of her binds.

Adam grabbed her hips and surged into her again. Sienna gasped as heat darted through her. She tried to meet each deep thrust, but the ties stopped her. The thick heat enveloped her body, clouding her mind until all she could think about was Adam and the pleasure building inside her, ready to explode.

Adam pulled at her hips as he gave a wild thrust, and then another. Sienna cried out as the sharp bite of the binds mingled with the pleasure, overwhelming her. They swirled and coiled inside her, transforming into something so intense that she couldn't breathe. She gasped for air, the burning sensations pressing in her chest.

She thought she was going to burst out of her skin. The pressure built faster and faster. The ache in her sex was almost too much to bear until suddenly the tight coil of desire deep in her belly splintered. Her mind tumbled and soared as the climax pulsed through her.

Sienna gulped for air, her throat rough, her lungs burning. She nestled deeper into a pillow and realized it hadn't been there before. She slowly became aware of her surroundings, along with every twinge and pain in her body.

She was hot and sore. Her wrists and ankles were raw, but she was no longer bound. She felt the mattress dip as Adam lay next to her. He turned her over and curled her body against his.

She closed her eyes, allowing Adam's soft praise to tumble over her. She sighed and gratefully accepted his body heat.

She only had seven more days of this. She wasn't ready to give it up. What made her think she would be strong enough a week from now?

CHAPTER ELEVEN

A dam looked at the wall clock high above the pool players and knew he had to leave. He felt bad about it, but not bad enough to ignore the fact that Sienna was at his front door, waiting for him.

He looked around the pool hall. It was busy for a Thursday night, and he shouldn't leave it all to Bill. The old, crotchety man might be able to deal with the patrons for a while, but he'd tire fast. Not that Bill would ever admit to the fact.

If only he and Sienna could have met at a different time. Adam looked at the clock again. Why didn't Sienna rearrange her schedule? What was more important than a scene with him?

It was hard for him to believe, but there was a lot he didn't know about Sienna Bailey. He knew her deepest secrets and how to make her purr like a satisfied cat, but he didn't know her friends or what she liked to eat.

He didn't know basic stuff about Sienna and that bothered him. Maybe that was why he barely got any sleep last night. Sienna was going to leave after the seven days were up. He might share a special connection with her, but it didn't hold up with the rest of her life.

He didn't think he would get the chance to strengthen the link between them. When they first met at the pool hall, Sienna wanted to hide the relationship with Adam. At the time, that was fine with him. He was used to being in the shadows, hidden like a dangerous secret. His forbidden presence in a woman's life made the trysts feel more taboo.

Now being a secret in Sienna's life bothered him. Soon he was going to be forgotten altogether. Adam sighed roughly and stepped away from the counter.

"Bill, I have to leave and I don't know how long it will take. Are you going to be able to handle this crowd alone?"

"No problem." He gave Adam a sidelong glance. "Have a hot date tonight?"

Adam stopped walking and turned to look at his employee. There was something in Bill's voice that made him pause. "Say what?"

Bill lifted one shoulder. "It's not like me to get in other people's business."

What he said was true, which was the deciding factor in why Adam hired him. The older man seemed to know everything that went on, which came in handy. He usually kept his mouth shut, which proved to be essential. "But?" Adam prompted.

Bill pulled off his baseball cap and curved it with his hands. "I notice Paul's little girl hanging around here a lot."

Adam frowned. Who was Paul's girl? For that matter, who the hell was Paul? "Paul's girl?"

"Bailey. Which daughter is she?" He looked off in the distance as he tried to remember the name. "Sienna! That's the one."

A tightness settled in Adam's chest. "What about her?"

"She's been showing up every Tuesday, but I don't see her play pool." Bill kept his eyes on his fingers as he bent the baseball cap. "That's fine by me."

Adam watched him for a moment. "Then why are you mentioning it?"

"The schedule changed this week." Bill put his cap back on. "Now she's showing up every day."

Adam didn't like how Bill tracked their movements. Were they that obvious, or did his employee have something more to it? Did he send the scarf to Sienna?

Adam studied the older man and immediately discarded the idea. Sienna received the scarf at work, which made it unlikely for someone like Bill to send it there. Anyway, Bill was not the chain-letter kind of guy.

"Sienna is a sweet girl," Bill continued, adjusting the brim of his cap. "Her dad and I go a long way back."

Adam stared at Bill. The man obviously had a point, but he was going around it in circles. "Do you have something to say?"

The older man dropped his hands and pierced Adam with a long, hard look. "Sienna is the type of girl you marry. Not the kind you fool around with."

"Is that right?" Adam arched one eyebrow. He thought Sienna was the kind to do both.

"Hell, everyone can tell that. She's not in your league, Adam. If you're not careful, she's going to fall in love with you and start talking china patterns."

Why did people think he was allergic to relationships and love? Because of the way he looked? Maybe he wanted her to fall in love with him. "What do china patterns have to do with anything?"

"Getting married," Bill clarified, slapping one hand over the other. "You know, mortgages, children, the whole shebang."

"Ah, got it." Adam had a very hazy image of being married to Sienna. The home would be warm and comfortable. She would stay in his bed all night and wake up next to him in the morning.

It wasn't all that bad, especially if they got to create a life together. In fact, he kind of liked the idea.

"All I'm saying"—Bill raised a gnarled hand—"is that you guys are getting serious. If you're not careful, you're going to get stuck in a shotgun wedding."

"Thanks, Bill." Adam gave him a pat on the back. "But you have nothing to worry about. I bet by this time next week, Sienna and I will be history."

"Why?" Bill frowned and the wrinkles seemed more pronounced. "Are you planning to dump her and break her heart?"

First the old man wanted him to stay away from Sienna, and now he was worried about how he was going to do it. Adam wanted to roll his eyes at it all. "No, that's not my plan. I have to go now."

"If I need you," Bill called after him, "I'll know where to find you."

"Bother me and you're fired." He walked away with the old man's knowing chuckle ringing in his ears.

So his rendezvous with Sienna had gained more attention than they realized, Adam thought as he left the building and went around the back. He should have known they wouldn't have gone undetected, but he was surprised that no one other than Bill had said something to him.

Maybe Sienna was wrong. It was possible that no one would bother her about her association with him since they were consenting adults. He would love to use this argument, but he thought it would backfire. If she knew anyone was aware of her secret, she would immediately stop coming around.

If he knew what was good for him, he should accept the inevitable with grace. Their relationship was doomed from the beginning, and it couldn't continue. The real world was going to crash in on them sooner or later. This way they controlled how it would end.

That didn't make him feel any better, Adam decided as he climbed up the stairs to his apartment. He wasn't ready to give up Sienna.

He stopped in his tracks when he saw Sienna waiting for him at his door. She looked different, and he couldn't figure out what it was that made him think that. She wore a navy blue hoodie and faded jeans. Her body was completely hidden from him.

That was the difference, he realized. Whether she was casually dressed or more formal, like yesterday, her clothing didn't usually conceal her curves. Why did she choose to wear something bulky today? He wondered about that. Was she already distancing herself? If that was the case, he was going to get those clothes off of her as soon as possible.

"Hi, Adam," she said with a smile, her hands tucked deep in her hoodie.

"Been waiting long?"

She gave a halfhearted shrug. "Not really, but it felt strange that you weren't here."

He bet it did. Knowing someone was waiting for you was seductive, but when that person was prepared to lavish attention and to pleasure you, the feeling was out of this world. Yet she was prepared to throw it all away because she thought someone knew about them.

He felt a flash of resentment and quickly banked it. There was no room for negative feelings in his plans tonight. He had to stay focused on pleasuring Sienna. Adam opened the door to his apartment and escorted her inside. He turned on the lights and closed the door, automatically locking it.

She stopped in the middle of the studio apartment. "Wow." She pulled at the neck of her hoodie. "It's warm in here."

He was surprised she had noticed right away. He had turned up the thermostat for their scene, but he didn't explain, not wanting to give her a hint of what was in store for her. "Take off your shoes," he said as he walked to the windows and pulled the shades down.

When he turned to her, he noticed that she hadn't followed his directions. She stood by the door, her hands still in her pockets. "Is there a problem?" he asked.

"Are you in a rush?"

He was, but he shouldn't be. He wanted to pack so much pleasure into seven days, and it was impossible. Adam closed his eyes and took a deep breath. "Take off your shoes and clothes. I have to get something from the kitchen. When I get back, I want to see you naked and lying faceup on my bed."

Adam pivoted on his heel and strode into his minuscule kitchen.

He didn't check to see if Sienna was following his directions this time. If she disobeyed, he wouldn't repeat them. He would send her home. He didn't want to, but he had to exert his dominance. He would give up his pleasure for that.

He went to the freezer and opened the door. He pulled out the popsicles he had made out of ice. He grabbed two and tossed them in a metal bowl that was set on the counter.

When Adam stepped back into the room, he found Sienna naked and lying on his bed. Satisfaction bloomed in his chest. This was what turned him on. He got a charge every time he told Sienna what to do and she followed it. Of course, it wouldn't be as much fun if she didn't have a strong will to match his own.

He walked to the bed and put the bowl on the table nearby. The clank of metal drew Sienna's attention. She frowned when she saw the bowl. It obviously wasn't what she expected him to bring.

"What's in there?" she asked.

"You'll find out."

She opened her mouth. He leaned over the bed and placed his finger on her lips to silence her. "No talking."

She pressed her lips together. Her eyes glittered with annoyance. Sienna never liked being told to be quiet.

He straightened to his full height. Bracing his legs apart, he told her, "Now get up and undress me."

Sienna scurried off the bed and stood beside him. Her eagerness humbled him. She reached for his shirt and pulled it over his head before tossing it to the floor. She stared at his chest and licked her lips.

"May I touch you?" she asked, unable to take her eyes off of his dragon tattoo.

"Yes." He sounded calm, but he was desperate for her touch.

She skimmed her fingers along the dragon before she explored every scar on his arms and chest. He hissed when her fingernail caught his nipple.

His cock was hard and ready. Her rapt attention and eagerness to please made his blood pump fast through his veins. He knew she would do anything he asked. A sense of absolute power flooded through him. The sensation was almost too painful for him to take his next breath.

"Take off the rest of my clothes." His voice sounded rough to his ears.

Sienna reached for his jeans and quickly pushed the denim and underwear down his legs. She crouched before him as she removed the clothes pooled at his feet.

After she pushed the clothes to the side, Sienna rubbed her hands along his legs. She followed the muscles and sinew up to his hips before grasping his cock. She caressed him with delicate strokes of her fingertips and then wrapped her hands around his length.

Adam placed his hand on her head. "Sienna, did I say that you could touch me again?"

She froze when she realized her error. Her hands squeezed his cock. Adam grimaced but remained still. There was nothing he would like better than to have Sienna jack him off or lick his balls, but tonight wasn't all about his pleasure. He was determined to show Sienna all she would miss.

"I'm sorry," she said meekly as she reluctantly dropped her hands.

He ached for her touch. He could cup the back of her head and plunge his cock into her mouth, knowing she would suck him dry. It took a monumental effort to focus on doing the scene he had planned.

"You need to practice your restraint," he told Sienna hoarsely. "Lie down in the center of the bed and face the ceiling."

Sienna followed his orders quickly, ready to make him happy after her mistake. She didn't even risk a glance at him because that was not included in his directions. His cock jumped with pleasure at this example of her obedience.

"Stretch out your arms and legs," he told her. She did so without hesitation. Adam grabbed the ropes dangling at the bed corners and bound her wrists and ankles with practiced ease.

He stepped away from the bed and surveyed his handiwork. With a few well-placed square knots, Sienna was spread-eagled on his bed, waiting impatiently for his next move. Her nipples were tight and hard, and he could see how wet her dark pink core was for him.

He looked at Sienna's face. She was watching him now, trying to predict his next move. Her gaze darted to the metal bowl on the side table.

"I have something special for you." He reached in the bowl and pulled out a popsicle. It was already melting, and the icy water splashed on his hand.

He held the cold treat over Sienna's mouth and rubbed it against her lips. "Lick it."

Sienna curled her tongue along the top. Adam's cock twitched as he watched her twirl her tongue along the rim. His balls wanted to curl up into his body at the sight.

"Now suck it," he said harshly.

Sienna wrapped her lips around the ice and suckled greedily. Her lips were wet and shiny. She moaned with contentment as she swallowed the icy drips.

He knew she was tormenting him on purpose. He loved how she teased. She might be bound and defenseless, but she was naughty, and flirted with abandon.

Adam's cock slapped against his belly. He pulled the ice from her lips, and it slid out with a loud pop. "Close your eyes, Sienna."

She pouted but reluctantly followed his command. He held the popsicle against her neck. She gasped and flinched, trying to dodge the ice. When he drew it down her breastbone she yanked at her ropes. Goose bumps prickled her flesh.

Adam swept the ice around her body. He didn't follow a pattern, to keep Sienna guessing. Sometimes he would swipe her skin with the popsicle, and other times he would linger. He had to constantly re-mind Sienna to close her eyes.

She arched when he rolled the melting ice on her nipples. She yelped as the slushy water dripped along her labia. Sienna kicked and lashed out when he swept the ice on the bottom of her feet.

Soon Sienna was shivering and twitching as she prepared for his next move. Her body was flushed as water trickled down her skin in tracks. Adam tossed the melting ice in the metal bowl and retrieved the second one. It was melting quickly, but he had just enough left.

Sienna's eyes widened as Adam positioned himself between her legs. He touched the ice against her soft inner thighs. She flinched, but didn't get very far.

"What do you plan to do with that?" she asked, her voice rising with each word.

"What do you think?" He circled the ice around the folds of her sex.

Sienna shrieked and tried to get away. The ropes tightened as they held her in place.

"No, Adam," she said, panting as she struggled to break free. "You have to be kidding."

"No?" He swiped the ice along her slit, watching her skin contract. He would use the ice unless she said the safe word.

"Adam, I swear—" She hissed as he slid the ice into her hot core. Sienna's hips bucked wildly as he pumped the popsicle within her. She screamed as he thrust deeper. He could see her muscles rippling from the cold.

Sienna took short, shallow breaths as she tried to master her re-sponses, but the sting of the ice was too much. She couldn't remain still.

She moaned with gratitude when Adam withdrew the popsicle from her and tossed it on the bed. He slid his hands under her hips and pressed the tip of his cock against her entrance. Her flesh was cold. He gritted his teeth as he sank into her.

The change from cold to hot sent Sienna over the edge. Her inner walls gripped him like a fist, pulsing around him. She cried out as she came, her body sucking Adam in deeper.

The waves of her orgasm ruthlessly milked his cock. He wanted it to last forever, but he couldn't hold on. He came in short, savage bursts.

Adam almost fell on top of Sienna. He leaned on his arms, which bracketed her shoulders. He lowered his head and kissed her cold, rosy lips.

"You are evil," she declared with a sleepy smile.

"I know," he said, his mouth curling into a slanted smile. "It's what you like about me the most."

CHAPTER TWELVE

"Almost done," Adam promised Sienna. He smoothed the plastic and took a step back to look at the masterpiece he had created. "There. Finished."

Sienna was mummified in cling wrap from the neck down. She had stood perfectly still as he wrapped yards and yards of the translucent plastic around her naked body. Her arms were crossed in front of her chest and bound so tightly that she couldn't move them. Her legs were wrapped together, reminding him of little mermaid fins.

"May I see in a mirror?" Sienna asked.

He noticed that she asked very politely. Almost sweetly. She really couldn't wait to see the results and was doing everything in her power for him to indulge her.

Adam opened his closet, where a full-length mirror hung on the door. He positioned the door so she didn't have to move. Sienna's mouth dropped open when she saw her reflection.

He watched her expression intently. He saw the pride glowing in her eyes, but he saw something more. Sienna was turned on by the sight of her complete incapacitation. She knew she was helpless and that he could do anything he wanted to her. She wouldn't be able to refuse.

Something in the mirror caught her eye. He saw her gaze move upward. She gasped and tried to turn around, but failed. "What time does it say?"

He looked at the clock on the wall behind her. "It's almost six o'clock."

"Oh, no," she wailed. "I'm going to be late."

Adam frowned at her words. He hated dealing with yet another intrusion from the real world. "I told you we were going to spend a lot of time today."

"Which is why I took off work early." She said it with a tight smile, but he could tell she was about ready to throw a temper tantrum. "Now come on, Adam. You have to help me out of this."

"Nope, you can forget it." He leaned against the wall and crossed one ankle over the other. "I don't like your tone."

"Adam!" Her cheeks mottled with outrage.

"In fact, I might sit down and watch you stand as still as a statue." He pushed away from the wall and headed for his recliner.

"Adam, please!" Her toes wiggled and he wondered if she was trying to stomp her foot. "Now is not the time to pull that on me. I'm going to be late."

He sat down and put up the footrest. He might as well get comfortable, because it looked like he was going to be there for a while. Sienna could never control her mouth. "What's more important than what we're doing right now?" he asked.

She closed her eyes and silently mouthed the numbers from one to ten. When she was finished, she opened her eyes and said, "It's not a matter of what's important."

"Then I see no reason to get you out of there."

Sienna glared at him. She tried to move her arms, but they were bound tight to her body. She wasn't going anywhere anytime soon. She watched her reflection as she struggled. Adam noticed that, in spite of it all, she found her helplessness arousing.

He propped his chin on his hand. "You're going to fall if you keep doing that."

She struggled harder and almost lost her balance. "Then . . . you'll have to . . . catch . . . me," she said in between grunts.

He would, too. He felt a grim satisfaction that she was aware of this fact. He might test her to her physical limits, but he would do everything in his power to prevent her from getting hurt or injured.

"Adam!" she yelled as she twisted and bent her body, trying to break free.

"Yes, Sienna?" he asked idly. "What is it?"

"Adam Nicholas Taylor!"

He froze. Had he read her responses all wrong? That couldn't be true, but she had just yelled out the safe word. She only used his full name when she couldn't handle the erotic activity. She had been exalting in the challenge until she found out the time.

"You can't use the safe word to get your way." He slammed the footrest down and vaulted out of the recliner.

"You can't break your promise," she threw back at him. She blew her hair out of her face and made one more unsuccessful try to break free. "I said the safe word and now you have to cut me loose."

She was right. He couldn't deny her once she said the safe word. It would mean breaking the trust that he had built with patience and gentleness. He wasn't going to destroy it so he could get his way.

He reached for the cling wrap at her neck and stopped. No, that was too easy for her. If she was really scared or in pain, he would rip the cling wrap clean off her body. But she used the safe word because she didn't want to be late for something else. She didn't even try to deny her real reason! He would not let her get away with that.

Adam grabbed a pair of scissors that he had kept nearby in case there had been an emergency. He reached for her waist and cut away the cling wrap. Within seconds, he had peeled the plastic from her hips to her ankles.

Her skin was flushed and dewy with sweat. He wanted to explore what he just uncovered, but that would give Sienna far too much pleasure for someone who had to be punished.

He balled up the discarded cling wrap and headed for the kitchen without saying a word.

"Uh, hello?" she called after him. Sarcasm dripped from her words. "Don't you think you forgot something?"

"No." He tossed the wrap in the trash can and went straight to the refrigerator. He could use a beer right about now, but he never drank during a scene.

Sienna appeared at the doorway. Cling wrap confined her from the neck to the navel. She was naked from the waist down. It was a delectable sight and Adam's cock grew heavy. He grabbed a bottle of water from the fridge and twisted the cap off.

"I said the safe word."

"And I cut you free." He took a long drink.

Her bottom jaw shifted to the side. "You're supposed to complete the job."

"That was never specified."

"Adam, please." Her voice was weak as she closed her eyes. She sounded like she was on the verge of screaming, crying, or both. "You have to unwrap me."

He had full intentions to do just that until she saw the time. He had wanted to unwrap her like a gift, tearing the clingy film from her breasts to focus all of her attention on her nipples, making them red and shiny with his mouth. Then he would have torn off just enough cling wrap to expose her ass. He would have teased her until she couldn't stand up straight. After that, he would have removed the plastic from her legs so she could wrap them around his hips.

Adam took another gulp of the cold water. It was no use thinking about it. She had ruined the scene.

"Okay, okay." Regret colored her words. "Adam, I'm sorry. I misused the safe word. I promise I won't do it again."

He narrowed his eyes. "Easy to say when we only have four days left."

She looked away from him. "I haven't decided that."

Hope filled his chest and he immediately squashed it. Sienna would say anything right now to get free. "Aw," he drawled, "now you're just saying that to sweeten my mood."

"Adam, please." She leaned against the wall, as if she were defeated. "I need you to take the rest off."

He strode toward her and cornered her against the wall. Her eyes widened with apprehension as he placed his hands on either side of her, blocking her from escaping. "Are you sure you want to go?" he asked with lethal softness.

She looked him in the eye. "I *have* to go."

"You didn't answer my question." He reached down and cupped her sex. She drew in a ragged breath at his audacious touch. "I don't think you want to go."

"Adam . . ." She closed her eyes as he caressed her wet slit. She spread her legs apart and sagged against the wall. "Oh, that feels good."

"I'm going to lift you up," he warned her. "Hook your legs around my waist."

"Adam, I can't. I have to—"

"I'll let you go soon. I promise." He waited, holding his breath until he felt her surrender.

"Okay," she whispered.

Adam held her hips and lifted her. Sienna opened her eyes and she glanced at the floor. She instinctively tried to grab him with her hands and couldn't.

"Hook your legs around my hips," he reminded her. Sienna's movements were clumsy but she did as she was told. She had no other choice.

"I won't drop you," he said as his cock pressed against the entrance of her tight, wet core.

"I know." She didn't look away from his face as he thrust inside her. The look of trust and pleasure on her face twisted his heart. He thrust into her again, holding on tight as he watched her chase the pleasure.

How could she give this up? The question floated in the back of his mind as he drove into her again and again. How could she give *him* up? He wouldn't have made the same choice, but then, he adored her.

His feelings cost him in the end, he decided as he gave one final savage thrust and pinned Sienna to the wall as he came. He was in the weak position of this power exchange, and Sienna was going to walk away without a backward glance.

Sienna's feet shuffled to a stop in the parking lot and she stared at the pool hall for the second time that day. "You want to go here?"

"Yeah," her date said as he looped his arm around her shoulders. "Lizzie told me that you're learning how to play pool. I thought it would be fun."

Fun? A hysterical laugh bubbled and dissolved in her throat. Try dangerous. Try suicidal. There was no way she could walk into Adam's pool hall *with a date*.

She turned to David and did her best to hide the panic clawing inside her. "That's a great idea, but I'm still not very good at it," she said in a low, confidential whisper. "Let's go somewhere else."

He gave her shoulders a good shake. "You're just being modest."

"No, really, I'm not," she said with a tight smile. "Anyway, it's Friday night. The place will be packed."

"So?" Understanding dawned on him. "Oh, you don't want people watching you try to play pool."

"No, I thought you would like somewhere more"—she wondered what would sway him to abandon this plan—"private."

David wasn't listening. "Don't worry. I'm pretty good at the game. I'll help you." He tightened his hold on her and escorted her into the building.

Okay, that's another strike against you. She had tried not to compare David with Adam, but she couldn't help it. Worse, Adam was the clear winner.

CHAIN REACTION   ■   109

David managed to run over her suggestions and make decisions without including her. Even when he did the gentlemanly things like opening doors and escorting her into buildings, she didn't feel cherished. David made her feel like she was incapable of crossing the parking lot by herself.

They stepped into the pool hall and the door slammed shut behind them. Sienna immediately felt trapped. She frantically looked around the crowd as David reserved a table. The balls clacked over the music blaring from the jukebox. Men and women of all ages crowded the hall. The lights were on full force, but the hall seemed dark and mysterious.

She didn't see Adam. Yet. She would not be so lucky if he had chosen to take the night off. She was going to have to play it cool. This was good practice. After all, she was going to run into him from time to time.

"Let's get a drink," David said. He draped his arm around her waist and Sienna jumped. She didn't like the familiarity David displayed, but it was really going to make Adam angry.

Practice or no practice, this was a bad idea. It was like dangling raw meat in front of a starving wild animal. She didn't want to cause trouble, and knew she had to convince David that this place was hazardous to his health.

"You know," she said, injecting as much sweetness and light into her voice as possible without sounding foolish, "it could be quite a while before we get a table. Let's go somewhere else."

"No, we're already here. Sit down and relax. What will you have?" he asked as he motioned to the bartender.

Arsenic? Straight up?

David frowned and leaned closer to her. "What?"

Sienna cringed. Had she said that out loud? "I'm not thirsty," she quickly recovered.

"I'll get you a Coke."

Sienna clenched her jaw before she said something sarcastic. David was seriously getting on her nerves. He was going to find out by the end of tonight that she was not as sweet as Lizzie had suggested.

She saw the bartender approach them. "Hi, Bill," she said to her dad's friend.

Bill stopped in his tracks when he saw her. He tugged at his cap and looked down. He gave an "it's been nice knowing you" shake of the head. She realized that Bill knew about her relationship with Adam.

How did he find out? What did he know? How much has he told her father? Her stomach twisted into knots as a thousand questions crashed through her mind.

As David gave their drink order, Bill gave a furtive look behind her. Her stomach cramped with dread. She knew right then that Adam was in the building—probably in the same room!

Adam hadn't seen her yet. At least, that was her assumption since an explosion hadn't occurred. She didn't want to be around when it did.

"Hey, there are some buddies of mine from work," David said. He hooked his arm tighter around her waist and gestured for the men to come over. He didn't catch their attention, so David called over the noise.

Sienna felt heads turn, and she knew the moment Adam saw her. She could sense the danger rolling over her like a black thundercloud. She felt his hot gaze on her back, right where David had placed his hand.

She couldn't help it; she had to look over her shoulder. Her gaze collided with Adam's. He was on the other side of the room, but the look of fury on his face told her that he was ready to leap over the tables, push people aside and claim her as her own.

Sienna slowly looked away as every alarm bell went off in her head. She had to get out of here before Adam caused a scene. But Adam was closer to the exit. He would block the door before she could leave. She had no doubt about that.

"David, would you excuse me?" She carefully stepped away from him. "I need to use the restroom."

"Now?" He reached out to hold her back, and she expertly dodged his hand. "But I want you to meet my friends."

"Let me freshen up my makeup. I'll be right back." She hurried to the ladies' room. If she could get a locked door between Adam and her, then she might have a chance. She felt him hot on her heels, but she couldn't look back. She had to focus on the door and pray no one was in the tiny restroom when she got there.

She saw the door to the ladies' room was wide open. She broke into a run and made a dash for it. Sienna stepped inside the bathroom and kicked the door. She whirled around, ready to lock it, when she saw Adam's hand snake around the edge and push the door open.

CHAPTER THIRTEEN

"You can't come in here!"

Adam ignored her remark and strode into the bathroom. She took a prudent step back. When he locked the door behind him, Sienna knew she was in big trouble.

"That guy"—his voice shook as he held back his anger—"is why you were in a hurry to get home?"

"No," she lied and watched him carefully. Darkness swirled around him, ready to lash out. For the first time since she'd known him, Adam didn't possess iron control over his emotions.

"How long have you two been together?" His voice was low, but was so sharp it could slice right through her. "As long as we have?"

"No!" She took another step back as malice wafted off of Adam like a poison. "It's a blind date. I didn't even want to go on it."

"But you did." He curled his hands into fists. "Right after I fucked you, you went straight to him."

She flinched at Adam's words. Was that how he viewed their stolen moments? She would never degrade them like that. What they shared was special. At least, to her.

Sienna tilted her chin up. "What if I did? What if I spent the evening with a man? You have no say in the matter."

Adam glared at her, his eyes flashing like chips of blue ice. She knew she was playing chicken with danger, and she couldn't stop. Her heart pounded against her ribs as excitement trickled through her, heating her blood.

"You are going to have to get used to seeing me with other men," Sienna continued, taking on a haughty tone that she knew she shouldn't use on Adam. "Our arrangement ends in four days. Do you think I'm going to spend the rest of my life without a man?"

"You might as well."

His arrogance ignited something hot and wild inside her. "There is no use talking to you, and I have better ways to spend the night."

Adam's eyes narrowed into slits as his face tightened. "I'm sure you do."

She ignored his lethal tone. "Now step aside. My *date* is waiting for me." She waved her small clutch purse at him, secretly wondering why she couldn't act meek and subservient. It was the only way he was going to let her out of this bathroom.

He leaned against the door and leisurely studied her from top to bottom. Her casual dress suddenly felt too short although it stopped right at the knee. Her strappy shoes were flirty and feminine, but at the moment they felt clunky. Her skin tingled as he slid his gaze along her bare legs.

"Take your shoes off."

Sienna sucked in her breath like she had been punched. "What?" she asked in a scandalized whisper, curling her toes as if that would keep her shoes on her feet.

"You heard me." He ensnared her gaze with his, and there was no tenderness in his eyes. "Take off your shoes."

"No! This is not a scene." Yet her body reacted like it was. Her sex heated as her nipples tightened and poked against her bra.

"Why can't it be a scene?" he asked as he stared at her breasts and slowly licked his lips. "You are at my place, which you come to for only one reason."

Her mouth fell open. Did he really believe that was how she saw him? She blinked back the sudden tears. "That is unfair."

"Don't forget that you rushed me earlier." His gaze drifted down to her legs. "You owe me."

"Let me repeat." Sienna's voice shook. "I am not going to do a scene with you. There are my neighbors outside, not to mention my date, who is going to be looking for me soon."

His eyes took on an unholy glow. "Even better. Take off your shoes."

Sienna crossed her arms, tucking her clutch purse against her chest like a shield. "No."

Adam reached out and yanked her against him. Her purse fell to the floor with a clatter. "You came to my place with a man and flaunted him in front of me," he said softly through clenched teeth. "You should know there are consequences for that."

"I didn't bring him here," she whispered fiercely. "It was his decision. I swear I tried to talk him out of it, but he dragged me in."

"You don't want to date him and you didn't want to come here." He clearly didn't believe her. "Do you see a pattern?"

"I'm telling you the truth."

"You follow his wishes." His expression darkened and the muscle in his jaw bunched. "Am I being replaced? Have you found yourself a new master?"

"What? No!" His question startled her and gave her heart a jolt. He could never be replaced in her life. She could never trust or adore anyone else this way.

She wanted to tell him that, but considering his mood, she was afraid he'd use that emotional power over her. She trusted him when it came to pushing her sexual boundaries. If he knew how much power he had over her emotions, he might flex those muscles to keep her.

Might? He would. She saw it in his eyes. The wildness, the instinct to keep what was his.

He had to give her up and now he was losing his power over her. It was a nasty surprise for him. Had he believed that, years from now, he could tell her to take her shoes off and she would submit? Did he think his power was so everlasting that she would do a scene with him whenever he felt like it?

Maybe he did, and maybe he wasn't wrong. She felt the pull right now. She wanted to obey Adam and have him reward her. She needed to please and comfort him, even though she should walk away and go back to her date.

"Take off your shoes," Adam said in a growl, "or I will take them off for you."

Whoa. Her eyes widened until they stung. He was breaking their rules left and right. "We can't do it here," she said, trying to placate him. "Someone will hear us."

"So what? Let them hear us," Adam said as he dragged down the zipper of his jeans. "I want them to hear you call out my name."

He did. She saw it in his face. He would love it if she claimed him publicly, but that was the one wish she could not grant him.

"It amazes me. You hate being thought of as Sweet Sienna," he said as he shoved his clothes down and revealed his cock, which was thick and hard for her. "But then you're afraid that people will find out that you aren't so sweet and nice."

He didn't understand, Sienna realized as she stared at his erection, the ache inside her intensifying. She played the role she was given by her friends and family. She had to meet those expectations or the consequences would be far-reaching.

"You and I know you aren't that sweet, and you aren't nice." Adam wrapped his fist around his cock and pumped it in front of her. "Other people's opinions matter to you more than they should. You wouldn't try to date me because nice girls wouldn't."

"I explained that," she said weakly. She stared at his cock, her core clenching with need.

"So I like my sex with a twist. So everyone knows that. Who the hell cares?" The crown of his cock was now wet and shiny. "You do.

You don't want others to know that you like sex, that you have sex, or that you really like to have sex with me."

He was right. She wanted to duck her head in shame. He made her sound shallow and mean. Hypocritical. Definitely not sweet and nice.

"Take. Off. Your."

She kicked off one shoe, then the other, and listened to them skid and hit the tile wall. She wished she could say she capitulated because she knew she wouldn't get out of the bathroom, but she knew the truth. She wanted to obey him. The risk of getting caught gave an extra kick to her pulse.

Adam showed no satisfaction when she followed his command. He pumped his cock, the sound of the friction echoing in the small room. "Get on your knees."

Sienna knelt in front of him. The floor was cold and hard against her bare knees. She tilted her head back and looked him directly in the eye, silently waiting for his next order.

"Suck me off."

She reached for his cock. It was warm and hard beneath her hands. She stroked him, enjoying every twitch and shudder Adam gave. Anticipation and pride swelled in her chest as his erection grew under her touch.

The noise outside the door was loud and too close for comfort. The air chilled and swirled around her. She inhaled his hot, aroused scent. She shouldn't linger or indulge in the sensory overload. She knew she had to hurry. Every extra minute increased her chances of getting caught.

Sienna licked the tip of his cock. She loved the taste of Adam. She enjoyed giving him head and could do it forever, but not now. Now her goal was to get the job done quickly and get out of here.

She laved her tongue along the underside of his cock and felt him flinch. She continued down the length, giving light, teasing licks. She cupped his balls and fondled them, prepared to use every trick she knew to get him off as fast as possible.

Adam leaned back heavily against the door and spread his legs wider. She glanced up at his face. He watched her with hooded eyes, but she saw their angry glitter. She didn't know if she could diminish his anger or replace it with pleasure.

Sienna gave his balls a good squeeze, but he didn't groan in response. His nostrils flared, but otherwise he didn't move at all.

He was going to make her really work for this. She wasn't sure how long he could hold off an orgasm, but she knew Adam's control over his body was monumental. She was going to be here until morning, with a tired jaw and bruised knees, if she wasn't careful.

Sienna pulled away from his cock and started to lick his balls. Adam's breath hitched as she nibbled and sucked the smooth, tight sacs. He placed his hand at the back of her head.

"I said, suck my cock."

She noticed that his voice wasn't blurred with lust. Sienna reluctantly returned her attention to his cock. She had been so sure that was the shortcut she had been looking for.

She curled her fingers around the base of his cock and squeezed. Adam winced but didn't buck his hips. Sienna wrapped her lips around the tip and started to suck.

She wished she could just suck as hard as she could to weaken his restraint, but she knew better. The only way Adam would come was if she overwhelmed him with attention. She flicked her tongue along the slit and sucked. She lapped and licked the head, and then gave a surprising twist with her hands at the base of his cock.

Her world centered on his erection, which was just what Adam longed for. It didn't take long for his hips to buck. His fingers gripped the back of her head. He slammed his back against the door, and she stopped when it rattled and shook under the impact.

"Don't stop," he whispered hoarsely as his fingers dug into her scalp.

"Step away from the door," she said. "Please?"

She was surprised that he did. Adam leaned toward her and drove his cock further into her mouth. She sucked him fiercely as he held her head immobile. Adam's breathing grew harsh as he rutted her mouth. She dropped her hands from his cock and held onto his hips as he thrust past her lips.

His fingers twisted in her hair. Sienna could tell from the choppy, untamed thrusts that he was about to come.

The knock on the door startled them. A scream caught in her throat as she froze. Adam's cock still pulsed in her mouth, but he didn't move. Sienna's eyes widened as the doorknob twisted.

"Sienna?"

David! Sienna slid Adam's cock from her mouth. She was going to stand up, but Adam's hands kept her still. She felt his power shimmering from his touch. He hadn't used force, but he was going to use it if necessary.

"Sienna?" The doorknob twisted from side to side. "Are you still in there?"

"I'll be right out." Her voice wavered. "I'll meet you at the bar."

She didn't know if David heard her or would do as she said. She didn't say anything, but the doorknob stopped moving. Sienna tried to listen for retreating footsteps, but heard nothing. She wondered if he was still by the door.

She gave another cautious glance at Adam, praying he wouldn't say anything or open the door. His expression was fierce. Fury leaped in his eyes and the muscle in his cheek twitched, but he didn't say a word.

Instead, he tilted Sienna's head back and pressed his cock against her mouth. She parted her lips and he drove in deep. She almost gagged but fought to control the reflex. Sienna's nose was buried in Adam's dark pubic hair as he thrust into her mouth.

His hands pressed hard against her skull when he came. She gulped and swallowed as he shoved his cock down her throat. Each savage thrust made it difficult to breathe. When he gave one final surge, she moved to retreat, but Adam kept her in position.

He held her against him and she inhaled his musky scent as she tasted his cock in her mouth. What was he going to do next? Sienna's heartbeat went into overdrive.

Just when she thought he was going to keep her like that indefinitely, Adam slowly withdrew from her mouth. He took a step back and leaned against the door, watching her intently.

Sienna wiped her mouth with the back of her hand. She didn't look at him as she got up from the floor. Her knees ached, but not as much as her sex, which clenched and unclenched, waiting for Adam's cock to burrow in.

Sienna wobbled as she picked up her purse and slid her feet into her shoes. She turned to check her appearance and tried not to flinch. It was a disaster. She looked like she had just had sex in a public bathroom.

Her face was pink and her lips were red and swollen. There was nothing she could do about it now. She smoothed down her hair and tugged at her dress.

Sienna took a deep breath and faced Adam. With more bravado than she felt, she unlocked the door and turned the knob. She tried to open it, but Adam didn't move.

She stared at the doorknob. "You're in my way."

He leaned down and whispered in her ear. "When you kiss that guy tonight, you'll taste me in your mouth." He stepped away from the door. Sienna escaped without giving a glance back.

CHAPTER FOURTEEN

It was Saturday morning when Adam heard the familiar tap on his door. It caught him by surprise, yet he had been listening for it for hours. Sienna was here for another scene.

He slowly exhaled as the tension left his body. After last night he could have sworn that he had ruined everything. He would not have blamed Sienna if she had never returned. It would have hurt, and it would have been a regret he'd carry for the rest of his life, but he would have stoically accepted it.

Adam opened the door and his pulse leaped at the sight of Sienna. There was nothing unusual about her T-shirt, denim jacket and jeans. She stared back at him, her chin jutting out defiantly as her eyes shone with attitude. Adam savored the moment, knowing in his heart that this was one of the last times he would see her at his door.

"Well?" Sienna put her hands on her hips. "Are you going to let me in?"

Sienna was in rare form. The corner of Adam's mouth twitched with a smile. "I didn't think you were going to show today."

"Why would you think that?" She sashayed past him and slipped off her jacket. "I always keep my promises."

And he didn't. She left that unsaid, but it hung between them. "I'm sorry about last night."

She tossed her jacket on a chair, making herself at home before she turned and looked him in the eye. "You should be."

"I broke the rules, and I know I broke your trust in me," he admitted. He wasn't going to make excuses or expect forgiveness. The most he could hope for was to fix what he had ruined before their deadline was up.

"You were provoked. I knew you would be, and I shouldn't have gone in the hall last night with my date." She thought for a moment and held up her hand. "Although I'm not excusing you for what you did."

"I didn't think you would."

Sienna shoved her hands in her hair and sighed. "I let David drag me in there because I didn't want to cause a scene or answer uncomfortable questions."

He didn't say anything as jealousy pricked his gut. Adam was not going to ask anything about the date, but he wondered. Did she sleep with this David? Was she going out with him again? More importantly, why did she go out with that guy and not give *him* a chance?

Sienna turned away and strolled around his apartment. "In case you're wondering," she said casually over her shoulder, "David didn't get so much as a kiss from me."

"You didn't need to tell me that," he said, but he was glad that she did. The not knowing was driving him crazy.

"A coworker set me up because she doesn't think I date," Sienna told him, trailing her finger along the back of his recliner. "Which, technically, is true."

Adam studied Sienna, wondering why she was being so forthcoming this morning. Despite appearances, Sienna was a secretive person. While he might be the biggest secret she kept from others, he was not privy to her deepest thoughts and feelings. She preferred to keep secrets from him as well.

Her reason for being chatty occurred to him like a slap on the head. She was trying to appease him just in case he had some tortuous scene planned. He reluctantly admired her cleverness.

"You wouldn't tell her that you hooked up with a man because that would lead to ... what do you call it?" He tilted his head as he pretended to recall his memory. "Uncomfortable questions?"

Her smile dimmed when she realized her approach wasn't working. "Right," she answered tightly. "Can we get on with whatever you have in store for today?"

"Are you in another rush?" he asked as he walked toward her. "Have another date lined up for tonight?"

"No, but I would like to leave before it turns dark," she answered, her voice taking on a sarcastic edge. She looked around the room. "No ropes?"

He shook his head. "Not today."

She gave a frustrated huff and made a face. "You know, in order to work toward an oriental rope dress, one needs to practice with ropes."

"Is that so?" he drawled. The woman's attitude was unlike anything he'd seen. Was it because of last night, or was there something else going on?

"How am I going to prepare for a rope dress when we only have"— she quickly counted on her fingers—"three days left?"

She was obsessed with the oriental rope dress, and she was in for a rude awakening. "I'm going to put this to you as plainly as I possibly can. We aren't working toward that goal." He rocked back on his feet and waited for the fireworks to explode.

"What?" she squawked, her mouth dropping open. "Since when?"

"Since you gave us seven days." He had never promised her they would fulfill that wish by the end of the week. He'd like to, but he wasn't going to risk her safety.

Sienna splayed her hands in the air, her fingers wide and tense with anger. "Why didn't you tell me?"

"You are not ready for a rope dress." No amount of pleading, cajoling, arguments or threats would convince him otherwise. "Maybe in another month."

Her eyes widened as she looked up at the ceiling. "Another month? I don't have—oh." Her mouth twisted. "Now I get it."

"I doubt it."

She glared at him. "This is all a negotiation tactic for you."

"I don't know what you're talking about."

"Maybe I should call it blackmail, because that's essentially what it is. If I want to accomplish my goal then I can't leave you after the seven days are up."

"That's not true." He didn't want her to leave, but he wasn't going to stand in her way. It had to be her decision, and his lack of control over her choice was killing him.

She pointed an accusing finger at him. "You are stringing me along. You act like, if I just hang on for a little while longer, then I'll get what I want. But that's not what will happen. If I stick around for another month, you'll still say I'm not ready."

"Are you done?" She had better be, because his patience was wearing thin.

"Have you been stringing me along all this time?" Her face reddened as she considered the possibility. "You were *never* going to give me a rope dress, were you?"

"I was, but that was before—"

"That's it!" she announced, tossing her arms in the air. "I'm out of here." She headed for the door.

He reached out and grabbed her arm. His restraint was holding on by a thread. He didn't like her accusations, but it was her threat that bothered him the most. She was ready to leave because he wouldn't indulge her.

"Listen to me." His tone was cold and sharp. "I want to make every one of your fantasies come true. The oriental rope dress was your goal and I was willing to give it to you, but you're not ready."

She rolled her eyes. "So you keep saying, but that doesn't make it true."

"I want to keep you safe," he insisted. She wanted to be reckless and wild, and he wanted her to feel that way while he held the safety net for her. "I want to make the experience everything you dreamed about. In order for that to happen, you must be ready."

"I am ready," she yelled.

"No, you're ready to *grab for it*." He knew it was time to give her the harsh truth. "You don't have the restraint you need. You think you've been patient and deprived. You don't know the meaning of those words."

"Are you kidding me? What about all those scenes we've done?" She gestured in the direction of the bed. "It's all about patience, control and deprivation."

They had been taking baby steps and now she thought she was an expert. It was time to demonstrate just how much further she had to go. Adam crossed his arms and stared her down. "Then let's see how good you are at it."

"Is this a challenge? Like an exam? I don't need it." She flattened her hand against her chest. "I can take anything you throw at me."

"You used the safe word yesterday," he pointed out.

"Oh, I can't believe you brought that up." She pressed her lips together and she fought back her temper. "I said I was sorry. You can't hold that against me. And I like to point out that before yesterday I hadn't used the safe word for months."

"Let's see how long you can last today without using it."

"If I pass, do I get the rope dress?"

The woman had a one-track mind. Fortunately, he was just as determined and tenacious as she was. "Take off your shoes."

Sienna followed his directions without hesitation. She kicked off her shoes and waited for his next order. Her eyes narrowed when she noticed that he didn't answer her question.

"Go lie on the bed."

Sienna frowned as she turned and walked to the bed. Why didn't he ask her to disrobe? That was different. What was he planning that required her to keep her clothes on? She couldn't imagine, but, knowing Adam, it would prove devious.

She crawled onto the bed and lay in the center, her arms at her sides. She tilted her head to watch Adam from beneath her lashes. He walked toward her and her stomach tightened with anticipation. Adam Taylor wasn't handsome, but there was something about him that made her go weak in the knees, especially when he had that look of intent.

"Don't move." He stood at her feet, but didn't touch her. Sienna did her best not to frown, but he was changing his methods again.

He had nothing set up, nor did he gather any props as he approached the bed. She had no idea what he planned to do and that rattled her. She liked his unpredictability, but at the same time she agonized over it.

Sienna forced herself to remain calm. If she was tense, she was more apt to make sudden moves or a mistake. When Adam finally grasped her ankles, she was very proud of herself for showing no reaction.

Adam stroked the tops of her bare feet with his fingertips. Light, teasing touches that a lover might bestow with affection, but not for someone as ticklish as she was. It was torture. She felt like her legs were on fire from the knee down.

She gritted her teeth when Adam slid his finger along the side of her right foot. Her skin tingled with warning, and she was horrified that her sex pulsed with anticipation. When he rubbed his knuckle along the arch of her foot, Sienna knew she was in trouble. It took all of her strength to remain perfectly still when she wanted to dodge his hand.

This was why he didn't bind her ankles to the bed. She should have known! She would have relied on the ropes too much, because they would have controlled and concealed her instinctive reactions.

Her legs trembled as Adam massaged her feet. She clenched her core as every touch sent darts of pain and pleasure through her body. She pressed her lips together as he dug his thumbs against the balls of her feet. The sensations pricked and bubbled just under her skin. She wanted to scream.

She exhaled shakily as he let go. Her muscles locked and a fine sheen of sweat coated her skin. She watched silently as Adam walked into the kitchen. When he disappeared from her sight, she sagged against the bed.

She could do this, she reminded herself as she regulated her breathing while her heart pounded in her ears. She had to pass this test. Rope dress or not, it was a matter of honor. Not ready? Ha! She'd show him.

Her next breath caught in her throat when Adam walked out of the kitchen carrying a small jar of honey. *Oh . . . no . . .* Sienna tried not to wince. She curled her toes in, praying that he wasn't going to use that on her feet.

Adam flipped open the cap and turned the bottle upside down. Sienna squeezed her eyes shut. A tremor swept through her legs as she kept her feet still. She almost jerked them away at the last moment. It took an incredible effort to keep them in the line of fire.

A stream of honey landed on her left foot. If she twitched her toes, she could flick off the thick, golden rope. She was so tempted to wiggle her foot, but she remained motionless.

As Adam put a dollop of honey on the high instep of her right foot, Sienna wrinkled her nose at the sweet scent. She normally liked honey, but not on her feet.

Adam put the bottle on the floor and Sienna relaxed a little. She had visions of her feet encased in mountains of sticky honey. She was glad Adam showed some sense of moderation.

She cringed when Adam smeared the honey on the top of her right foot. It felt gooey. She tensed and almost kicked out when she felt

Adam's tongue on her foot. Her sex flooded when he lapped the honey from her skin.

Oh, God . . . Oh, God . . . Sienna tried to breathe. His tongue tickled, but worse, she felt every lick in her clit. She pressed her legs together, wishing the sensual ache would go away. Okay, that wasn't true. She wished he would put that tongue to good use and lick her clit.

Adam moved his attention to the other foot. This time he didn't smear the honey. He captured her small toe in his mouth. Sienna gasped at the moist heat and the touch of the edge of his teeth. He gently sucked the honey off her toe. The insistent pull went straight to her breasts. Her nipples stung as they tightened.

A moan escaped from her mouth when Adam paid attention to the next toe. She slowly curled her fingers, pressing her nails into her palms and welcoming the bite. She needed the pain to divert her attention from her feet.

By the third toe, the deep indentations of her nails weren't enough. She wanted Adam to abandon her feet and suck on her nipples. Her sex ached for his mouth. She was desperate for him to lick her wet slit as if it was covered in honey.

As his mouth engulfed her big toe, Sienna fought to remain still. She didn't twitch her hips as moisture leaked down her slit. She kept her hands at her side when she really wanted to grab Adam by the neck. She longed to press his mouth against her breast before sinking onto his cock and thrashing her hips from side to side.

When Adam let go of her big toe, Sienna's breath was shallow and choppy. The folds of her sex were slick and puffy. She knew she would shatter the moment he plunged into her.

"Very good, Sienna," he said as he stood up. "You may go now."

At first the words didn't make sense. She stared at him until his words jarred her. She propped herself up on her elbows. "What?"

"The scene is over," he explained as he picked up the bottle of honey. "You did well."

She looked at the bed and then back at him. She could tell that his cock bulged under his jeans, but he showed no interest in doing anything about it. "But . . . you . . . we didn't . . ."

"Come back tomorrow and we'll continue."

"Tomorrow!" He expected her to function in this state of arousal for a day?

"That's right," he said, disappearing into the kitchen. "Tomorrow."

"But I—"

He peeked around the corner of the kitchen doorway. "Don't try to get yourself off before then. I'll know."

She glared at him, her body throbbing for completion. She didn't want to follow that last order, but she would. She would be disappointed in herself if she failed.

She could wait until tomorrow. She'd show him that she was more than just ready. He'd find out that she was his equal.

CHAPTER FIFTEEN

Monday evening and Sienna was back at Adam's place. She paused at the stairway leading to his apartment. A part of her wanted to sprint up the steps. She felt alive and free when she was with him, and she was eager for more. The other part of her wanted to cancel for the day. She wondered what Adam had planned for her today, but she didn't think she had the strength to find out.

For two days he had teased her and tantalized her senses. One touch and she would melt. Now he only had to look at her and she would start to sweat. Countless times she had been close to climaxing, but Adam had denied her satisfaction.

She glared at the door, knowing there was a strong possibility he would not let her orgasm today as well. The last two days had left her on edge and grumpy. She was so aware of her body. Her workday seemed to last forever as every move ached. Her clothes felt tight and scratchy. Even now her jeans rested heavily against her skin.

She couldn't take another night of this. If he didn't let her come today, she would not return tomorrow.

Yeah, right. Sienna shook her head in self-disgust and climbed up the stairs. She would be here for tomorrow, and not because it would be her last day.

Something inside her drove her to meet Adam's challenge. She had to exceed his expectations. She used to think the visits to his apartment would teach her more about herself. She thought she would find out what made her interested in bondage. Instead, all she managed to discover was that she had barely pulled back the first few layers.

The basis for her needs and desires would remain a mystery to her. She guessed some secrets were destined to reside inside herself. She wasn't happy about it, but if she didn't have Adam, she couldn't imagine anyone else taking the journey with her.

She didn't want to stop. She was just beginning to learn more about herself. This week should have answered all of her questions, but all it did was make her long for more.

Then don't give up. Sienna stopped at his door as the words boomeranged in her head. *Keep Adam in your life.*

That was impossible. Sienna covered her face with her hands and took a long, shuddering sigh. She dropped her hands as she faced the truth.

It wasn't impossible, but she could tell that it would be a lot of hard work. Yet she wouldn't face it alone. Adam would be at her side and backing her up. He was the kind of guy a woman wanted in her corner. He had the tenacity and raw power to see anything through. That is, if he wanted to.

He'd protected and taken care of her in the past, but that was for sex. His interest in her would wane, especially when her real life interfered with the fantasy. Would he still be at her side then? She didn't think so. It wasn't as if he was in love with her.

In all honesty, she had never said she loved him. She didn't love him, but she could easily fall for him, if she let herself. But did they have enough in common other than sex?

"Sienna?"

She jumped at Adam's voice and looked up. The front door was wide open and he stood on the threshold wearing nothing but a pair of jeans.

"I'm sorry. I was thinking of something." She drifted off as she stared at his chest. The dragon tattoo seemed particularly ferocious today.

He frowned and studied her face. "Are you okay?"

"Yes, thank you," she said with a determined smile. "May I come in?"

He silently gestured for her to enter. She stepped inside and did a quick glance around the apartment. Once again, he had nothing set up. Sienna pressed her lips together and kept her expression blank as disappointment billowed inside her.

So it was going to be another day of teasing. She honestly didn't know how much more she could endure. She was so deprived of his touch that she would probably come the moment he thrust into her. Sienna winced and squeezed her legs together. The mere thought of having him mount her was enough to make her ache.

"Take off your shoes."

Her body quivered at his command. She stared at him, but his back was turned. She didn't understand why he had started the scene all of a sudden, but she wasn't going to talk back. She wasn't going to give him any reason to think she couldn't rise to the challenge.

She toed off her flat shoes and assumed her position. She laced her fingers and held them in front of her. She bowed her head slightly and watched Adam from beneath her lashes.

Adam walked to his desk and opened a drawer. He pulled out a purple silk scarf. Her heart gave a jolt of recognition. It was the scarf that came with the chain letter.

Sienna's head snapped up. "What are you going to do with that?"

Adam turned and faced her. "I'm going to use it on you."

He knew exactly what that scarf represented to her. It was sent to her as a warning. It started all of the trouble she was dealing with now. She didn't want to see it ever again, and he wanted to use the strip of silk in a scene? "Why?"

"Take off your clothes," Adam said, acting as if she hadn't spoken. Sienna wanted to repeat her question. Yell it out until he answered. Instead she clenched her teeth and slowly undressed. Her hands shook with anger as she watched him twist the scarf into a tight rope.

When she tossed her bra and underwear to the side, Sienna stood before him naked. She felt at a disadvantage while Adam still wore his jeans. Desire and panic spiraled in her belly as her gaze never left the scarf.

"Put your hands behind your back," he told her as he covered the ends of the scarf with electrical tape. She silently did as he said. Adam approached her carrying the long, twisted scarf with both hands. "Stay perfectly still."

She obeyed him, inwardly flinching as he draped the scarf over her neck. Sienna felt him folding and pulling some of the silk at the back of her neck. "What are you doing?" she couldn't help asking.

"I'm making an overhand knot," he explained.

She didn't know what that signified. Why was he adding a knot at the back of her neck? Why an overhand and not a simple square knot? What was he going to do?

He draped the scarf over her shoulders and the twisted silk fell between her breasts. "Now be quiet and remain still."

Adam grabbed the sides of the scarf between her breasts. She watched him make another overhand knot at the center of her chest. His hands bumped and brushed against her breasts and her nipples tightened. If only he could cup her breasts, then she would stop vibrating with need. She was sure of it.

He took the ends of the scarf and twined them under her breasts. She winced as she felt the gold threads scratch the soft skin, but didn't complain. She watched Adam's intent expression as he worked the knots, and her sex grew slick with lust.

She was surprised when he stepped behind her and bound her upper arms. The position was uncomfortable, and she couldn't shift her arms to find relief. Her skin flushed and chilled as the sense of helplessness swirled around her.

Adam wound the rope along the top of her breast. Her posture was tall and erect as he tied the ends of the scarf at the center of her back.

He then circled her several times, very slowly, as he studied every inch of her body.

She felt the tension of the scarf behind her neck and at her breastbone. The twisted silk rubbed under her breasts and at the center of her back. When she tried to move her arms, the bindings tightened against her.

Adam stood in front of her. His eyes sparkled with dark pleasure as a satisfied smile pulled at his mouth. "Do you want to see what I've done?"

"Yes, please," she whispered, her throat thick with emotion. It was not the rope dress that she wanted, but it was a compromise she hadn't expected.

He led her to his closet and opened the door. Shock slammed in her chest as she stared at her reflection. The purple scarf contrasted sharply with her pale skin. It was no longer a pretty, delicate accessory that could hide a flaw or give her a ladylike appearance. It was now a dangerously sensual rope that outlined her breasts, squeezing and protruding each curve from her body.

"Do you like it?" Adam asked as he stepped behind her. He looked at her eyes in the reflection.

"Yes," she replied in a breathy sigh. "Thank you."

"You're welcome." He leaned down and nuzzled her neck with his mouth. She watched him in the mirror as his hands came around and plucked her nipples.

Her breasts looked different bound against the purple silk. They appeared smaller, but her nipples looked huge. The illusion was mesmerizing. She couldn't look away as Adam kissed down the length of her neck. When he played with her breasts and captured her nipples between his fingertips, Sienna preened under his attention.

As he fondled her breasts, he slowly slid one hand down the center of her stomach, her muscles twitching under his touch. Sienna spread her legs farther apart for him. She paused, praying that he wouldn't stop and chide her for her presumptuousness. Instead he cupped her sex, pushing back the wet folds with his fingers.

He growled against her neck and caught her skin between his teeth. The fire inside her flared from the bite. Adam rubbed her clit hard and she gasped for her next breath. Sienna's knees buckled as he pinched the stiff nub at the same time he pinched her nipple. The brilliant fire streaked through her, leaving her light-headed and shaky. She wanted to lean back against Adam, but her arms bound behind her made it impossible.

"Lean forward," Adam told her. It was the opposite of what she wanted, but Sienna did as she was told. She would do anything to keep the pleasure buzzing through her veins and heating her body. Adam held her hips and tilted her more until her ass jutted out to him and his erection pressed against her.

"Watch your reflection," he told her hoarsely as he unzipped his jeans. She stared at the mirror as Adam entered her from behind. She heard her juicy flesh suck him in as her jaw slackened with pleasure.

She watched a flush creep up her skin and pleasure soften her features. She was unable to believe her transformation from Sweet Sienna to this tousled and tethered creature. It went beyond anything she'd imagined.

Her breasts jiggled and weaved with every hard thrust, and she knew Adam was watching each move. She could feel his hot gaze on the tips of her breasts. She bent down more and the scarf tightened, digging into her skin. She groaned as the sting colored her pleasure.

Her breasts swung as Adam plunged into her. She closed her eyes as she concentrated on the sweet ache between her breasts and thighs. She felt dizzy and out of control as the first climax rippled through her pelvis, clenching Adam's cock.

She winced as pain suddenly lanced through her arms. Heat flashed through her and her legs shook to remain upright. Sienna dragged her eyes open and her gaze connected with Adam's. She knew the stark need that burned inside him, and she understood his pain. He wanted his torture to end, but more than anything, he wanted it to last.

Adam's fingers bit into her hips as he drove inside her. His thrusts grew faster and she couldn't take her eyes off of her breasts as they bobbed and swayed. The purple scarf held her back, pinching her skin, but she felt like she was breaking free.

It was like nothing she'd ever seen, Sienna realized as heat inside her exploded and spun wildly. She struggled to keep her eyes open, wanting this moment to last. Her mind felt sluggish as she chased after every lick and spark of bliss. She wanted to hold on to and contain the sensations whizzing through her limbs.

Sienna couldn't, but she vainly hoarded this feeling. Even as the aftermath pulsed through her womb, she knew she'd never experience this pleasure again.

CHAPTER SIXTEEN

"**H**eading to the pool hall?" Sienna asked as she slipped on her shoes. She had showered and dressed, but found herself lingering.

"Soon." He now wore jeans and a sweatshirt. Adam stood by the door, and she got the sense that he was hanging back. "I want to give you something before you leave."

"Really?" That was unusual, but she made a point of keeping her double life separate. No memento from Adam was tucked away or on display in her house, and nothing of her real life was brought into the scenes they did.

"Here." He held the purple scarf out to her. "I'm returning this."

She took an instinctive step back and kept her hands to her side. "I don't want it. You can keep it."

The scarf dangled between them. "I told you that by the end of the seven days you would have earned it."

Panic kicked in her gut. "It hasn't been seven days." She still had one more day. One more time with Adam. He couldn't stop now.

"What's one more day going to do?" He lifted a shoulder. "It's not going to change anything."

Sienna hunched her shoulders, surprised by his callousness. She should have known that the binding of her breasts was a send-off present. "So that's it? We're done?"

"Yeah, we're done."

She took the scarf, when she wanted to snatch it from his hands and rip it. Instead she carefully folded it into a small square. "Thanks," she said softly, unable to look in his eyes. "For everything."

He slid his hands in his jean pockets. "Yep. Take care."

She didn't want their good-bye to be like this. She wanted to hug him, but she was afraid she would hold on and never let go. She longed for another kiss, even though she knew one was not going to be enough. Sienna wanted to leave with just a hint of sophistication and a smile, but if she was going to be completely honest, she didn't want to leave at all.

"Well, I'll see you around." Her final words seemed so lame. Adam had showed her more than a good time—he had showed her what she truly was. She was a woman who enjoyed sex with a twist.

She looked down at the scarf in her hands and realized she had a lot in common with the silk. The scarf could be seen as pretty and refined, or it could be dangerously sensual. It could be both, but not at the same time.

She was both sweet and spicy, but never together. She didn't want Adam to know just how wholesome she could be. He wouldn't have allowed her in his apartment if he knew that she had a traditional, romantic streak.

Yet, at the same time, Sienna didn't want anyone other than Adam to know how sensual and daring she could be. She might be able to handle the sting of ropes, but her feelings were easily hurt. The people in her life didn't understand the allure of bondage, and it was safer to keep that part of her private.

Maybe one day she wouldn't care, or perhaps she could go through life keeping her fantasies a well-guarded secret. Whatever she decided, she'd wish Adam was there by her side.

She stepped over the threshold and out of the apartment. Sienna slowly turned around as Adam held the door. She knew she should keep walking, preferably with a swagger, but she couldn't. She felt that if she let this moment go, she wouldn't get another opportunity.

"Adam?" she asked as her heart thumped against her chest. "Would you like to come over to dinner tomorrow night?"

He frowned and tilted his head as if he hadn't heard her correctly. "Say what?"

"Come over to my place tomorrow," she said, injecting a little more confidence by turning her question into a suggestion. "I know you don't have anything planned since I was your usual Tuesday night."

"Sienna," he said with a fierce scowl, "this is not how to make a clean break."

"I'm trying to ask you over to my place." She flattened her hand on the stair banister. "For a date."

His eyebrows shot up. "A date?"

"I should warn you, I never have sex on my first date," she said with a straight face.

"You're kidding." An emotion she couldn't decipher flamed in his blue eyes.

"No." Guys never tried to have sex with her on the first date. They didn't think she was that sort of girl. She might break tradition for Adam.

"Sienna, the whole point of these seven days was because you were worried that someone knew about us."

"I know." She dipped her head and noticed that his hands flexed against the edge of the door. If she didn't know better, she'd think her invitation had rattled him.

"We made it. No one discovered you here."

"Well, Bill seemed to know," Sienna argued, gesturing in the direction of the pool hall.

"He can imagine what goes on between you and me, but he doesn't know," Adam said. "Bill keeps his mouth shut."

She couldn't argue with that, and she wasn't going to try. Adam didn't seem interested in taking this relationship to a new level. Or, rather, a level that didn't focus on sex.

"You can leave now and no one will ever know what happened in here. Why are you trying to mess that up?"

"I'm not." She should have remained quiet and kept walking. Adam seemed insistent on getting rid of her.

"We're done," Adam continued relentlessly. "We called all the shots. We got to say when and how we ended this relationship."

"I was given that final choice," Sienna said loudly, cutting through his objections. "In case you have forgotten, the deal was that after seven days I would choose either to end what we have or to continue. I've made my choice."

"The choices were either to continue what we're doing or stop altogether. Making our relationship public was not one of the options."

"Well, it should have been."

He leaned against the door frame, his mouth slanted in a mocking smile. "Don't tell me that you've gotten over your fears of being found out."

She couldn't admit to that. "No, but I'm tired of living a double life. I want my fantasy guy in my real world. Is that too much to ask?"

"Yes," Adam said without hesitation. "It's never going to work, and you'll live to regret it."

"I didn't say it was going to be easy." She knew he was going to argue about this all night. It was time to take charge. "So how about it, Adam? My place at seven o'clock? I'll cook for you," she promised in a sweet voice.

Adam's expression hardened. "I never agreed to this."

"It's not up for discussion," she said breezily while her nerve endings were shredding. "It boils down to this: Do you want me? If so, you're going to have to work for it."

"What the hell?" He pushed the door all the way open and it bumped against the wall. "I have worked my ass off for you this past week."

"Good night, Adam."

"Why are you doing this?" he asked as he stepped out of his apartment. "Because you're going to miss sex?"

She rolled her eyes. "Fine, be that way." She started down the stairs.

"I didn't say no."

Sienna smiled, but kept walking. "I know," she said over her shoulder.

"I don't even know where you live," he admitted.

She paused at the end of the stairs and looked up. Adam was leaning over the banister. He looked frustrated and confused, which she decided was much better than the cold, indifferent good-bye she'd received earlier. "If you really want to find me, you'll figure it out."

His eyes widened. "You're not going to tell me?"

"Ask around," she said as she headed out the main door. "Someone is bound to give you directions."

"Ask around? Are you insane?"

Probably. She felt like her instincts were taking over and she was along for the ride. "I want you to ask everyone you know where Sienna Bailey lives."

"They'll know you're dating a man who likes to tie his women up," he warned her.

He knew exactly what would shake her up. She couldn't let him see it if she wanted to pull this off. "Good-bye, Adam. See you tomorrow."

"I didn't say yes," he called out.

"Your loss, then." She closed the door and heavily leaned against it. Her arms and legs trembled as she felt like she had just made the riskiest gamble of her life. She had no idea if it would pay off. She couldn't stop the feeling that the loss was going to be hers.

✲　✲　✲

This was a bad idea, Adam decided as he stood in front of Sienna's apartment door, clenching a wine bottle. He didn't know why he had pursued this. He should leave.

He gently shook off the raindrops that clung to his bouquet of roses. The weather was vicious. Rain had slashed across his windshield and gusts of wind had pulled at his car, but he managed to get here. Nothing would have kept him from arriving on Sienna's doorstep. As much as he argued against it, as much as he knew it was a bad idea, he wanted this date and the promise it held.

Adam reached out to knock on the door, but it swung open before his knuckles made contact on wood. The scent of spices and home-cooked food hung in the air, but his gut twisted at the sight of Sienna. She stood in front of him, wearing a light yellow sweater, jeans and a welcoming smile.

"Hi, Adam." She stood on her tiptoes and brushed a kiss against his mouth. It was not nearly enough for him, but she turned her head just as he leaned in for a deeper kiss.

Sienna looked over his shoulder. "Hi, Mrs. Lowenstein," she called across the hall. "Have you met Adam Taylor?"

Adam glanced around just in time to see the door slam shut. Now that's the kind of welcome he was used to. "What was—"

"Ssh," she said out of the corner of her mouth. "She'll be watching you through the peephole. Once we go in, she'll call my mother with a full report. Come on in."

"You sure you don't want to give her something to report?" Anticipation drummed inside him as he considered a few possibilities.

Sienna's dark eyes took on a wicked gleam, but she pressed her lips to prevent a smile. "No, thanks. My mother's vivid imagination will keep her occupied."

He stepped inside and looked around Sienna's apartment, taking in everything from the handmade afghan tossed on the girlie sofa to the collection of family photos. Sienna's home suited her, but it was an exotic world to him. He was never going to fit in.

Adam thrust out his hand and offered the flowers to her. Her face brightened as pleasure flooded through her. "Thank you," she said as she took them.

The tightness in his chest began to relax. He was glad he had listened to Bill's advice about the flowers. The guy wouldn't give him Sienna's address, but he had plenty to say about treating a good girl right.

Adam watched Sienna turn to the table next to the door, and noticed that she had a glass vase filled with water. The size of the vase would fit the bouquet perfectly. It was too much of a coincidence. "How did you know that I was bringing flowers?" He didn't even know he was going to do it until the last minute.

Sienna gave a guilty smile while she unwrapped the protective paper from the flowers. "One of my friends works the corner store. She called right after you left her counter and told me that you were bringing wine and roses. She was disappointed you didn't buy condoms."

"Don't worry, I have enough."

Her cheeks turned pink as she placed the flowers in the vase. "Considering your reputation, she also wished you'd buy something like duct tape."

"I didn't bother since you brought the scarf home." It was already beginning. People were getting into their business. Her real life was encroaching on their fantasy. Was he ready for that?

It was too late to pull back. It had been from the moment she took the leap and invited him into her world. Or maybe it was the moment he saw her with another man.

No, it was the first time she walked into his life. He took one look and knew he would never be the same again.

"I don't have the scarf anymore," Sienna said as she studied the bouquet and adjusted one of the stems. "It was part of a chain letter, remember? I sent it off."

"Why? You earned the scarf." He thought she would proudly display it in her bedroom or tuck it away where she could feel pride every time she saw it.

"I didn't spend that week with you to get the scarf," she reminded him as she helped him off with his wet jacket and hung it up. "Anyway, it wasn't mine to begin with."

"Who'd you send it to?"

"My hairdresser," she said as she took the wine bottle from him. "The woman is always talking about sex with her clients, so I know she'll put it to good use."

"So could we." There were many things they could have done with that scarf, but he'd only had seven days to work with.

"I'm not asking for it back," she said as she walked toward the kitchen. "Dinner's almost ready. Oh, and Adam?" She stopped at the kitchen doorway.

"Yeah?"

She looked at his rain-splattered jeans and wet oxfords. "Take off your shoes."

Take off your shoes? His jaw dropped as he stared at Sienna's naughty smile. If she was looking for trouble, she had found it. He kicked off his shoes and strode toward her with lightning speed.

Sienna shrieked as he cornered her in the kitchen. He pinned her to the refrigerator and plucked the wine bottle from her hands before he held them above her head. He leaned into her and claimed a long, wet kiss.

"Adam!" She gasped when he ground his cock against her.

"Ssh," he mimicked. "Mrs. Lowenstein will hear you."

Sienna eyes danced as she bit her lip.

"That's better." The real world might be right outside their door, but that could also work in his favor. He reached for the dish towel hanging from the oven door. "You need to be absolutely quiet . . ."

CHAPTER SEVENTEEN

As Tiffany closed up her hair salon for the day, she heard the familiar hum of the garage door. Excitement sharply twisted in her pelvis. James was home.

Tiffany turned to her office nook and opened her bottom desk drawer. Anticipation licked through her veins as she heard James drive his car into the garage next to her tiny shop. She reached in her secret toy box and retrieved the new vibrating cock ring.

She looked at the new purchase in her hand. It supposedly came highly recommended, with a vibrating bullet on the top to stimulate her clitoris. Considering how much she paid for all the watch batteries she put into the vibe, it had better be an amazing experience.

However, the ring looked too small. The jelly rubber would stretch around James's cock, but it could still be a tight, uncomfortable fit for someone his size. Not to mention that she wasn't sure how he would feel about a bright pink jelly ring around his cock.

Tiffany hesitated, closing her fingers around the toy. Should she try it on James so soon after the mishap with the bathtub of Jell-O? Only one way to find out. Tiffany grabbed her Magic 8 Ball.

"Okay, Magic 8 Ball, do your stuff." She shook it hard. "Should I try this new toy out on James today?"

Tiffany rolled the 8 Ball and looked at the answer. *Most definitely.*

Good, she decided with a sly smile. Tiffany set the Magic 8 Ball down and left her shop, but not before checking in the mirror by the back door.

She smoothed down her long brown hair. The sleek-cut style was deceptively casual, just like her red blouse and her fake alligator-skin skirt. James had no idea how much time and effort she put into her appearance. And she had no intention of him ever finding out.

Tiffany fixed a few wispy hairs and decided she was presentable. She closed her hand around the cock ring and stepped out of her shop. After locking the door, she turned the corner and stepped into the garage.

James was just returning from the mailbox, carrying a few catalogs and a small package. His light blue shirt was opened at the neck, his tie long gone. The charcoal trousers he wore emphasized his impressive stature.

The cool autumn breeze had ruffled his black hair. The style was ultrashort and did nothing to hide his receding hairline, but it worked on James.

Whiskers shadowed his jaw, and the lines on his forehead were more pronounced. She saw the dark circles under his eyes that never seemed to disappear, even after a lazy weekend. James was good when it came to kicking back and relaxing. His sense of fun was the first thing that attracted her to him.

She never understood why her friends had been so surprised when she hooked up with James. He had fit all of her requirements, namely single, employed and treated women well. Okay, so he wasn't classically handsome like her ex-husband, but as far as Tiffany was concerned, that was a plus!

James looked up when she hit the button to lower the garage door. His expression brightened when he saw her.

Tiffany felt herself melt a little. She loved the way James looked at her. Like she was the brightest spot of his day. She never wanted that to fade, and made a point of looking sexy and beautiful for him. It wasn't an easy accomplishment since they lived together and had been a couple for the past two years.

"Hi, James," Tiffany said with a seductive smile. She tossed back her hair and strode toward him. "I missed you."

James slowed to a halt. His hopeful expression made her heart turn. She felt stronger and sexier just from his eagerness.

Tiffany stood in front of him and looped her arms around his shoulders. James was very tall, well over six feet. She stretched against him, her small breasts pressing against his lean chest. She tilted her head up and waited for his kiss.

That was the only thing she didn't like about his height. Usually she enjoyed the sensation of James surrounding her, but when she wanted a kiss, she had to wait for him to lean down and bestow it.

Of course, she could always climb up him and get that kiss. She hadn't tried that yet, but then James never refused her, and he never held back.

James leaned down and swept his mouth against hers. She loved his mouth and found James's kisses addictive. A brief touch wasn't enough for her.

Tiffany darted her tongue past his lips, tasting and urging him for more. She heard the mail fall to the floor before he gathered her into his arms and held her tight.

The toy she held bit into her palm, an insistent reminder of her goal. Tiffany tipped her head back, reluctantly pulling her lips from his. "I have something for you."

James arched his eyebrow. "Tell me it's not Jell-O."

"No, but it's close," she admitted.

"I'm scared," he teased.

Tiffany lowered her arms and opened her hand, revealing the powder pink cock ring. She held it up for his inspection.

James eyes widened. "You're kidding, right?"

"They only had pink left. Sorry." She patted his chest. "Don't let the color throw you off. I'm told men rave about this toy."

He took a step back.

She followed him. "Come on, James. Try it. You might like it." She pressed her hand against his growing erection.

He held his hands up, as if warding off the ring. "I'm not going to fit in that thing."

"It stretches," Tiffany promised as she pulled at his belt and slid the leather strap from the buckle.

He looked around the garage. "Are you saying you want to do it here?"

"Sure, why not?" True, it wasn't the most romantic spot. The garage was dark and utilitarian. There were stacks of boxes and holiday decorations tucked in the corners, but the place was clean.

Come to think of it, how was it possible that she hadn't seduced James here before? She must correct that oversight. Tiffany pulled his belt free and went for his zipper.

Tiffany grabbed for James but her hands flailed in the air. She was suddenly sitting on the hood of his car. The metal was still warm from his commute.

He stepped between her legs and pulled her close, angling her hips to fit snugly against him. Her short skirt bunched up her thighs as his cock pressed against her core. She felt his body heat through the layers of clothes.

"That thing is never going to fit me." He motioned at the sex toy with a tilt of his head. "Let's forget about it and do without."

"Hmm . . ." Tiffany reached down and slowly pushed aside his clothes to reveal his cock. "I bet you it will."

"What are you trying to say?"

She pressed her lips to prevent her laughter. "The instructions swear it will fit every man."

"I bet you that piece of rubber will break before you can get it around me."

"You're on." Tiffany smiled at his confidence. She thought it was the sexiest thing about him.

She massaged his testicles before she pumped her hand up and down his cock. She liked the feel of him. Strong and hot. She shifted her hips and anticipation pulsed inside her.

Tiffany gently worked the pink jelly ring around his cock. It was difficult to believe, but the ring only made James's length look bigger and more intimidating. The pink rubber stretched tight, threatening to tear. The vibe bullet on top was minuscule. She absently wondered if she would feel any pulse coming from it.

"Told you," Tiffany said in a singsong voice. When he didn't reply, she glanced up at his face. James's eyes were squeezed shut and his jaw clamped tight.

"Does it hurt?" she asked, gliding her hands against his arousal, ready to rip the ring off.

"No," he said hoarsely. "I wouldn't call it that."

Oh, great. Now he was going to act tough and ignore the possibility of being castrated by something small and pink. "What would you—whoa!" Tiffany found herself flat on her back against the hood of his car. Her legs dangled over the side.

James stripped the undies down her bare legs and over her wedges. Desire wrapped tight inside her when she saw the dark intensity in his eyes. He slid his finger in her wet sex and she arched her neck back, giving a throaty purr.

He rubbed his thumb against her stiff clit as he thrust a finger in her core. Tiffany groaned and wiggled impatiently against the hard surface of the car. "Come on, James." She wanted him in her now.

"Not yet."

She gasped and arched her spine when he slid another finger inside her. Tiffany hooked her legs around James's lean hips. She clamped her thighs against him, desperate to get him closer.

The slow, lazy circles he drew around her clit were nothing like the purposeful and fierce strokes of his fingers. She felt the moisture sliding down her slit, her body on fire as she rocked against the car.

"James, please," she said in a growl.

He withdrew and slid his hands between her and the car. He gripped her buttocks hard, holding her steady, before he made his first powerful thrust.

Tiffany's eyes shot open as he plunged into her. Her mouth sagged open, but her breath caught in her chest. James filled her, slowly stretching her to the point of discomfort. She felt something small and metallic bump against her.

The vibe. She reached down where they were joined together to start the vibrator, but she fumbled against the button. James brushed her hands aside and with one flick of his finger the powerful vibrations racked Tiffany's body. A moan dragged out of her mouth as she twisted and rolled against the churning. James thrust in her, each stroke long and deep.

She felt an intense heat building inside her, layer after layer. Her skin felt hot and tight. Sparks of pleasure crackled just beneath the surface. She felt like she was going to burst after each thrust.

The metallic buzz started to slow. Tiffany frowned as she heard something like gears grinding. She opened her eyes, confused. She looked at James, who seemed just as perplexed as she was.

A bolt of understanding hit them at the same time. They looked down at the cock ring. The batteries were running out.

"Hurry," Tiffany begged. There was no way she was going to stop everything and change batteries.

James's deep strokes grew faster and faster. Tiffany could barely keep up, meeting each thrust. She moaned as hot, thick sensations swirled inside her. She wanted the whirlwind to gain speed, grow hotter and break free.

James seemed closer to his climax. His movements were rough and wild, as if he couldn't master the lust pounding inside him. When his hips matched the breathtaking rhythm, she knew he was going to come.

The fierce, pulsating movements ignited inside her. Her hot coil of desire spiraled out of control. She cried out, her voice echoing in her ears, as the pleasure washed over her.

As the intense heat faded, Tiffany slowly became aware of her surroundings. The dark garage felt cold, but she had a warm, heavy man slumped on top of her. James pinned her to the unyielding car hood, the metal poking in her spine.

"Tiffany," James murmured against her neck, "you screwed my brains out."

She ducked her head and hid her smile. She knew she shouldn't be *proud*. What they had was supposed to be sacred, transcendental and all that other stuff.

But she did what she set out to accomplish. She had come up with yet another wild experience for her man. No complaints coming from him about how unimaginative or clueless or . . .

Tiffany shook her head to clear the thought. She wasn't going down that memory lane. That was years ago. She was a much different person.

Anyway, whatever her ex-husband thought, he was now wrong. She hoped he was gnashing his teeth with envy somewhere while his bimbo girlfriend scrambled to come up with something "imaginative."

James lifted his head. "Are you okay?"

He must have felt the tension invading her body, and she forced herself to relax. "Never better." She speared her fingers in his mussed hair.

He slowly withdrew from her. She sat up and watched him struggle to remove the cock ring from his erection.

"You know, you can ice that and the ring will come off easier." Should she mention that if the ice didn't work, there was always the emergency room?

"Ice?" James gave her a look of horror.

Hmm. She'd mention the emergency room as a last resort. "I'll go get some from the freezer."

James stopped her before she could move. "I can handle it."

"Okay. If you say so." She looked away and her gaze caught the stack of mail on the floor. There was a small package among the catalogs and bills. A *discreet* brown package.

Another toy. She was sure of it. She couldn't remember what she had ordered, but Tiffany knew she had to hide it. At least for a little while, until James got over the cock ring.

"Honey," she said sweetly, trying not to look at the mail, "why don't you go on ahead and take a nice, hot shower? I'm sure that would help."

He kept pulling at the pink jelly ring. "Yeah, good idea." James slowly walked out of the garage. Tiffany waited until she heard the creaking of the stairs before she hopped off of the car. She ignored her undies on the floor and scooped up the small package.

"I got it off!" he called down, sounding victorious and somewhat relieved.

"That's great!" Tiffany flipped the package over but didn't see a return address. Okay, some sex toy boutiques took "discreet" just a little too far. She frowned when she saw the cancellation stamp in the corner. There was a sex shop in town?

She tore the package open, getting excited. She liked surprising James with something new and different. It gave her an edge and kept him on his toes.

Purple silk toppled out of the brown envelope. "No . . ." Tiffany stared at it. It can't be. There had to be some mistake.

"Tiff?" James called from the stairwell. "Are you okay?"

"Nooo!" she wailed. She picked up the letter, vaguely hearing James running down the steps. The paper was lucky it was laminated or she would have torn it into a million pieces.

James appeared in the doorway, zipping up his pants. "What's wrong?"

She looked up from the letter and held it out to him. "I got it. *Again.*"

CHAPTER EIGHTEEN

"**G**ot what?"

"The damn fantasy chain letter!" Tiffany picked up the scarf and shook it in her fist. The gold thread seemed to dance gleefully. "Someone else sent it to me. Isn't there a rule against this sort of thing?"

James pressed his lips together. It looked like he was trying hard not to smile. "James," she said as she narrowed her eyes, "this is not a laughing matter."

"Sorry." He coughed back a chuckle before rubbing his hand over his face. "Maybe it's a different chain letter."

She didn't think so because she recognized the scarf. It was a beautiful shade of purple with gold threads dotting it. But she scanned the letter, hoping she could be wrong.

"It says: 'Dear Friend, I'm offering you the chance of a lifetime. You can live out your ultimate fantasy within one week of receiving this gift, provided you pass it on. All that is required from you is this: You must use the scarf during a sexual encounter in the next seven days.'" She looked up from the letter and glared at James.

He shrugged and leaned against the door frame. "There could be a new rule."

"'Mail the scarf and this letter to a female acquaintance within one week of receiving this package.'" Tiffany continued to read, lowering her voice into an exaggerated, ominous tone. "'Do not tell or discuss it with the woman. Those who follow these instructions will continue a fulfilling sensual odyssey. Those who don't will never find satisfaction for as long as they live.' "

"That's it? Nothing added?"

"Nope. The same Kali signed it." She slapped the letter against her hip and looked up at the ceiling. "Why are people always sending me these things?"

"Because they know that you're superstitious."

"That doesn't mean I *like* chain letters. I hate them!" She shook the laminated note and wanted to growl her frustration. "The only reason I follow them is because I respect their power."

James watched her silently as she picked up everything from the floor. "So what are you going to do?" he finally asked.

"What do you mean? Haven't you been listening?" What was she asking? Telling James anything immediately after sex was like eating before swimming. She should wait at least thirty minutes before she made the attempt. "I'm going to have to follow those rules again."

"Oh, poor baby," James teased, his brown eyes taking on a wicked glint. "I really heard you complaining last time."

Tiffany remembered how James had tied her to the bed. She paused as a quick flash of desire scorched through her. She remembered that night, letting James have his way with her and being unable to do anything to stop him. That night had been wild and she wasn't against repeating it.

"Well, guess what we'll be doing tonight?" She sashayed past him and started up the stairs.

"Hold on," James said at the bottom of the stairs. "We're going to do the same thing again?"

"Yeah." She bristled at the question and stopped. She hadn't heard him complain about sex, but then, she made sure they rarely repeated. Surely he could handle that for one night. This was special circumstances!

James followed her up the steps. "Are you sure you want to do that?"

She was only sure of one thing. "I want to get this scarf out of my life as quickly as possible."

"I understand that, but we shouldn't repeat what we've already done."

"Why not?" she asked as she continued to climb up the stairs.

"Obviously it didn't work," James argued.

She stared at the scarf. Had she somehow broken the rules and that's why it came back?

"The letter says that using the scarf would send you on a sensual odyssey," James said, standing right behind her. "You got the scarf again because you haven't started it."

Tiffany shook her head. "No, that can't be. I used the scarf and I followed the directions."

"Okay, the wrong odyssey."

James had a point. Tiffany didn't believe in coincidences. She had gotten the scarf again for a reason. She was all for the lifelong satisfaction the letter promised, but couldn't this Kali person offer an instruction manual? Some ideas on how to use the scarf?

Because, as much as Tiffany would love to think she was as creative as the next person, her ideas were not spawned from her imagination or needs. She got them from books and sex-toy sites. She relied on her clients talking about their adventures rather than devising one on her own.

Maybe her ex-husband was still right about her. Maybe she wasn't instinctively sexy. Sure, she wore the seductive clothes and had a good business transforming her clients from frumpy to fabulous, but she wasn't as sensual as she looked.

Tiffany sighed as the doubts pricked at her. She couldn't let her ex-husband's hurtful words find their target. She was just as sexy and sensual as any other woman out there.

So what if she relied on other people's ideas? Who cared? At least she was adventurous enough to try them. And that was all that mattered.

Now she only had to come up with another idea on how to use the scarf. She stuffed her fingers in her hair and groaned. This stupid chain letter was really putting her through the paces.

"Tiffany?"

"I'm fine, James," she said wearily as she headed toward the dining room table. "But I swear, there should be a cosmic law against this." She gave the scarf another shake, hating how the gold streaks caught the fading sunlight and sparkled.

James wrapped his arm around her shoulders and gave her an encouraging hug. "Think of this as an opportunity. Look at the positive side to this."

She slanted a look at him. "Like, since I got this twice, I should get twice the pleasure?"

His smile was downright naughty. "That's the spirit."

"Easy for you to say," she mumbled as she dumped everything she held onto the table. "You don't have to come up with an idea."

"Then let me."

"You?" His offer came as a surprise. She must have misunderstood. "You want to come up with an idea?"

He gave another shrug. "Yeah, sure. Why not?"

She might as well let him. It would be one less thing to worry about. "Okay, but there's a time limit."

"I know."

"I have to mail this scarf out in seven days. So think fast." She gave him a pat on his arm and stepped away, but James wrapped his hand around her wrist, requiring Tiffany to stand where she was. She glanced up at him and saw the excitement glimmer in his eyes. "You already came up with an idea?"

"How about if you tie me up?"

Tiffany froze as her instincts went haywire with James's suggestion. Something dangerous and troubling curled inside her, nestling in the dark region of her mind, ready to strike.

It was a bad idea. She didn't know why she thought that, but she wasn't going to question her instincts. They'd never let her down before. Now wasn't the time to poke at her worries and investigate. Tiffany knew she had to distract James from pushing that idea.

"Well, that's one option," she said as she cautiously removed her wrist from his hand.

James frowned. "What's wrong with it? You have to admit, we've never tried it."

"True, but I know you're feeling rushed because of the time frame. I'm a firm believer that you should never go with your first idea. So keep trying," Tiffany said with a bright smile. "You'll come up with something great. I just know it."

James lay in bed later that night, flipping the TV channels with the remote control as he waited for Tiffany. He wasn't paying much attention to the screen. The canned laughter sounded like it was in the distance, and the bright colors didn't mesmerize him. His mind was still wrapped around what had happened when he asked to act out his secret fantasy.

He couldn't believe Tiffany had dismissed his idea out of hand. It was a good thing she didn't know it was one of his deepest, darkest fantasies. He didn't think it was ridiculous or way out there. Considering how he got to tie Tiffany to the bed last time, she should have been all over his suggestion and eager to play it out immediately.

Granted, she would have to do all the work while he lay there and enjoyed the attention, but seriously, how was that different from any other day? Tiffany preferred to take charge and be in control. Or at least, she liked the illusion.

James turned off the TV and tossed the remote control on his bedside table. Was Tiffany so used to deciding what they were going to do that she couldn't give it up? Not even for one night? It was unfair, and he wasn't going to put up with it.

Most of her ideas were less than successful, but he never complained. Toys malfunctioned, potions and lotions didn't live up to their promise, and he was still sporting a scar on his big toe after their last Tantric experience. As strange as it might seem, he wouldn't change a bit of it.

James smiled as fragments of the most sensual memories flickered through his mind. He had never expected to find someone as demonstrative and affectionate as Tiffany. She was everything he longed for and he couldn't believe his luck in finding her. He was more than willing to risk a few bruises and permanent food-coloring dye if it meant being the recipient of her eager attention.

But he honestly never thought she would deny him this one wish. James rolled to his side and looked at the bathroom door, waiting for Tiffany. Why did she say no? Tiffany *never* said no. She was willing to try anything once.

He knew this, and yet he had never suggested getting tied to the bed before. It was like he had predicted she would reject it out of hand. How did he know?

He had liked tying her to the bed the last time they received the scarf. He remembered that she couldn't stop laughing, but her giggles turned to shrieks when he tickled her. The wrestling got wicked very quickly, and while he enjoyed it, there was a moment when the image flickered in his mind of their roles reversed. The possibility had fueled more than one wet dream since then.

When he saw the purple scarf in Tiffany's hand today, he knew he had to make the most of this opportunity. This was his one chance to fulfill that fantasy.

Or so he thought.

Maybe he had rushed the idea. He didn't present it at the right time. He should have waited until she wasn't annoyed about the chain letter.

But something told him that there would never be a perfect time to convince her. Not a request from her fiancé or an ancient curse. She wasn't interested in tying him up.

James heard the bathroom door open and he inhaled the steamy cloud of Tiffany's tantalizing bath oil. She was framed in the doorway, wearing a short lace nightgown that left nothing to the imagination. He swallowed roughly when he saw the dusky nipples peeking through the lace. His cock stirred when she shifted her legs, revealing the trimmed strip of hair covering her sex.

Tiffany turned off the light and chuckled at his groan of protest. She loved to tease him and he bet she'd strut the rest of the way to the bed. James could barely see the outline of her figure, and the white, lacy nightgown took on a bluish tinge.

She slid between the sheets and curled up against him. Her breasts pressed against his chest as she wrapped her arms around him. "James," she said after she gave him a soft kiss on the lips. "I was thinking..."

"Yeah?" He caressed the curve of her hip and his fingertips skimmed the short, flirty hem of her nightgown.

"We shouldn't use the scarf tonight."

He held the disappointment at bay and continued to stroke his hand down the length of her leg. He couldn't get enough of her warm, soft skin. "Are you sure?" he asked. "The chain letter doesn't give you a lot of time."

"But you know how bad luck comes in threes."

He frowned, wondering what that had to do with the chain letter. "I'm not following you."

"Well..." She sounded distracted as she drew lazy designs on his chest with her fingers. "First there was the Jell-O fiasco, and then there was the cock ring incident."

"Incident?" His hand paused at the back of her knee. "Nothing bad happened with the cock ring."

"You couldn't get it off," she reminded him.

"I had trouble removing it," he corrected as he hooked her knee over his leg, "because it was too small to begin with."

"As I was saying," she continued a little louder. "It's obvious we shouldn't try to use the scarf at this time. We need to try something new. Then, when we use the scarf, we won't taint it with bad luck."

It was the most convoluted piece of logic he had ever heard, James decided as he reached down and stroked her slit. She was hot, slick and ready for him. His cock swelled in response.

But he wasn't going to have her in the way he wanted. He bet Tiffany had worked on her excuse all during her bath, which meant she was doing her best to stay away from the scarf. She really didn't want to face the possibility of tying him up.

But she couldn't stay away for long, he mused as he played with her stiff clitoris and enjoyed the way her hips swiveled in response. Tiffany was too superstitious. He could afford to back off for now and be patient for one more day.

"What do you suggest we do instead?" he asked, sliding his finger into her sex. He was so ready to burrow his cock into her.

"Hopscotch," she said in a hoarse whisper.

He squinted in the dark and stared at her face as his eyes adjusted to the dark. "Hopscotch?"

Tiffany closed her eyes and nodded. "Beth, one of my clients, told me all about this position called the Hopscotch."

"Why?"

She swiped her tongue along her bottom lip. "Why did Beth tell me?"

"No." He reluctantly withdrew his finger from her wet sex. "Why is it called Hopscotch?"

"No idea, but that's not the point. Basically I lie down"—she turned on her back—"and I put my feet against your chest." She waited a moment. "This is where you come in."

"Where am I?"

"You kneel in front of me."

He reluctantly got up and knelt in front of her, her ass resting against his knees. He didn't know what he was supposed to do with his hands. He decided to hold her right ankle with his left hand and her left knee with his right hand. He didn't want to get too fancy. "Now what?"

"What do you think?" Her tone was saucy.

"That's it?" That was too easy compared to some of the new positions Tiffany discovered. "No sudden rotating? No back bends?"

"None of that, I promise." She bucked her hips against him, urging him on. "This position is supposed to be good. Beth raved about deep penetration."

"I really don't want to think about what Beth likes." But he liked the deep-penetration part. A lot. His body shook with anticipation.

"Of course, we could always try the one where I do a head-stand—"

"Hopscotch." He wasn't up to anything that was too dangerous. "I vote for Hopscotch."

He gripped her ankle and knee before he slowly drove inside her. Her flesh clutched him and sucked him in. He almost didn't want to leave. James retreated and thrust again, penetrating even deeper. His knees shook at how good it felt.

He could tell that Tiffany liked the new position. She rocked against him, matching his pace and urging him to go faster. Her whispered pleas barely reached his ears as her feet pushed against his chest.

Suddenly her sex gripped him hard and pulsed around him. It was the most incredible sensation and he didn't want it to end. He drove his cock into her several more times before he came. James couldn't have held on any longer if he tried, with her tight core ruthlessly squeezing his ejaculation out of him.

James hissed between his teeth as he withdrew from Tiffany's warmth. His body ached and the cool air stung his skin. He lay down next to Tiffany and tucked her against him.

"Thank Beth for me," he murmured against Tiffany's hair.

Her laugh was languid. "Will do. It was nice trying something new that worked the first time."

James murmured his agreement when the thought occurred to him. "Does that mean we broke the 'bad luck in threes' rule?"

Tiffany yawned. "Not quite."

Which meant she'd try something new tomorrow. And if that went perfectly, she would try something else. Something that wasn't the scarf because she didn't want to "taint" it with the bad luck.

Damn. He should have seen that coming.

CHAPTER NINETEEN

Tiffany woke up before her alarm clock went off Saturday morning. She blinked her eyes open and found herself up close to James's smooth, muscular chest. She sighed as his heat enveloped her and snuggled deeper in his embrace.

She closed her eyes, wishing she could have another hour or two of sleep. James slept soundly; she had spent most of the night worrying. How was she going to use the scarf without tying him up?

The scarf had to be used within the week. That was a no-brainer. She couldn't ignore the threat of a curse. Unfortunately, James knew how superstitious she was and would use it to his advantage.

He had to know that she would use the scarf within the week, so he was biding his time. When she did bring it to the bed, he was going to insist on being tied up. Unless she came up with a solid reason not to use his suggestion, she would be stuck doing just that.

No excuse came to mind. She couldn't lie and say she had a bad experience with bondage. That would have been brought up when he had tied her up with the scarf the last time. She couldn't tell him why she didn't want to tie him up. She wasn't quite sure herself, and she didn't want to delve into it.

Even if she was inspired with a good lie, she had no alternative idea on how to use the scarf. She thought of everything from binding her feet to using the scarf as a trapeze. Yet bringing a Cirque du Soleil element into her bedroom was not going to make James forget what he really wanted to do.

She should never have complained in front of him. Tiffany sighed, her ribs shuddering as she exhaled. She should have never suggested he come up with an idea.

What possessed her to do that? She liked being the one who came up with the ideas. She wanted to be the best lover James ever knew. She wanted to be so good that he would think twice before wanting another woman. He needed to know that he had the best sex waiting at home.

Best sex? Tiffany scrunched up her nose. That sounded so unromantic. Best lover? That didn't sound right, either.

Maybe the right term was best sex partner. She was all about pleasuring him. If he was satisfied, then so was she. She made sure she climaxed, and James was a thoughtful lover, but her goal was to make *his* mind melt and toes curl backward every time.

There were a few times when she wished James would surprise her with sex. Do something that made her know that it wasn't just the sex, or that he had a willing partner. She needed to know that he wanted *her*.

She didn't know what he could do to prove that. If she had to come up with the plan, then it wouldn't be that much of a surprise! But if she let James come up with the idea, he'd still want to be tied up.

The alarm went off and Tiffany jumped in surprise. She twisted around in James's arms and reached out to hit the clock button. She'd have to think about her pleasure later. Right now she had to come up with ways to distract James for six more days. It wasn't going to be easy.

James stirred and groaned, just like he did every morning as the alarm ripped him from his sleep. His hands glided up her rib cage, his movements hiking up her short nightgown. "Don't go," he said drowsily.

She smiled as he squeezed her breasts, the lace biting into her skin. The sting flashed through her body and desire pressed low in her belly.

She rubbed her legs together, but that only made the spark of lust flare brighter. Tiffany glanced at the clock and decided she could fit in a quickie before her first appointment.

She leaned back, signaling her surrender. His low growl of triumph made her sex heat and swell. He shoved aside the straps of her nightgown and fondled her nipples. Tiffany arched her back, thrusting deeper into his hands. His thick cock pressed against her ass. She wiggled against him as her pulse quickened. Her chest rose and fell as anticipation gripped her chest.

"Turn around," James said against her ear. His voice was still husky with sleep.

She did as he requested, her breath hitching in her throat as her tight nipples rasped against his chest. She scooted up and placed a soft kiss against his mouth. His whiskers grazed her lips and she liked the bite. Tiffany pressed her hands against his jaw, the stubble poking her skin as she deepened the kiss.

James's hands roamed along her back, the lace slithering under his palms. Tiffany thought he was going to grab and knead her ass, but instead he held her tight and rolled on his back, carrying her with him.

She lay on top of him, her hair falling over their faces like a curtain. Tiffany straddled James's hips, his cock nestled against her slit. She sat up straight and grabbed the hem of her nightgown. Slowly shimmying out of the lace, Tiffany rocked against him with each move before tossing her nightgown onto the floor.

She flipped her hair back and gave James ample time to stare at her. She knew her smile was victorious when she felt his cock leap underneath her. Tiffany caught his gaze and her smile dipped. The intense, loving look in his eyes told her what she needed to know. He wanted *her*.

Tiffany ran her hands along her face and neck down to her breasts.

She moaned and whimpered as she plucked her nipples until they became tight and red. She enjoyed watching his expression harden. James's hands slid up and down her legs, his grip tightening as he encouraged her to keep going.

"Tiffany..." His voice was so rough and low that it gave her goose bumps.

"Hmm?" she asked, tilting her head back, her long hair swinging against the base of her spine.

James's hands tightened on her thighs. "Where's the scarf?"

His question was like a slap of cold water on her skin. She froze. "Scarf?"

"The one with the chain letter," he said, his hips bucking gently under her. "We could use that now."

She was flaunting her body to him and he was thinking of the scarf? "No, James."

James squeezed his eyes shut. "Why not? What do you have against tying me up?"

She didn't want to get into it. "I don't have time," she said as she swung her leg over and got off the bed. "I have to get ready for work."

"Do you know," he said harshly, "that this is the only sexual favor I've asked from you?"

Tiffany stiffened under the accusation. That couldn't be right. She was sure he had asked her to perform sex acts, although she couldn't think of any at the moment. What man wouldn't when he had a woman who made a point of always being ready and available for him?

"I have to get ready for work." She ducked her head and made her way to the bathroom.

"I didn't hold back when you were tied up," James pointed out. "In fact, I've never denied you."

He made it sound like it was a chore having sex with her, when she made a point of giving him pleasure. Tiffany pivoted on her heel. "Why do you want it so badly? Why do you need to get tied up? It's not like you're always in control and need a break."

James abruptly sat up. "You think you're in charge? Every time?"

"Why does that sound so shocking?" She put her hands on her hips and stared back at him. He had no idea all the work she put into this relationship. "I come up with the ideas. I tell you exactly what to do, and then we do it."

"Tiffany"—he slowly shook his head—"you are in for a big surprise."

She rolled her eyes. "Whatever. I have to get ready." She hurried into the bathroom. She didn't know where James got off complaining, but she was sure about one thing: He was not going to give up the idea of getting tied up.

He was *never* in control? *He* was never in control? What planet was Tiffany living on? James was still reeling over her revelation that morning. He had spent most of the day pacing and stewing. It usually took a lot to get him mad, but it felt like nothing was going to calm him down.

If Tiffany really thought that she was always in control when they had sex, then she needed to learn from her mistake. Right now, James decided as he marched down to the garage. He would teach Tiffany that not only was he often in charge, but that he let her get away with a lot because he liked to spoil her.

He didn't feel like spoiling her now. He wanted to teach her a lesson. James strode to the back of the garage and tried the door that led to her hair salon. He was glad to see it was unlocked and he quietly stepped inside.

The scent of chemicals and fruity hair products hit him first. Next was the sound of the radio. He turned the corner, walked past the minuscule bathroom and saw Tiffany alone in the salon, sweeping the floor.

He smiled with appreciation at her light blue cheetah-print shirt. It fit snugly, emphasizing her small curves. Her skintight jeans accentuated her ass, as the low waist revealed a hint of skin.

James quietly walked behind her and, with one swift move, he curled his arm around her waist. Tiffany screamed and he clamped his other hand over her mouth. He pressed her against his body as the call of the hunt echoed deep inside him.

She kicked and twisted, and he was surprised by her strength. James ducked as she swung the broom at his head. He shifted his stance and saw their reflection in the mirror.

Whoa. Tiffany looked small and defenseless against him. He had never seen her like that before. He looked dark and dangerous, which he'd never been accused of. He wasn't sure if he liked it or not.

"James?" she asked, her word muffled against his hand. She sagged as relief poured through her. "What are you doing?"

He ignored her question and wrestled the broom from her grasp. James tossed it to the side, letting it drop to the floor with a clatter.

"James?" she said louder, giving a hard jab with her elbows. James winced, but drew her closer. He walked backward, carrying her with him. Tiffany resisted, her heels dragging against the hard floor.

He passed the bathroom and belatedly remembered the step up to her office area. He stumbled but stayed upright as he turned the corner. No one walking by the windows would see them. Tiffany must have realized the same thing, as her spine went rigid.

He slid his hand from her mouth and down her throat. James tilted her head back against his shoulder. He was tempted to kiss her and drive his tongue deep into her mouth. He wanted it so much that his lips tingled, but her kisses always drove him crazy. He had to stay focused.

"If this is about what I said this morning . . ." She trailed off as his hand went to the metal button of her jeans. She swatted at his fingers. "Fine, you have just as much control as I do. There? Are you happy?"

He didn't answer as he dragged her zipper down. The sound of metal scratching metal was loud to his ears.

Tiffany grabbed his fingers, trying to pull them away from her clothes. "My next client is going to show up any minute." Urgency pulsed in her voice.

"Then you better get on your hands and knees now."

Her fingers froze against his. "No way."

"This is the second time you've denied my request, and all on the same day. If you plan to withhold sex from me altogether because I asked to be tied up, you better tell me now."

She didn't say anything, and fear shot through him. Was that her plan? Should he pull back, damn his pride, and continue to let her think she had absolute control over him?

"No," she said slowly. "I wouldn't do that. Why would I punish myself?"

James wanted to sigh with relief, but the fear still burned in his chest. "Get on your hands and knees."

She let go of his hands. "Your timing sucks."

He needed to see her face. He couldn't tell what was going on in her head. James whirled her around and pressed her against the wall. "*My* timing sucks? Did I complain when you gave me head at my office?" he asked.

"I was under your desk when your boss came in," she was quick to point out. "He never saw me."

"But you kept going down on me the whole time he was talking." He remembered that moment with perfect clarity. He had fought to form coherent sentences as Tiffany had deep-throated him. His boss had looked at him like he was a moron, but he hadn't cared at the time. He had done everything he could not to come until the man left his office. It had been a near thing.

"What are you complaining about?" She seemed genuinely at a loss. "Most guys would pay for an experience like that."

He shoved her shirt and bra up, revealing her breasts. Her nipples were already tight and erect. He leaned his head down and licked them as he pulled her jeans and undies down her legs.

James inhaled her aroused scent and cupped her sex. She was slick and ready for him. He sucked one of her nipples hard. Her guttural groan set off a spark of white heat in his blood. Tiffany gripped his hair in her hands. "Hurry," she begged.

He rose and towered over her, frowning. "What makes you think you can tell me what to do and when?"

"I'm sorry"—she gasped as he pressed his thumb against her clit— "for when I said you were never in charge."

"You're just saying that," he drawled as he drew small circles against her clitoris. "You don't really think I was in control. I let you have your way, but you never saw that."

She whimpered and closed her eyes. "Come on, James."

"I spoiled you. Whatever you wanted to do, you got it," he informed her as he trailed his finger along her slit. His cock pressed against his jeans, ready to sink into her. "I was your personal playground."

"You enjoyed it." Her eyes flashed with anger.

He dipped his finger past the folds of her sex and her flesh gripped him hard. James paused, fighting back the need to drop his jeans and slam his cock into her hot, wet core.

"I'm telling you right now that those days are over," he said hoarsely as he pumped inside her, his cock throbbing with need as he watched Tiffany ride his hand, chasing her pleasure. "If I'm not going to get my way, neither are you."

The bell over the door chimed. Tiffany's hips stopped moving, but he kept pumping into her. He stared into her eyes, which were blurry with lust.

"Damn you, James," she whispered, her body shaking.

He knew how she felt. Tiffany wanted him to continue, but she knew she should make him stop. She licked her lips as he thrust his fingers quickly, picking up the pace. He knew her body ached to ride his hand fast and get a quick release, but every other instinct told her to pull back. She was probably wondering if he would stop if she asked. Or did she think he wouldn't listen to prove a point?

"Hello?" It was a feminine voice. "Is anyone here?"

"Just a minute," Tiffany called out before she gave James a pleading look. He pumped harder and watched her eyes roll back.

"Okay. I'm Grace Russell," the woman called out, her voice sounding nearer than before. "I'm a neighbor, and a bunch of us are planning a networking party for all the entrepreneurs in the complex."

"Hold on a second," Tiffany said.

James noticed the frantic note in Tiffany's voice. Despite what she might think, he didn't want to embarrass her. He reluctantly withdrew from her wet heat. Her disappointed groan went straight to his cock.

He stepped away and let her go before he went with his instinct to throw her over his shoulder and take her to bed. "Did you hear what I said?" he said softly. "If I don't get my way, neither do you."

"Yeah. I got your message loud and clear," she whispered fiercely as she zipped up her jeans. "I tried to be your fantasy girl, but because I won't fulfill one lousy request, then I can forget about it."

"I didn't say that."

She adjusted her bra and pulled down her shirt. "Next you'll tell me that you'll go elsewhere to get what you want."

James staggered back. He felt like he'd been sucker punched. "What?"

"You men are all alike." Hurt shimmered in her eyes. "You desperately want what you can't have, even if it means ruining a good thing."

He reached out to yank her back and tell her how wrong she had it, but Tiffany dodged his hand. She placed a smile on her face as she stepped around the corner. "Hi, Grace, I'm Tiffany. What can I do for you?"

James leaned his head against the wall, tempted to knock a hole through it. She did all this because she wanted to be his fantasy girl? Why didn't he notice that?

How was he going to show her that he wanted her, and only her? He didn't know, but it was obvious that he was ruining a good thing. He needed to fix it, and fast.

CHAPTER TWENTY

After work, Tiffany avoided James and skipped dinner. She headed straight to their room, claiming a headache, which wasn't too far away from the truth. She soaked in the bath until her fingers and toes resembled prunes, but she finally had a plan.

She would surrender and tie James to the bed. She didn't feel like she had any other choice. For once, she didn't control their sex life, and she didn't like it.

Tiffany did what she could to boost her courage. She dressed in her slinky tiger-print nightgown. The spaghetti straps and high hemline should make her feel exposed, but the color and stripes reminded her to act like a fearless predator. She needed to assume that role tonight, especially since she didn't feel like it.

She heard James walk into the room. He leaned against the doorway and she felt his gaze on her. Tiffany's movements became choppy and disjointed, but she pressed on. She did her best to ignore him as she searched her drawer of lingerie.

"What are you looking for?" he finally asked.

"The scarf," she said in a mumble as she opened another drawer and riffled through her socks. She knew she had hidden it so James wouldn't stumble upon it, but she didn't think she hid it that well.

The tension rolled off of James. "*The* scarf."

"Yeah." She slid the drawer closed and opened the one below it. "The stupid purple one that came with the chain letter. How many scarves do you think I have?"

"Uh, why are you looking for it?"

She looked up at him. Wasn't it obvious? "I'm tying you up to the bed."

There was no change in his expression. No smile. No jolt of interest or immediate tearing off of his clothes. His eyes were hooded as he studied her. "What changed your mind?"

"Oh, don't get all thrilled on me." The man had no idea how much it was costing her to do this. He should be grateful and throw himself on his knees and thank her.

"I'm thrilled on the inside."

"What happened?" She shoved all the neatly folded silks and cottons to one side of the drawer. "You've been drooling over the idea and, now that I'm giving it to you, you're not happy. Make up your mind."

He shoved his hands in his jeans pockets and crossed one foot over the other. "I would have liked it more if it was something you wanted to do."

Now he was asking for too much. "James, get over it. I want to make you happy. If this makes you happy"—she slammed the drawer shut—"then I'm happy."

"You don't sound happy."

"I'm ecstatic," she said through clenched teeth as she pulled the bottom drawer open. "Yes! Here's the scarf." She grabbed the purple silk and clenched it in her fist.

"Are you mad because of what I did in your salon?" he asked, watching her intently. "Are you plotting revenge?"

She made a face. "I'm not the vengeful type." She was angry over what he had said and done, but honestly, was it anything different from how she jumped him and had her wicked way?

As much as she'd love to tie him up and torment him to within an inch of his sanity, she wasn't going to do it. Not only did she want to get this over and done with as quickly as possible, she knew any form of revenge would backfire.

James tilted his head. "This wouldn't have anything to do with your horoscope today, would it?"

Tiffany didn't look at him as she slid the drawer closed and slowly stood up. "You read my horoscope?"

"It's helped me on many occasions," James admitted. "Today yours suggested trying something new because the day 'favors broadening your horizons,' or something like that."

She twisted the scarf around her hands, not daring to look him in the eye. "I might read my horoscope, but that doesn't mean I base all my decisions on what it says."

"Really?" He drew the word out. "So we're no longer waiting for the most auspicious day to get married? Good to know."

Tiffany's jaw shifted to one side. "I already did my new thing for the day, so this doesn't apply."

"What was the new thing?" He sounded suspicious.

Tiffany looked at him and batted her eyelashes. "I said no to you when you wanted sex," she revealed sweetly. "I must say it has broadened my horizons."

His face darkened and he pushed off from the door frame. "Don't plan to make it a habit."

Tiffany wanted to take a step back, but she remained where she stood. "Sure, you can sound tough now, but when you're tied up"—she dangled the scarf in front of his face—"there's not much you can do about it."

James snatched the scarf and gave it a fierce tug. She pitched forward and stumbled before bumping into him. James wrapped his arm around her waist, holding her tight. She still refused to let go of the scarf.

"You're really going to tie me up?" he asked. "To the bed?"

"That's right." There was something different about him tonight. She had seen glimpses of this hard side of James, and it made her nervous. Not scared, but it set her on edge. She couldn't predict what he would do, and the volatile atmosphere crackled between them.

His eyes narrowed into slits. "What's the catch?"

She frowned at his line of questioning. Why did he suspect her actions? She had never given him reason before. "There's no catch."

James stood silently, watching her until the tension between them felt like it was going to snap. He dropped the scarf and took his hand away from her. "I'll take a rain check on the offer. Thanks anyway."

Rain check? Her eyes widened as she stood still. She hadn't expected that. She was giving him what he wanted and he wasn't raring to go. Why?

The only thing she could think of was her attitude. She was prickly and obviously not eager. She needed to work on her presentation, be more of a seductress than a martyr if she wanted to get over this hurdle.

And that was exactly what this was. All she had to do was tie him up once. Just once, and then she would have given him what he wanted. He wouldn't go looking for another woman who would do what she refused.

Of course, he could still go to another woman. The possibility made her want to double over from the pain. Or maybe he would discover after tonight that he wanted to get tied up again and again. What if this one night inspired a full-fledged fantasy that knew no bounds?

"James, this is your only chance." She placed her hands on both sides of the scarf and stretched the silk. "You either get tied up with the scarf tonight, or I will never tie you up."

Tiffany regretted those words the moment they left her mouth. She saw the dark thunder roll in James. His expression darkened as the muscle bunched in his tight jaw. She knew she had gone too far, but she couldn't pull back.

"Is this an ultimatum?" he asked, his voice raspy.

Tiffany bit her lip. It did sound like one. So much for her seductress role. She didn't want to make threats, especially if he tossed an ultimatum right back at her. "I am informing you that there is a small window of opportunity."

James stared at her like he didn't know what had happened to his affectionate fiancée. The woman who adored sex and wanted nothing more than to give him pleasure. He didn't realize that the woman had her limits until he slammed against them.

"The window is closing," she said.

James moved his arm. Tiffany held her breath, not sure what he was going to do. Would he take away the scarf? Would he grab her like he did in the salon and flaunt his physical power?

He reached for his shirt and pulled it up and over his head. He didn't look away as he reached the snap of his jeans and shucked them off. "Where do you want me?" he asked coldly as he stripped off his underwear.

Tiffany drew in a ragged breath. He was meeting her challenge. She didn't know if she should feel triumphant or beaten at her own game. Tiffany wanted to get this over and done with, but most of all, she wished she had the power to erase his wish altogether.

"I want you on the bed, of course." She didn't sound as nonchalant as she would have liked. It was difficult to sound detached when she was too nervous to breathe.

James strode to the bed and Tiffany couldn't help but watch him. His back was broad with solid muscle, tapering down to his lean waist and compact buttocks. Her stomach did a naughty flip as she watched his ass move with each step. The muscles rippled in his powerful thighs as he knelt on the bed and lay down.

She noticed that he took his side of the bed out of habit. Every move he had made since he decided to take her up on her offer was too smooth and leisurely. She wanted to take him out of his comfort zone in any way she could.

"In the center of the bed, please," Tiffany said, strolling toward him. She let the scarf drag on the floor behind her.

The corner of his mouth twitched with impatience, but he slid to the center of the mattress without saying a word.

Tiffany crawled on the bed and knelt at his side. Her gaze wandered along his naked body. He didn't move, but she felt the power and strength shimmering off of him. His cock jutted up proudly.

"Hands above your head," she said.

He gave her a sidelong glance. "Are you going to participate during any of this?"

"Of course." She held up the scarf. "I'm going to tie you up. Unless you would like to do this on your own."

"No, thanks. The honor is all yours."

She ignored the sarcastic edge to his words and reached for one hand. She tied the scarf around his wrist, noting that the purple silk looked fragile next to his hand. She tugged the knot a little harder before threading the scarf through the headboard and tying his other wrist.

"Comfy?" she asked with an ultrabright smile.

He gave the scarf a tug. She gave a quick check at the headboard when it rattled, but he didn't break free.

She slowly exhaled with relief that she had tied him up correctly, and straddled James's waist. She leaned down, bracketing his face with her hands.

"Aren't you overdressed for the occasion?" he asked, lifting up one eyebrow.

The man didn't show any signs of being at a disadvantage. She pretended to ponder his question for a moment. "No." Tiffany leaned down and kissed him. Short, teasing kisses as he tried to capture her mouth with his. What made him think he could catch her? she wondered. Did he think he was just as quick as she was, even when he was bound to the bed?

She slid her hands along his arms and chest. She liked the thud of his heart under her palm as much as watching his muscles flex under her hands. But something was wrong. James didn't show any signs of excitement. He watched her with an icy expression as she drew designs on his body with her hands.

His skin was warm, not hot or slick with sweat. Why wasn't he getting turned on? Did he really need her to be naked? That was never a requirement before.

She tried to remember what James had done when he tied her up. That had been a wild night. She had gotten so turned on so fast that she came several times.

What did James do exactly? She dotted kisses from his chest to his stomach, but she couldn't remember much of that night other than how he made her feel. Tiffany dipped her tongue into his navel, watching his muscles contract.

She moved down to his cock and hesitated. Usually by this time his cock would be shiny wet and slapping against his stomach. He was erect and aroused, but not by much.

Maybe he was nervous. She glanced up at his face and found him watching her. If James was nervous about having his fantasy fulfilled, he hid it amazingly well. His chest rose and fell in a calm, regular pattern. His skin wasn't flushed. His eyes didn't glitter with need, nor did his nostrils flare as he held onto his restraint.

The man didn't need any type of restraint. If he was any calmer, he would be asleep. *Terrific.* She was trying her best to give James his dream and instead he was nodding off.

There was one thing that he couldn't sleep through, Tiffany thought with a sly smile. She grasped the base of his cock and gave him a good squeeze. James's hips vaulted off the bed.

She encircled his length with both hands and gripped him as

tightly as she could, slowly pulling her hands upward. Her first hand went over the tip and she moved it to the base of his cock, under her other hand. She continued to squeeze and tug upward, over and over, milking his cock. He was erect and thick, but she could tell his arousal wouldn't last long.

"Tiffany . . ." James bucked his hips as he groaned out her name. It wasn't a groan of passion. More like an "enough."

She wasn't going to give up. She gave a sharp twist with her hands and he hissed. She had given him a fantasy sex life any man would long for. She wasn't going to break that streak now. Tiffany lowered her head and took his cock into her mouth.

James bucked his hips against her face. Tiffany was determined not to notice how still his cock felt against her tongue. She swirled the tip along his length, but she wondered what she was doing wrong. How could she fix this?

It wasn't as if they'd had perfect sex every time. She handled their mishaps with aplomb. She—

A collage of fragmented memories flickered before her eyes. She slowly withdrew from James's cock as the realization struck her. James tossing aside the *Kama Sutra* handbook and making up their own position that swiftly brought them both to shattering orgasms . . . James, whose quick thinking saved her from a demonic sex toy. He used it for something else than its intended purpose with amazing results. . . .

James, who guided her through every new adventure and took care of her . . . James, who made her feel like a sex goddess . . . James, James, James.

She sat up as she wrestled with the truth. James was right, once again. He was always in charge, quietly controlling their moments, letting her think she was doing it all until something went wrong. All this time she had thought she was his fantasy girl when in fact she was only as good as he made her.

It wasn't all her. It never was. Tears stung her eyes. Their successful sex life was all James. If he found another woman, he wouldn't miss a thing.

"Tiffany?"

She ducked her head. "This isn't working," she whispered. "I'm sorry." She scurried off of the bed and ran to the bathroom. She had to get away before he saw the tears spilling from her lashes.

"Tiffany!" he shouted, the bed creaking violently. "Damn it, Tiffany. Get back here."

CHAPTER TWENTY-ONE

"**T**iffany!"

He grabbed the silk above his hands and ignored the fierce bite in his wrist. James pulled, but the scarf didn't tear. He jerked his arms, the bed creaking and shifting underneath him, but he couldn't break free.

"Tiffany," James growled. "Untie me right now."

She didn't respond and panic clawed at his chest. He wrenched his arms against the bindings. He couldn't believe she had left him tied up. Had it always been her plan to leave him hanging?

No, that wasn't like Tiffany. Something else was going on here, but all he could think of was, how long was she going to leave him? He couldn't remember a time when he had felt this stuck.

How long *was* she going to leave him? Dark excitement slithered and coiled in his chest. He was at Tiffany's mercy and there was nothing he could do about it. His blood pounded through his veins as his cock twitched.

James called out to Tiffany again, only this time he heard a running faucet. He frowned. If she was ignoring him to reapply her lipstick or make a costume change, she was going to be in so much trouble.

He clamped his teeth around the knot at his wrist. He bit down and pulled, but nothing happened. He was stuck. James yanked against the scarf with all his might. Fire streaked down his shoulders and arms, and the bed creaked ominously, but the bonds didn't weaken.

When Tiffany finally opened the bathroom door, James stopped pulling against his bindings and flopped back onto the bed. He glared at her as his chest rose and fell rapidly from his exertions.

"Don't leave me like this again." His arms ached and the skin at his wrists felt like they were rubbed raw. He slowly uncurled his fingers from making fists.

"I'm sorry." His warning didn't register on her blank face. She walked over to him, and only then did he notice her red eyes and nose.

James's frown deepened. "What is going on?"

She shrugged and worked the knot at his wrist. "I don't know." Weariness seeped into her voice. "I tried, but it wasn't working."

She loosened the knot but, to his surprise, the sting in his arm didn't go away. Tiffany unwound the silk from his wrist and grimaced when she saw the deep red marks on his skin. She delicately stroked the inflamed skin with her fingertips before bringing his hands to her mouth. Tiffany pressed kisses along his wrist.

This time, a kiss wasn't going to make it all better. James sat up and ripped the scarf free from the headboard. Tiffany didn't look at him. Either she was too embarrassed about leaving him strung up to the bed, or she innocently assumed he would deal with his other wrist. Instead, James grabbed the end of the scarf before capturing Tiffany's hand.

Her arm went rigid as her tense fingers splayed in the air. "What are you doing?" she asked, trying to back away. She didn't get far. James held on tight, ignoring her yelp of shock as he quickly wound the purple silk against her wrist.

She struggled to break free, but he easily held her arm still. "This isn't funny."

He didn't reply and showed no sign that he heard her. James concentrated on tying the silk around her wrist. When he was done he pulled back and gave the scarf an experimental tug. Grim satisfaction filled his chest when the silk tightened against her delicate wrist. Tiffany had no chance to escape and run away again. "There."

Tiffany stopped struggling and stared at her wrist. She frowned and looked at her free hand. He knew what she was thinking. Why did he only bind one hand? It didn't take long before she followed the length of the scarf and discovered that he was still bound to the other end.

Her eyes widened when she realized that he had tied them together. "You have got to be kidding." She plucked at the knot with her free hand, but he held both her wrists and pulled her against him, her breasts flattening against his chest.

"Now tell me what is going on in that mind of yours."

Her eyes shuttered and lost their sparkle. "No. I don't feel like talking about it."

"What scares you about tying me up?" It didn't make sense to him. The woman was sexually adventurous and his request seemed tame considering what they'd done in the past.

Her mouth pinched, and he knew she didn't like to appear cowardly. "If anyone should be scared, it should be you."

James raised an eyebrow. "Exactly."

She looked away and her shoulders hunched forward. "I didn't know why I was against this," she admitted.

Didn't? "But now you do?" he asked carefully.

She pressed her lips together, but didn't reply for the longest time. She finally gave a sharp, reluctant nod.

He waited for her to say something more, but she seemed satisfied with her answer. He wasn't. Not by a long shot. "Plan on telling me?"

"You were right." The words seemed to drag from her throat. "It's all you. You're the one who's in charge, whether it looks like it or not."

James winced. He should have known his angry words would create a power play. He wanted to be honest, but instead he caused more harm than good.

"You make the sex better," she went on, stopping only to give a shuddering sigh. "I'm just along for the ride."

Her words sent a jolt of shock to his system. "What?" He rolled them over and pinned her to the bed, ignoring how good she felt beneath him. "Where did that come from?"

"You said so yourself." She covered her eyes with her arm. "You spoiled me and let me have my way. I didn't believe it until I tied you up."

"It's not all me," he insisted, pulling her arm away so he could see her face.

"It might as well be," she grumbled.

Did she want him to compare her to his past lovers? That topic was a minefield and he wasn't going anywhere near it. "Why is this so important to you?"

"Are you kidding me?" She tried to sit up, but failed as the scarf jerked taut between them. "Do you know how much time and effort I put into looking sexy? Or how much planning I've done to give you a special night?"

"I can imagine."

"It's a sham," she admitted, a blush creeping up her neck and flooding her cheeks. "I created a look, but that's all it is. A look. I'm only as sexy as you let me be."

James slanted his head to the side and stared at Tiffany. He had something to do with how sexy she was? He didn't think that was true, but if it was, how could that be a bad thing? "I'm confused."

"It doesn't come naturally. It never will. I need to face the facts." She closed her eyes as if the possibility were unbearable. "There will always be a woman who will be sexier than me. Your true fantasy girl is somewhere out there, not here."

He stared at her. That was what she'd been thinking all this time? How could she think so poorly of herself? Or of him? Anger flickered deep in his gut. "Now I get it."

"About time," she said under her breath.

"You're comparing me with your ex-husband." The anger inside him felt as destructive as acid.

She gasped in outrage. "No, I'm not."

He grabbed the scarf and, with one yank, she was sprawled back on the pillow underneath him. James settled deeper between her legs and trapped her arms with his. "You think I'm going to sleep with every woman who turns my head. Thanks a lot."

She studied him with narrow eyes. "How many women turn your head?"

"You think I'm that shallow?" The anger rolling inside him was dangerously close to flash point. "That I would risk everything we have together to screw another woman?"

Tiffany rolled her eyes. "Oh, like the thought never crossed your mind. It crosses every man's mind."

"Not mine." Not since he found Tiffany. She was everything he wanted in a woman. Loving, funny, loyal, sexy, affectionate . . .

A thought suddenly occurred to him. "Wait a second." He drew his head back and studied her face. "All of those new toys and positions you kept wanting to try out . . ."

She tilted her head back. "What about them?"

"You did that to wear me out." All this time he had thought she couldn't get enough of him. "You made sure I wouldn't have the energy to look at another woman."

"No." She shook her head vigorously. "I did it to make you happy."

That might be true, but it wasn't the motive behind all those exhausting sex marathons. Tiffany wasn't simply interested in the latest gadgets or recommended sex toy. She made sure that he was aware of the constant possibility of sex.

James slowly rolled away from Tiffany and lay back on the bed. He stared at the ceiling, almost wishing he didn't know the truth. The most affectionate woman he knew had an ulterior motive behind every touch. He absently rubbed the ache in his chest, but the knowledge still hurt.

He didn't want to ask, but he had to know. James took a steady breath, bracing himself for the worst while hoping for the best. "Do you like having sex with me, or is that all to keep me happy?"

Tiffany's sharp intake of breath was his first sign that he was in for it. He didn't regret asking, but it was going to take some time to calm her down.

"I resent that!" Tiffany bolted up from the bed, and he winced as the scarf tightened, cutting into his wrist. "If I didn't want to have sex with you, you would never have gone on a date with me. I don't believe in wasting my time."

"How do I know that?"

Tiffany frowned. "How do I know five years down the road you won't shack up with a young, sexy thing?"

He shrugged. She didn't know, and nothing he said would change that. "You'll have to take my word for it."

"Same here." She folded her arms across her chest.

James hissed as her movements pulled at the scarf. "No, it's not that simple. You know what? No more sex toys for you."

Tiffany's jaw dropped. "Excuse me?" The words stretched and hung in the air. "Did I hear you correctly? Are you *grounding* me from playing with toys?"

"You've been hiding behind them." The moment he made that accusation, he knew it was true. The sexy look, the pursuit of the newest vibrator, and even the outrageous positions, were all smoke and mirrors. She didn't want him to notice that she was working hard to give him pleasure.

"Hiding?" she repeated in a squawk. "I have not! They are sex *aids*. They *enhance* the sex."

"No sex toys, no new positions," he began to list. He was denying them both, but he truly believed it would help their relationship in the long run. "No sexy lingerie . . ."

"What?" She looked down and gestured at her sleek nightgown. "What kind of man would want that?"

"Your man."

"You are going overboard." She held her hand up as if to stop him. The sharp movement sent darts of fire coursing down his arm. "I'm not going to let you do this."

The discomfort didn't distract him long enough to keep him from recognizing that Tiffany wasn't going to give up her habit easily. He didn't know if it was because she was so attached to her accessories, or if it had more to do with his take-charge behavior. "It's time to get back to the basics."

She drew her head back when she saw the glimmer in his eye. "Now?"

"No time like the present." He rolled back on top of her, settling between her legs. "Tiffany, let me introduce you to the missionary position."

"Have you forgotten something?" She raised her hand and motioned at the scarf that bound them together. "This is considered extra, isn't it?"

The scarf would keep her in line and prevent her from surprising him with a trick maneuver. "You're keeping that on," he decided. "Think of it as a teaching device."

"Right." She wasn't going to believe him for a second. "You just don't want me to take over."

"That, too." He braced his arms on either side of her head and tenderly brushed her hair from her face.

"Good luck on getting me naked," she said with a smile. "My nightgown is against your new rules, remember?"

"Don't worry, leave everything to me." He studied her face. He thought she was beautiful and perfect. James lowered his head and gently kissed her. He outlined the edges of her lips with his own, slowly making his way to the center. His mouth tingled, eager for more.

He couldn't get over how soft her lips were underneath his. Sparks of white-hot need pricked against his skin, swirling just beneath the surface as he kissed Tiffany. She tried to deepen the kiss, but he ruthlessly denied himself from accepting her seductive invitation.

James slipped his tongue along the seam of her mouth. Tiffany parted her lips, welcoming him inside. He slowly explored her mouth as she melted against him. She swirled her tongue against his before sucking him in deeper.

His cock leaped and beat against Tiffany's thigh. A tremor swept through him as he held onto his restraint. His body ached to sink into Tiffany. He yearned to claim her swiftly and soundly.

Was he so jaded that he couldn't enjoy a kiss for what it was? Maybe he needed to pull back as much as she did. Tiffany arched against him and moaned against his mouth. She wanted him to hurry to the finish line as well. James retreated and placed soft, loving kisses along her forehead and on her eyelids. He brushed his lips along her cheeks and chin before drifting down to her neck.

Tiffany arched her throat back, ready to give him full access. She expected him to be soft and tender, but he couldn't hold back for much longer. James kissed her hard and grazed the length of her throat with the edge of his teeth. He enjoyed hearing her long groan as he sucked the pulse point.

James reached up and pulled her spaghetti strap over her shoulder, peeling her nightgown away from her breasts. He felt his balls tighten, his cock curving upward, as he stared at her small curves.

He cupped her breast, his hand tingling from the contact. It always amazed him how she fit perfectly in his large hands, as if she were made just for him. Tiffany murmured with pleasure as he fondled her roughly. He swiftly took her nipple into his mouth.

He chewed her nipple and pinched the other one as Tiffany writhed under him. Tiffany's bound hand knocked his, but she didn't push him away. Her wanton movements flared his imagination. He wanted to watch her break free as much as he wanted to channel that wildness toward him.

James whispered encouragements to Tiffany as he caressed and tasted her breasts. He could spend hours suckling and licking her nipples. He loved hearing her little pants as he tugged hard or lapped gently.

Yet if he waited any longer, he would ignite and explode before he penetrated her. He felt the sweat beading on his hot skin. The fire swelled in his blood. His balls were tight and ready to burst.

Licking and kissing down her flat stomach, James inhaled Tiffany's aroused scent. He grazed his hand along the slope of her hip and trailed his finger along the jutting pelvic bone. Tiffany's hips bucked when he cupped her sex. She was hot and slick for him. She gripped his bound wrist and he didn't feel the sting of his skin as she pressed him closer.

He traced her slit with his fingers as the head of his cock swelled with anticipation. He needed to sink into her and start pounding. He couldn't hold off for much longer.

Dipping his fingertips past the wet folds of her sex, Tiffany's flesh clamped down on his finger and drew him in. He felt ripples of Tiffany's gentle climax and her breath hitched in her throat.

James withdrew from her hot core. He laced his fingers with hers and raised them above her head as he drove his cock into her. Tiffany moaned and arched to accommodate his erection, but this time she wrapped her legs around his waist.

He smiled as her heels dug into him and began to thrust. He liked her possessive act. Tiffany didn't realize that he wasn't planning on going anywhere. This was where he wanted to be most of all.

He watched her face as she came. The dazed, wondrous expression made his cock expand painfully. He tossed back his head as he drove into her tight core. James squeezed his eyes shut and gritted his teeth. A shudder swept through him. He felt a chill, then started to sweat as he tried to hold on.

The scarf pulled at his wrist. James opened his eyes to see Tiffany stretch languidly as an orgasm rippled through her flushed body. The sensuous roll of her hips was too much.

He tried to control his thrust, but a white-hot sensation kicked him hard. He drove wildly into her as the fire seared through his arms and legs, billowing through his chest until the last thrust. James grunted through clenched teeth as he came, stealing his breath away.

James collapsed against Tiffany. He knew he was too heavy for her and should roll off, but he couldn't bring himself to leave her soft curves. He barely had the energy to smile as she cupped his face with her hand.

Tiffany had an uncanny knack for making him feel powerful and weak. Loved and desired. She was the most sensual woman he had ever known, but she wouldn't believe him. It was going to take a lot of convincing, but he was willing to spend a lifetime proving it to her.

CHAPTER TWENTY-TWO

Tiffany woke up early the next morning and groaned with frustration. It was her day to sleep in, but she saw the lavender and salmon streaks of dawn in the sky. She frowned before she realized she was once again tucked against James's chest. His arms were wrapped around her.

She sighed and snuggled deeper, feeling protected and cherished. She knew she shouldn't take this moment for granted. She wasn't much of a morning person, but waking up like this should bring a smile to her face.

Tiffany also knew she shouldn't have been so afraid of tying James up. She winced with regret for putting him through that, but she was glad she had told James how she had felt. It wasn't going to fix everything, but it was a start.

She might even look at the scarf in a whole different light. It was no longer something to avoid or hide. The next time she saw it, it could remind her of the fun, intimate moments she shared with James.

Where was the scarf? She raised her head and looked around the bed. Tiffany vaguely remembered James untying it and gently removing it from her wrist. He had inspected the creases on her skin with infinite care before tucking her hands against his chest. She didn't see him throw the scarf or where it landed.

At the time she couldn't have cared less, but now, in the light of day, she felt different. She needed to find the scarf, and if she had the courage, she wanted to try and tie James up to the bed again.

It might turn out to be a disaster, she thought as she carefully disentangled herself from James's embrace. The negative but honest thought made her pause. She was tempted to nestle back into James's arms. It was safer there.

No, she wasn't going to let one mishap set her back. If something went wrong, this time she wouldn't run off and leave James bound to the bed. He'd have trouble trusting her if she did that twice.

She wanted to do this, she decided as she got out of bed. Not because she failed the first time, and it wasn't because she believed in the power of the chain letter. It wasn't even about being his fantasy to keep him happy at home and by her side.

Tiffany wanted to give James the one thing he asked of her. He was right that he never asked for sexual favors. He didn't need to, considering all the possibilities and ideas she threw at him.

When it came right down to it, she wanted to give him pleasure. There were no ulterior motives or expectations. She saw this simply as an act of love.

Tiffany crept around the room and found the scarf on the floor close to where James slept. She picked it up and stretched it in her hands. She wondered if she should wake him up before she bound him to the bed.

Hmm . . . A sly smile tugged at her mouth. Let the man sleep. She bet James would remember that stupid ultimatum about no sex toys. He would change his mind once she showed him how fun they could be.

She slid the silk under his reddened wrist and carefully tied it in a knot. Her heart leaped when James shifted, but he didn't wake. She was somewhat surprised by her luck.

Tiffany threaded the silk through the headboard and made her way to his other wrist. The scarf yanked short. She looked at the headboard, thinking the scarf had gotten caught, but that wasn't the case. She didn't have any more silk.

She looked back at his free hand and realized she would have to move his hand toward the head of the bed. Tiffany bit her lip as she very, very gently maneuvered his hand. She hovered over James, her nightgown brushing against him as she raised his arm above his head. James stirred awake as she wrapped the silk around his wrist.

"Tiff?" he asked, his voice rough and groggy.

"Morning, James." She quickly tied the silk into a knot, her fingers fumbling in her haste. "Sleep well?"

He blinked. James tried to move his hand to rub the sleep from his eyes, but his arms didn't move the way he expected. Confused, he tried again, but got the same results. "What's going on?"

She patted his shoulder. "Just lie back and enjoy."

"What?" He tried to prop himself on his elbows, but the scarf yanked him back. James struggled to look behind him, and his eyes narrowed when he saw the purple silk.

He pulled hard, but the knots didn't unravel. Tiffany breathed a sigh of relief. This stunt just might work.

James turned his attention back on her and cast a sizzling glare. "Tiffany," he warned.

"Yes?" she asked innocently as she straddled his naked body. She pressed her knees against his sides as she rubbed against his stirring cock. "Stop pulling, or you're going to hurt yourself."

"I told you no more toys." He gave the scarf a quick jerk. The bed rattled like ominous thunder.

"Can't do anything about it now." She spread her hands on his chest and rubbed every angle and dip. There was something to be said about having absolute freedom to touch him any way she wanted.

"Just wait until I get my hands free," he said in a growl.

"That is not an incentive to untie you." She grasped his short brown nipple between her fingers and gave it a sharp pinch. His muscles bunched in response and a heady sense of power flitted through her veins.

"Didn't you listen to anything I said last night?" Exasperation tinged his words.

She leaned forward until her face was a kiss away from his. "I did, and it made a big difference."

"You don't have to do this." His eyes were stormy. He didn't want her to do this, but at the same time, he kind of did. He wasn't going to enjoy this if she felt like she had to give him this one fantasy.

"I want to." She brushed her lips against his.

He turned his head away as if her kisses were too addictive. "You already fulfilled the chain letter," he reminded her harshly.

She sat up. "That's right. We did." She could send the scarf away and out of her sight, knowing that she had done everything the letter instructed.

"So you can untie me." He moved his hands, letting the rasp of silk punctuate his command.

She looked at his hands, bunched in fists as they lay waiting. She scrunched up her nose. "No, I don't think so."

"Tiffany!" He yanked the scarf hard and the bed shook beneath them. She ignored his display of restrained power and linked her arms at his shoulders. She lay on top of his naked body, chest to chest, hip to hip.

She smiled at him, watching him struggle. She'd never seen him vulnerable, and she had never felt so totally in control. Suddenly her world flipped. Tiffany stared at the ceiling and James was on top of her.

An angry, aroused James. She glanced at the scarf, which was still attached to the bed. The purple silk had twisted when he rolled over.

Apprehension curled around her chest. "You don't play fair."

James's eyebrow arched. "This from a woman who tied me up while I was sleeping."

She pouted and looked at him from beneath her lashes. "I'm sorry."

"Sure, now you are." He flexed his hips and prodded his cock against her sex.

Tiffany bit her bottom lip to stop a moan from escaping. He was going to tease her until she begged for his cock. She might have full use of her hands, but somehow she felt she was at a distinct disadvantage.

She needed to make the most out of her hands. Tiffany wrapped her arms around his back and held on tight. She bucked her hips to meet his. James gave a short thrust, giving her a sample of what she was missing.

Tiffany's sex flooded with need. She wanted him deep inside her. She needed his cock to fill and stretch her until she thought she would shatter.

She skimmed her hands along the length of his spine to the hard, sculpted buttocks. She clenched his ass with her hands and tilted her hips until the folds of her sex covered the tip of his cock.

James's groan echoed in the bedroom. He nuzzled his face against her neck before he surrendered to the need whipping through him. Tiffany stilled as he plunged his cock into her. The sudden invasion left her breathless as heat flushed her body.

Clenching his buttocks with all her might, Tiffany pushed him in deeper, desperate for more. James didn't need any encouragement. He thrust into her with a fierce, primitive rhythm, and she met each move with a wild tilt of her hips.

She relaxed her grip to circle her finger around his anus. The flirty, teasing touch was like strumming a raw nerve. James flexed his body like a quivering bow. The headboard shook as he tried to move his arms.

"Tiffany," he said in a hoarse whisper. "Don't even think—"

She massaged his hole. James's arms and legs shook before he slammed his cock into her. The bed shook and pitched as he thrust into her again and again.

She pressed her finger hard against his anus. James shoved his cock inside her, rubbing that magical spot. Tiffany's mouth sagged open, her eyes fluttering shut as she felt herself splinter into pieces.

James came with a series of long, powerful strokes. Her heart was pounding in her ears and against her ribs when he slowly withdrew. His breath came in gulps as he flopped onto his pillow.

He faced the ceiling and winced as he tried to move his hands. "Are you going to untie me now?"

Tiffany smiled tiredly as she rolled on top of him. "Not just yet."

It was Monday evening when James stood in the middle of their bedroom and surveyed the mess he had made. After two days of playing with the purple scarf, he suddenly couldn't find it. What had happened to it?

"James?" Tiffany called up the stairs.

He grimaced and glanced at his watch. Tiffany was already home. There was no way he could spring the scarf on her now. His evil plan had been thwarted. It was a shame, because she would have deserved every wicked, delicious moment of it.

Man, he had been planning all sorts of things to do with her. At work he didn't hear half the stuff people were telling him because he was fantasizing about all he could do to Tiffany with the scarf. He didn't concentrate on the road during his commute home, his mind filled with images of the purple scarf and a naked and willing Tiffany.

Damn. He reluctantly headed for the stairs. It was just as well. He had meant what he said about no more sex toys, and that included him. Tiffany needed to go cold turkey, even if it meant he would go cross-eyed with lust in the process.

He walked down the steps and saw Tiffany waiting for him. Her sensual beauty hit him like a well-aimed punch. He felt dazed and short of breath as his gaze traveled from her mane of brown hair to her long, stunning legs.

James wrapped her in his arms and gave her a long kiss. His heart swelled as she clung to him. He hoped she'd never stop being so affectionate. "Miss me?" he asked when she drew away.

"I did." She glanced up in the direction of the bedroom. "What are you doing upstairs? Moving furniture?"

Had he been that loud trying to find the scarf? So much for being sneaky about it. "I think I lost the scarf," he admitted, refusing to tell her the real reason he was looking for it. "We need to find it before your deadline."

"Oh, you are so sweet." She cupped his face with her hands and gave him a lingering kiss. "But you don't need to worry. I mailed the chain letter."

"You did what?" He dropped his hands as disappointment shook him to the bone. He tried to quickly regroup. "We had a few more days left."

"First you're in a rush to send it off, and now you think I mailed it too soon." She rocked back on her heels and cast him a suspicious look. "What gives?"

"Nothing." He tried to look innocent, but from the deepening suspicion gleaming in Tiffany's eyes, he knew he was failing. "I'm surprised, that's all. Who did you send it to?"

"Grace Russell," she answered as she headed for the kitchen, her hips swaying provocatively.

James frowned and rubbed his hand over his jaw. The name didn't sound familiar. "Who the hell is Grace Russell?"

"One of our neighbors," she informed him as she picked up the mail he had left in the basket by the phone. "She's the one who interrupted us in our salon."

"Oh, her." He hadn't caught a glimpse of her, so he still didn't know who she was. "Why did you send it to her?"

She looked over her shoulder and smiled. "Because I barely know her."

He stepped behind Tiffany and wrapped his arm around her waist. "I don't understand."

She turned in his embrace and looked up to him. "The last time I sent the chain letter to one of my clients, never dreaming that it would be sent back to me. But it did, and do you know why?"

He shrugged. "No."

"My business relies on referrals. Chances are most of my clients know one another. The circle of friends and acquaintances is small, so it was only a matter of time before the scarf found its way back to me."

"That made you give the scarf to a stranger?"

"Exactly." She turned and sorted through the mail. "I will never have to see that horrible purple scarf again."

"Come on, you had fun with the scarf." He pressed a kiss against her neck. "Admit it."

"I did, but I always have fun with you. Honestly, I hope I never see that chain letter again."

She always had fun with him. The words echoed in his head. Tiffany said it so casually that it was obvious she didn't realize how important those words were to him. Or maybe she always felt that way, so she didn't think it needed to be said as a proclamation.

He was still reeling enough that he almost missed Tiffany's sleight of hand. First he saw the small brown package and then he didn't. "What's that?"

She tensed under his hand. "Hmm?"

"That package under the catalogs," he clarified. "Are you trying to hide something from me?"

Tiffany grabbed the package before he did. "What, this?" she asked in a light, breezy tone. "It's nothing. Just an electronic device."

"Electronic device?" He read the return address and recognized the name of the sex shop. "As in vibrator?"

"Maybe."

"Tiffany"—he firmly turned her around to face him—"I said no sex toys and I meant it. We are going back to the basics until you aren't hiding behind smoke and mirrors."

"I understand"—she held up a hand in defense—"but I ordered this before you decided that."

James shifted his bottom jaw to the side. He was fully aware that she said she understood. She had never mentioned anything about agreeing with his choice. James took the box from her and shook it. "What's in it?"

"I don't know," she admitted as she took the package away from him. "It could be one of three things."

"Three?" Did the woman have revolving credit at all the online sex stores? Her habit was more expensive than he thought.

She opened up the box and smiled. Anticipation glowed in her eyes. "I've been waiting months for this! It was on back order."

"What the hell is it?" The device had wires attached. It looked small and probably didn't give a lot of buzz, but he didn't care. It had *wires* attached. He knew electrocution was in his future.

"It's a vibrator you connect to your MP3 player," she explained. She clutched it to her chest and gave an excited jump. "The pulses go with the beat of your favorite music."

"You're kidding me."

"Come on, James." Her voice dropped to a seductive pitch as she grasped the collar of his shirt. "Let's try it out."

"No." He needed to sound firm, especially since he felt himself weakening.

She pouted. "Aw, come on, James."

He didn't know how much longer he could hold out. The MP3 player jump-started his imagination, but it was Tiffany's pout that always got him. She had no idea that was her secret weapon, and he wasn't going to let her find out just yet.

"I'm going to hide the MP3 player." He pivoted on his heel and ran toward the stairs.

"James!" She hurried after him. "Be a sport."

He dashed up the steps and into the bedroom. He turned the corner and grabbed the MP3 player off his chest of drawers. Desire pulsed in his veins as he waited for her to catch up.

As he listened to her footsteps pounding down the hallway, he realized Tiffany was half right. She might always have fun with him, but it went both ways. Whenever he was with Tiffany, she gave him the time of his life.

CHAPTER TWENTY-THREE

She had to stop peeking in her neighbors' windows.

Grace Russell knew she shouldn't. Bad manners. Bad habit. Bad idea. She needed to stop.

It shouldn't be so difficult. After all, the people in the townhouse complex were boring. Most worked from their homes and spent way too much time hunched over their computers.

And then there were a few neighbors who were hunched over other . . . things during the day.

Grace curled her shoulders up and focused on her computer screen, determined not to look out her window. She should really lower her blinds. Close the windows. Lock them. It was the only way to resist temptation.

She shouldn't be tempted. She purposely chose to set her office in the second bedroom, which overlooked the unheated swimming pool. No one ever used it, even in the height of a Seattle summer, so she shouldn't find any distractions. Yet one unusual move from a neighbor's window and her focus was kaput.

From the corner of her eye, Grace saw an odd flash of movement. It was from her new neighbors on the left side. She had already met them and, while she found them nice, there was nothing fascinating about them.

Still, she had to look.

Just one glance and then get back to work, she ordered herself.

The neighbors were two women. Olivia, now swaddled in a terry robe, was extremely skinny and tall. She had worn an outrageous outfit when she moved in, which matched perfectly with the streaks of red and orange in her short brown hair. Olivia had a loud laugh and an aggressive walk, even when carrying boxes four times her width.

The other neighbor was Lynn. She was quiet but friendly. Pretty, but kind of nondescript. There was nothing dramatic about the woman's long blonde hair and gentle curves, which strained against the damp towel wrapped around her.

Grace couldn't help but compare the women. While Lynn's personality glowed like a light from a reading lamp, Olivia's charisma was like a laser.

She watched them pad barefoot into their kitchen a floor below, and could hear a snippet of their conversation. They were the oddest pairing of roommates, Grace decided with a shake of her head. She expected to hear lots of arguing from that townhouse. What could those women possibly have in common?

Olivia reached over to Lynn. Her fingers gripped the towel tucked between her breasts and snatched it off.

Grace blinked. *Uh, whoa.* Her eyes widened as she stared at Lynn, from her bared breasts to her shaved mons. From this angle, Grace realized that Lynn was almost as voluptuous as she was.

Olivia walked behind Lynn, possessively cupping the blonde's large breasts. She slowly stroked Lynn, as if savoring the lush curves, her hands sliding from the soft undersides to the very tips. Grace felt a tug deep in her belly as Olivia played with Lynn's pale nipples.

Lynn arched back and Olivia kissed the length of her neck. Lynn's smile was very seductive. Nothing at all like the sweet, almost shy grin Grace had seen the day before.

Olivia glided one hand down Lynn's stomach. Grace was mesmerized by the sight of bright red nails drifting down Lynn's pale flesh. She shifted in her chair as her sex tingled with anticipation.

Olivia rubbed Lynn's clit. The blonde closed her eyes and rocked her hips. Grace heard Lynn's growl of pleasure from her open window. The groans from Lynn pulled at something deep and hidden inside Grace. She wanted to look away, but found herself tilting her head even more to the side, trying to see *everything*.

The brunette pulled away from Lynn and stepped in front of her partner, her back bumping up against the sliding door. Grace felt a flash of annoyance about the blocked view until she saw Olivia kneel in front of Lynn.

I really shouldn't be watching this.... Grace couldn't help herself. She leaned closer to her window as the naughty sensations coiled tighter and tighter.

Lynn pressed her arms against the glass door, her breasts smashed against the pane as Olivia crouched before her. The blonde's curves now looked indecently large, her rosy nipples rubbing hard against the window.

Olivia parted Lynn's labia and rooted for her clit. Lynn's mouth sagged open and her rapturous gasp surprised Grace. She watched as Lynn's hips bucked and swayed. Grace couldn't stop staring at the rhythmic movement of Olivia's head. The tension in Grace's body was building fast, to the same beat.

Lynn's hips bucked and swayed. A flush crept from her chest to her face. The look of pure pleasure on her face stabbed Grace with envy.

Lynn dropped her hands from the window and gripped the back of her partner's head. Her fingers were tense and white at the knuckles as she dug into Olivia's brown hair. She rode Olivia's face at a ferocious pace, her whimpers and moans filling the air. Grace shifted in her seat as the sounds tapped against her swollen clit.

Grace knew the moment Lynn came. Her body quivered like a taut bowstring before she released, hard and long. Her body reluctantly squeezed out the pleasure as it rippled from her core.

The look on Lynn's face was painful to Grace. She had to look away. She closed her eyes, but the vision was firmly stamped in her brain. She flinched and hunched her shoulders as she heard the blonde's sense of wonderment.

She had never felt like that. Ever. Grace crossed her legs as her clit throbbed for satisfaction. It was going to be a long wait. Sure, she'd had plenty of sex, and she had no problems climaxing. But never had she experienced rapture.

She wanted to. Grace winced at her silent admission, knowing she was being greedy. But it was true. She longed to have a spectacular sexual experience. Experience such heights that she would fly to the sun and melt.

Only to come crashing down.

Hmm. Grace slowly opened her eyes and stared blankly at her computer screen. There was a downside to the great heights: great falls.

She looked back at her neighbors' window and did a double take. Olivia was now sprawled on the kitchen island. The brunette's robe parted open, cascading down the sides of the cabinetry as her legs draped Lynn's shoulders.

Grace looked away abruptly. She rubbed her hand over her stomach, trying to erase the hollow ache. What was wrong with her? She didn't want either of those women. She didn't want to join them. So why did she feel jumpy?

She abruptly stood up. She didn't want to think about this. Grace hurried out of her office as if something dangerous were nipping at her heels.

Marching down the flight of stairs to the first floor, Grace tried to purge the thoughts and images from her mind. It wasn't working. She felt on edge, and her cheery home, which often brought her peace, offered little comfort.

Sunlight spilled into the quiet living room and kitchen as a gentle breeze tugged on the curtains. She had the windows flung open to bring in the last warm days of September. The tinkling sound of fountains and the fresh smell of flowers beckoned her to go outside.

That's what she needed to do, Grace decided as she walked down the next flight of stairs. Get out of the house and find a different view. She reached the bottom floor, grabbed her keys and opened the door. She paused when she remembered that she wore nothing but navy blue yoga pants and an oversized bright orange T-shirt dotted with coffee stains.

She looked sloppy. *Oh, so what?* Grace slipped her feet into flip-flops. She never made a point of dressing up. As long as the important body parts were covered up, who was going to care?

She crossed the small driveway with a touch of defiance, heading for the wall of locked mailboxes. Grace froze when she saw someone was already there, but when she saw the bright pink cheetah print, she knew it was Tiffany Martin, the friendly hairdresser a couple of townhouses away.

"Hi, Grace." Tiffany's gaze automatically went to Grace's hair. Grace had to fight back the impulse to stuff her fingers in the short blonde tufts and fluff it up.

Grace nodded her hello. "Hey, are you going to be at the party tomorrow?" Grace tilted her head at the flyer stapled to the lockboxes. Anything to distract the woman from her hair, which was in desperate need of a trim.

"Absolutely," Tiffany said, gathering her mail into the crook of her arm. "I don't know most of the neighbors. What better way to find out?"

"And, for all you know, they can provide a service for your business that you don't know about." The more Grace found out about her neighbors, thanks in part to watching out her window, the more she realized that they were like her: working at home and in need of getting out from time to time.

"Do you need any help getting ready?" Tiffany asked, giving a covert glance to Grace's stuffed mailbox.

"No, we have everything." Although the idea was the spur of the moment, Grace was experienced at throwing parties. It didn't matter the size or the occasion; in her wide social circle, her house was the place to go. "Just bring your business cards."

"I better get going." Tiffany took a step back, her gaze darting from Grace's packet of mail to her face. "I have an appointment coming in a few minutes."

"Okay, see you later," Grace called over her shoulder. She closed her mailbox, removed the key and turned, almost bumping into a solid wall of muscle.

Matthew Collins. Grace closed her eyes for a brief moment. She knew it was him before she even saw his face. Whether it was the lean, muscled body or the spicy scent, her body was already responding to his close proximity.

"Sorry." She mentally prepared herself before she looked up and faked her surprise. "Oh, hi, Matt."

"Grace." Matt's voice poured over her like thick honey, clinging to her skin and unable to be shaken off.

She smiled as casually as she could while her pulse kicked up a beat or two. Wow, the guy was hot. She could tell even though his white polo shirt only hinted at the lean, muscled torso and shoulders. His faded jeans hugged every tight, compact muscle, but she had a good idea what he would look like naked. She mulled over the idea far too often.

Matt looked like your average hot guy, but she had seen him exercise when she looked out her bedroom, down one level, and into his living room. This life coach had moves that made her sweat. He had a level of strength and flexibility that she would love to bring into her bedroom.

Not that she was only interested in his body. He had a secret tender streak that she'd seen on occasion. Matt also possessed a sense of humor that always made her smile. She appreciated those attributes, but they didn't make her twist and turn in her bed at night or spawn X-rated fantasies.

"What time do you need me?"

Heh. What a leading question. The possibilities were endless, but she knew what he was really asking. Guys such as Matthew Collins did not see women like her in *that* way. It was as if her sexual allure gene didn't compute to the male brain. That is, if she ever had it in the first place.

She was the kind of woman men and women felt comfortable around. And that was fine with her. It didn't cause a problem. But, then, she had never tried to go for the likes of Matt.

And she wasn't going to start. She knew her limitations.

"Grace?" Matt prompted with a concerned look. "Are you okay?"

She was undoubtedly staring at him with her tongue hanging out and panting with lust. He probably thought she was a mouth breather or something. *Really attractive! Why don't I add drool while I'm at it?*

"Yeah, I was trying to remember the schedule. Meet me at the main building around four, okay?" She gave a brisk nod and headed back to her home, where she could at least drool in private.

But she couldn't help looking over her shoulder once she got to her door. Grace bit her lip and looked away. This friendly one-of-the-guys persona was going to kill her. But that was all she was ever going to be. She was not a size zero, not all that experienced in sex, and didn't have anything to attract the likes of Matthew Collins.

Accept what you have and just be friends. Don't hope for something more. Grace sighed and kicked off her shoes. She hung up her keys and climbed the stairs, wishing the ways of the world worked in her favor once in a while.

But that kind of wishing would get her in trouble. How many times did she think Matt was saying something suggestive until she realized her mind was playing tricks on her? Or when he was asking about restaurants, and for one infinitesimal moment she thought he was asking her out.

She didn't need that kind of embarrassment or misunderstanding, thank you! She had to keep it cool and friendly. Matt didn't need to know that one of his "buddies" fantasized about him.

Grace walked over to her kitchen island and immediately remembered how her neighbors used that type of cabinetry. She set her mail down and automatically sorted through the envelopes and packages, trying not to picture Olivia spread-eagled on the granite countertop. She glanced at her kitchen window, wondering if Olivia and Lynn were still at it. *No, don't even think about looking!*

She returned her attention to the mail. There was a small brown package, and Grace couldn't remember ordering anything. The lack of return address surprised her. She pressed her fingers on the envelope. It wasn't hard. She shook it. She didn't hear anything. It was suspiciously light.

Grace opened the package and pulled out a deep purple silk scarf. The gold threads interspersed within it captured her attention. It was a celebration of the senses.

But who had sent her such a gift? It wasn't her birthday. Grace frowned when she saw the laminated letter. She squinted as she read the faded words on the paper.

Dear Friend,

I am offering you the chance of a lifetime. You can live out your ultimate fantasy within one week of receiving this gift, provided you pass it on. All that is required from you is this: You must use the scarf during a sexual encounter in the next seven days.

Mail the scarf and this letter to a female acquaintance within one week of receiving this package. Do not tell or discuss it with the woman. Those who follow these instructions will continue a fulfilling sensual odyssey. Those who don't will never find satisfaction for as long as they live.

Kali

Grace slowly set the letter on the table and looked at the scarf. Tears pricked her eyes. Her nose stung as her throat constricted.

She didn't know why she felt the need to cry, or why the presence of the scarf scraped at her. It was a stupid gift. Not even that. A dumb chain letter.

Grace rubbed the tip of her nose with her knuckles, warding off the urge to cry. She should be laughing. After all, she was supposed to use the scarf during a sexual encounter in the next seven days? Ha!

Why didn't they include a sexual partner in the package? Grace wondered, rolling her eyes. Because she didn't have anyone up for the running to take to bed. She hasn't had one in weeks . . . months . . . years.

Grace stilled, her body tightening with shock. *No, that can't be right.* A sharp sensation twisted in her chest as dread seeped into her.

How long had it been? Grace considered the question and her mind clanged shut on the answer. Too long. She didn't want to know *exactly* how long it had been since she had sex.

How could this have happened? True, she wasn't a highly sexual person, and yes, she didn't have a lot of chances to meet men, but that didn't mean she'd taken a vow of celibacy!

She had to do something about it. Right this very minute. Grace made a fist and tapped it on the table. She was going to find a sex partner, take him to bed and use the scarf in the next seven days.

Grace refused to listen to the warnings that blared inside her head. As far as she was concerned, she was already living the "no satisfaction" part Kali warned of in her letter. She was ready to go on a sensual odyssey, no matter what the consequences.

CHAPTER TWENTY-FOUR

She hated shopping. Grace wrinkled her nose as she passed a perfume store and kept walking, her sneakers squeaking on the floor. She hated shopping for clothes, for necessities, and now here she was shopping for men.

She was ready to go home empty-handed.

Grace never understood the fun in retail therapy. While her friends and family got a great buzz from a sale, and a day at the mall was a reward or celebration, she saw it as a pilgrimage to endure.

It had always been that way. Going to the mall as a teen was an exclusive corner of hell. Nothing ever fit. Nothing looked good. Even trying on the accessories was touch and go. Would she be able to get the bracelet around her wrist? Was that hot new color going to make her look sickly? Did the belt have enough notches?

Her friends would always go in the boutiques that catered to the extremely thin and trendy crowd. Grace would long to wait outside, but that would make her look even more out of place. So she would trail behind her friends, preparing for the inevitable "Are you lost?" question from a snobby salesclerk.

These days weren't much better. She might have lost weight, but she would never be accused of being slender. She was no longer a teenager whose world was heavily influenced by fashion dos and don'ts, but it still felt like she was an outsider. The designers of the world definitely forgot about her.

Stop looking at the itsy-bitsy clothes. You are shopping for a man. A lover. It should be easy. One size fits all.

Grace looked around the second floor of the mall and saw an attractive man step out of an electronics store. She froze and squeezed her fingers around her purse strap. She was very aware of the purple scarf nestled in the corner of her purse.

The guy strode toward her. He glanced in his shopping bag, checking the contents.

She swallowed roughly, wondering how she was going to strike up a conversation. She frowned at the thought. What was wrong with her? No one ever accused her of being shy.

But she had never tried to proposition a man before. Grace's heart pounded against her rib cage as the man looked up. She twisted the purse strap around her finger, imagining the scarf uncoiling, ready to strike.

The man looked at her—through her—as he walked past.

Grace's eyelashes flickered as she stayed perfectly still. She was numb at the man's dismissal. Of course he didn't notice her. Why did she think men would react differently to her today than on any other day?

Maybe the mall was a bad idea. Grace walked to the nearest store and stared at the window display as she considered her strategy. She might have better luck at a local bar, where drinking was involved.

But through the years she had heard that the mall offered the best place for quick sex. If not the swingers club that supposedly met at the food court every Thursday night—which she refused to consider checking out—there were men who trolled the mall during the day, approaching women for quick, anonymous sex.

Or so she had been told. No one had ever approached her.

Maybe she was approaching the hunt for sex in the wrong way. She needed to wear war paint, or at least some lipstick. She should dress provocatively. Grace stared at the ultrasexy display in the store window, trying to imagine herself in those outfits.

She didn't have anything remotely like those clothes. Definitely nothing sexy. She went for comfort. She didn't dress for others; she dressed for herself.

When was the last time she dressed for someone? Grace stared at the skimpy red dress in front of her, trying to remember. Had she ever?

She looked at her reflection in the window. Her face was clean of makeup, and her blonde hair was short and spiky. She wore an olive green shirt and camo pants. Loose-fitting and monotone, the outfit allowed her to blend in.

But she didn't *want* to wear anything attention-getting. She couldn't put herself out there and on display. She couldn't exude sexual confidence knowing there was someone watching her, listing her attributes and deficiencies.

Anyway, it wasn't fair. Why should *she* dress up? She didn't expect a guy to dress up for her. Jeans and a T-shirt were fine. Perfect, really.

Matthew Collins always looked terrific in jeans and a T-shirt. She sighed as she remembered how his shirts teased her, hinting at solid, warm muscle. He would be equally hot and sexy if he wore something formal.

She looked at the man's suit in the window. If Matt wore that . . . Grace's cheeks warmed as she imagined him standing at her door, wearing that, waiting for her. And if she knew he wore it for her . . . to impress her . . .

Okay! Okay! Grace rolled her eyes. There was something to be said about dressing up for someone else.

She should play along, even if it meant squeezing into a sexy dress. Grace held her purse more firmly against her and took a step toward the door. Her determination wavered when she saw the other women shopping in the store. They were exotic creatures, their sensuality overwhelming without even trying as they browsed the racks.

She couldn't go in there. It was too intimidating. This store was for later. When she had more confidence, not to mention more money.

She pivoted on her heel and kept walking. Grace kept an eye out on her fellow shoppers. There weren't that many men. Maybe the rumors weren't true. All she saw were young mothers with strollers, a few packs of senior citizens and some pairs of teenagers who were probably skipping school.

Okay, it was a stupid plan anyway. She wasn't up for nameless sex with a stranger. It was dangerous, it was not her and she wasn't going to let a scrap of silk make her do it.

She walked to the far end of the mall, her stride increasing to a brisk clip. It was time to abandon this strategy. Grace took the escalator down, her gaze sweeping a lingerie store.

She'd never been in there before and, quite honestly, never had the inclination. Grace didn't see the need for the bold colors or aggressively feminine designs. But today was different. Today she needed every weapon she could get her hands on.

So what if she bought something that no one else would see? She would know, and that was all that mattered. If she wore sexy underwear, or beautiful lingerie, it might make her feel sensual. She would start to walk and stand like one of those exotic creatures, and before you knew it, become just like them.

At least, that was the plan.

Grace stepped off the escalator and approached the store. It looked dark and mysterious, probably for ambience's sake. She hesitated, hating the need to do so. The lingerie store was even more intimidating than the trendy boutique.

Just walk in there like you belong. Grace stepped inside and paused at the first display, as if the dark purple and hot pink merry widows had caught her interest. She wasn't sure why there were black satin elbow-length gloves and a riding crop on the table, but she wasn't going to ask.

She made herself go to the next table, showcasing bustiers and corsets. *Never in a million years*... They looked uncomfortable. Sexy, but uncomfortable. Grace was beginning to wonder if putting the two adjectives together was redundant.

She slowly walked from one table to the next. The bras promised to enhance while the panties offered to diminish curves. Each style guaranteed a sleeker, sexier version of herself. Grace wasn't too sure about that. She had a feeling that if she wore the lingerie for a day, once she removed the tightly engineered silks and satins, her skin would be decorated with angry red marks.

There had to be something that she'd like. That would fit and be comfortable. Something that would—*Ooh, flannel pajamas.* Grace rushed over and picked up a striking blue pair before she realized what she was doing.

No! Step away from the pj's. Grace dropped the colorful pajamas onto the table. No flannel. No covering up the cleavage. Definitely no cartoon prints. Find something silky. Revealing. Sexy.

She scanned the sleepwear section and saw the baby doll nighties. Well, she had never thought she'd try one on. They were extremely feminine. Fragile, and sometimes transparent.

But they weren't form-fitting. Always a good thing in her book. This might be something to start with, even if she slept by herself. Grace flipped through the styles on the rack. No, no, no—oh, God, no!—no, no and no.

She grabbed a white, lacy baby doll and checked the size. It might work. She walked over to the salesperson, who was chatting on the phone. The woman didn't acknowledge her as Grace headed for the fitting room. From now on she wouldn't wear camouflage prints. It really did make her invisible.

She was going to the first available dressing stall when she heard a thump. Grace stopped and looked around, noticing that someone was in the last stall.

The curtains twitched, but they weren't fully closed. Grace heard a rough whisper and a giggle. She took a step closer, wondering if there were two people in there.

A woman was straddling a man sitting on a chair. Grace couldn't see anything of the man but the back of his head. But she could see plenty of the woman. She wore a black flyaway baby doll, the lace parted to the side and revealing her flat stomach and lace thong panties.

Grace knew her baby doll choice was a mistake. She was never going to look like that woman.

The man reached for the knot nestled between the woman's breasts and slowly untied the string. He peeled away the lace, revealing her pert breasts. The man lowered his head and Grace could hear him licking the woman's nipples.

Grace's mouth sagged open. The woman gave a husky growl and arched her head back. She speared her fingers in the man's thick, dark hair and pressed him closer. Grace's eyes widened as her skin went hot and tingly. For crying out loud—was everyone in the world having sex but her?

The woman pulled away abruptly. Grace tensed, her stomach twisting. Had she moved? Made a noise? Had she been seen? She was standing right there, in the aisle, with no place to hide.

Grace wanted to run out of there. Turn around and put one foot in front of the other. But she remained still, rooted to the floor as she caught the woman's gaze.

Grace couldn't breathe. The woman's eyes glittered as she rose from the man. Her nipples were wet and red, her breathing loud and choppy in the quiet fitting rooms. The woman reached down and pulled at her panties.

What? The word reverberated in Grace's head. She wasn't stopping? They wanted an audience?

The man fumbled with his trousers as the woman kicked off her panties. The man grabbed for the woman's naked hips and guided her back down. The woman's gaze collided and locked with Grace's as she held onto the man's shoulders.

Grace felt like the naughty one, the guilty one for looking at them. Watching with anticipation as the woman slowly sank onto the man's cock, and listening to the slide and slap of skin against wet skin.

The woman let go of the man's shoulders and cupped her breasts. She pinched and pulled at her reddened nipples, watching Grace's reaction. The woman licked her lips and moaned, seeming to be more aroused by Grace's stunned expression than the man's cock inside her.

The man stood up abruptly, carrying the woman with him. The chair was knocked over, and the man tripped on the tangle of clothes left on the floor. They slammed against the wall, the woman calling out more with surprise than pain.

"Shut up or—" The man looked over his shoulder and caught a glimpse of Grace. He froze, his eyes widening in horror. The woman's throaty laugh echoed in her ears. Every instinct in Grace's body screamed for her to run. She took a step back and stumbled.

The man grabbed for the curtains. To pull them shut or to launch out of them and at her? Grace didn't wait to find out. She dropped the baby doll nightie she had crushed in her hands, and rushed out of the lingerie store at full speed.

Ohgodohgodohgod... She couldn't believe she had stood there and watched them. That she got turned on! She couldn't believe she got caught!

Her stomach cramped with embarrassment. Grace placed a hand on her face, her cheeks sizzling hot. That's it—no more watching! She had learned her lesson. Not that it was wrong to watch. She knew that all along. But this time she was discovered. This time she knew she had been seen.

Maybe she wasn't as invisible as she thought. . . .

CHAPTER TWENTY-FIVE

Grace stood at the edge of the cocktail party and slowly sipped her drink. She took advantage of the quiet moment to relax. She watched the guests mingle and listened to the hum of conversation. The event was winding down, but she knew she could claim that it was a success.

And once again, I clearly missed the true meaning of the party. Grace slid a look at two women vying for the attention of the personal trainer who lived in the complex. The businesswomen usually wore sharply tailored pant-suits, but tonight they wore tight skirts, plunging shirts and dangling earrings. Grace sighed and slid her foot out of her shoe. It had been a while since she had dressed up, and she had forgotten how much high heels hurt.

Grace was beginning to wonder what was wrong with her. She had approached the cocktail party as a networking opportunity for her computer-support service. Others saw this as happy hour. While she was looking for leads, they were looking to get laid.

Maybe she put too much emphasis on work. Or perhaps she saw the world differently. It was true that she didn't see the sensual side. She didn't feel sexy. Tonight she had gone so far as to toss the scarf over her dark blazer to feel confident and pretty, but the purple silk wasn't cooperating. It silently let her know that this duty was not in its job description.

Grace scanned the party that had spilled out onto the courtyard.

She immediately found Matt. He was taller than most of the men, but if she had really needed to find him, all she had to do was look for the largest group of women. Matt would always be in the center.

Matt turned his head and their gazes collided. Grace forced a smile to her lips as her heart lodged in her throat. She raised her cup in a salute and looked away, her pulse skipping fast.

Could she have lusted after a more out-of-reach guy? Grace rolled her eyes in self-disgust. Matt could have his choice of the most sensual and fascinating women. From the gossip she had heard around town, he had done just that.

What made her hope that he would wake up and pick her as his next love? Because she picked him? Grace felt the corner of her mouth twitch with wry humor. If only it were that easy. He was her fantasy, but she knew she was nowhere near his list for a dream lover.

If she was going to find a sex partner by the end of the week, she had to look at alternatives. She didn't like the idea. The disappointment jarred inside her, but she had to face facts and move on. Grace absently stroked the purple silk between her fingertips as she considered the single men at the party.

The choice had little to be desired. She wrinkled her nose as she studied a cluster of men posturing and bragging in a corner next to her. *Too metro . . . too macho . . . too blah . . . too blech . . .*

Okay, maybe the problem wasn't the men. It was her. She was plain and plump, and she should look for a guy who didn't mind that. She should settle for what she could easily get. Or, considering how shaky her confidence was at the moment, she should go for the guy who would be thrilled to have her.

Why couldn't that be Matt?

A shadowy figure blocked her vision. Grace blinked and focused on the person in front of her. One glimpse of the cow-print vest—or was that dalmatian?—and she knew who it was without even looking up.

"Great party," Tiffany said as she dragged her fiancé behind her. "Thanks for inviting us."

"Leaving so soon?" Grace asked, silently wondering how Tiffany could look sexy wearing bovine prints. If she wore that vest, she would look like . . . a cow.

"Yeah. Early appointment." Her scarlet red lips puckered for a moment. "Nice scarf."

"Thank you." She couldn't help but stroke the silk again.

"Where'd you get it?" Tiffany jumped as if she had been startled before glaring at James.

"Someone gave it to me," Grace answered.

Tiffany looked like she wanted to say something more, but her fiancé interrupted. "Good night, Grace," James said as he cupped Tiffany's shoulder with his hand and held her against him before guiding her back to their home.

"Good night." She watched them walk away, their movements in sync with each other. She liked how James had his arm around Tiffany's shoulders. It wasn't an act of possession as much as it was one of protection and intimacy.

Intimacy. That was what she was missing from her life. That was what she wanted more than random sex. Which is probably why she wasn't going to the nearest bar and finding a one-night stand.

She wanted a connection. Something that went past the physical touch. A connection that rippled through every aspect of her life. She wanted a relationship that made her feel like she was living every day to the fullest.

Grace turned her head as if watching Tiffany and James was too painful. Maybe it was. Or maybe it was a simple reminder that one night at a party wasn't going to change her life. It wasn't going to change *her.*

Her shoulders slumped as a wave of tiredness crashed over her. She suddenly felt weary, her spirit snuffed out in an instant. She walked to the trash can like she was on autopilot and tossed her drink before heading back to her house. She didn't look back at the party, suddenly craving to be alone.

The cocktail party was only a few feet from her front door. She entered her townhouse quietly and closed the door, sagging against the wood for support. The dark stillness enveloped her, but the muted sounds of the party filtered in.

Grace trudged up the two flights of stairs, her steps growing heavy and slow. She walked into her bedroom and only then remembered that she had left her bedroom windows open to let in the cool breeze. She walked over to close out the sounds of the party, but she paused when her hand rested on the sill.

Her eyes were drawn to Matt again. The circle of women hadn't diminished since she last looked. One woman in particular was getting bold, leaning against Matt and brushing her breasts against his arm.

It irritated her. She was jealous of the woman's proximity to Matt, but at the same time she was envious of her boldness. Matt seemed to be oblivious to the woman fastening onto him. Then again, he was probably used to it.

As much as she'd like to raise a haughty nose at those women, she knew how they felt. She'd like to think she was above all that, but the truth was that she knew she couldn't compete, so she didn't even try. If she thought she could gain Matt's attention, she'd be doing a whole lot more than rubbing her breast against his arm.

Not like that would ever happen. Grace turned away from the window and walked over to her bed. She silently stripped, letting the clothes fall in a heap on the floor.

She felt a reckless streak as she took her clothes off with the windows open. The shades were partially drawn, but she knew she was safe. No one at the party would see her up here in the dark. No one had a reason to look up here anyway.

She headed for the bed, more than ready to curl up in the warm covers, when she stepped on the luxurious strip of silk. Grace looked down and saw a faint glimmer of gold.

What was she going to do about that scarf? She was already behind schedule on finding a lover. At least, it felt that way. Yet she felt oddly reluctant to give up on the chain letter.

Then again, it said "sexual encounter." Her first thought was Matt, but that's because she dreamed about it. This scarf didn't promise Matthew Collins. It wasn't very specific about having a partner, now that she thought about it.

Grace sat on the bed and shook her head. Great. If that didn't bring home how pathetic her situation truly was. How many women had received this chain letter and considered having solo sex? Grace was pretty sure she was the first.

The possibility made her cringe. She wanted to run back to the party and grab the first man she saw. She was ready to yank him into her bed and do him to complete the rules of the chain letter.

Okay, maybe not.

She had to feel comfortable with a guy before he saw her naked. She knew she wasn't skinny or a bombshell. She wasn't going to fulfill any fantasies or make a man sink to his knees with reverence. He was going to have to be so far gone with lust or in love to not see her flaws, and that just wasn't going to happen with a one-night stand.

And it wasn't going to happen in seven—make it six—days. That meant she was going to have to do it herself and indulge in some solo sex. At least she knew exactly what she liked. She could get this over in no time and get rid of the scarf fast.

Grace folded the scarf, ignoring the ritual feel of her movements. She firmly tied the silk over her closed eyes. The material felt cool and slick against her face. A gold thread scratched her left eyebrow.

She gingerly lay down on the bed, her movements clumsy. She felt awkward and silly. Why did she feel silly? No one could see her. Okay, sure, she didn't usually blindfold herself, but the doors were locked, the room was dark and her neighbors were two floors below in the courtyard.

The voices seemed louder. She stilled and tilted her head toward the window. The voices sounded closer. Grace knew her senses were compensating for the lack of sight, but it didn't stop her twanging nerves or the shiver sweeping across her skin.

She picked up on Matt's husky chuckle. A mix of joy and excitement seeped into her blood. His voice was like a caress, her nipples tightening at the sound.

Grace cupped her breasts, rubbing her palms over the sharp peaks. She rubbed her thighs together when she heard his voice coming closer, almost directly below her window.

If only she had the courage to invite him in. Invite him? She wanted more bravado than that. She wanted to be like those sex workers she had once read about. The ones who stood by a window and enticed customers inside.

How would she entice Matt? She bit her bottom lip as a naughty sensation pressed heavily in her belly. If she had the courage, she would pose by her window and flaunt her body before boldly gaining eye contact with her sexy neighbor. Then she would slowly undress herself.

As she removed her clothes, Matt would be standing still, spellbound. When she was completely naked, Grace would tempt him more by cupping her breasts and feeding them to her mouth, licking her nipples with the curl of her tongue.

Grace fondled her breasts, hissing when she pinched her nipples. She imagined Matt's eyes, narrowed and smoky with lust, his cheekbones ruddy, but he wouldn't move. He'd be too scared to break the dream.

Yeah, she liked that.

Grace's hand slid down as she considered her next move. She cupped her mound, the heat wafting over her fingers. Dropping her knees to the sides, Grace imagined spreading her legs for Matthew, showing the glistening, dark pink folds of her sex.

She imagined the sharp rise and fall of his chest. His hands would be at his side, flexing and fisting, as he fought for restraint, his throat moving as he struggled to swallow and breathe normally.

Grace would know exactly what would make him forget how to breathe. Sliding her longest finger along the puffy, wet slit, she rubbed her fingertip against her clit. Grace hummed as intense pleasure radiated from the hard nub.

In her mind's eye, she could see Matthew drawing closer. The voices of the neighbors seemed to be closer, too. Louder. Harsher. Strangers saw her, too. They were gawking and whispering, but she didn't care.

No, she did care. Her sex flooded at the idea of people seeing her. Staring. Wanting her. Grace arched off the bed, capturing her swollen clit between her fingers, the same way she held her nipple. She pinched them hard, gasping as fiery sensations darted through her.

She imagined the strangers and neighbors watching her even more intently, waiting to see her come. But she wasn't watching them. Only Matthew, who walked to her window like a sleepwalker, his eyes on her damp fingers as they rolled her clit.

Grace rocked her hips as the orgasm gained strength, pressing against her pelvis. She let go of her nipple and rubbed furiously at her clit. With her other hand she dipped her finger in her sex, meeting the fierce moves with a buck of her hips. Her bedsprings protested with a squeak.

It suddenly became too much. Grace flinched and jerked as pleasure flooded her body, drowning her senses until she was in a dark and silent cocoon, her muscles pulsing with gratification.

She slowly became aware of the noise from the party. Grace

flinched, her senses in overdrive, when she heard Matt's sharp bark of laughter. Grace reached up and pulled the blindfold off. She curled her legs up and wrapped her arms around her knees, when a realization hit.

Even in her fantasies, she didn't get the guy.

CHAPTER TWENTY-SIX

Matthew Collins stepped out of the exercise room and onto the stone courtyard. He paused, allowing the crisp autumn air to caress his aching muscles. He took a deep breath and looked up at a scatter of stars. The swing of a door interrupted his thoughts. When he saw Grace exiting the complex's main building, his breath stuttered out of his lungs.

She was his living, breathing fantasy. Lush and curvy, Grace Russell had the kind of body a man wanted to grab and hold on to. She concealed her hourglass figure underneath shapeless shirts and baggy jeans, but she couldn't hide that she was a knockout. Not from him.

He watched her walk across the courtyard, balancing a tower of packages and boxes. He liked the way she moved, fluid and unrushed. He watched as her breasts and ass swayed with each step. God, he wanted her.

C'mon, you're a life coach. Helping others set and achieve goals is your career. You can do this. Visualize.

"Need some help?" Matt asked as he hurried to meet her. He grabbed a box just as it began to teeter.

Grace looked around the tower of packages. Something dark and mysterious flared in her eyes before she banked it. She smiled back at him. "Thanks."

Her smile twisted at his gut. His mind went foggy and he struggled to think of something to say. "What did you think about the cocktail party?"

"I thought it was great," she replied as she walked with him. Her clean scent was driving him wild. He didn't know what it was, but it made his mouth water. "It was a brilliant idea of yours," she continued.

"Thanks." Of course, when he had suggested it, he meant drinks for just the two of them. He wasn't sure how Grace misunderstood. Suddenly an intimate drink became a networking opportunity for the entire living complex. "But I didn't see you at the end."

"Oh, yeah." Grace frowned. "I . . . forgot to do . . . something. And it had to be done right away."

"Well, I had missed you."

She darted a look at him. She seemed startled and uncertain. Matt silently cursed at himself and drew back. "Let's do coffee sometime."

"Sounds good."

Great. He was getting somewhere. Coffee is nonthreatening. Had no sexual overtones. She couldn't possibly object. "How about tomorrow? Say around nine?" His chest tightened as he considered the possibility of pushing his luck.

"Sure. Oops, no. I take that back." They arrived at her townhouse. "I'm already meeting someone tomorrow."

"Oh." The woman's social life was always getting in his way. "That's too bad."

"But come with us," she suggested as she slid the key into the lock and gave it a twist. "My friend might need a guy like you."

"Is that right?"

"I don't think she's considered talking to a life coach." She opened the door and set the boxes down before she reached for the ones Matt held. "So we'll see you at Starbucks down the street at nine."

"Sure." He reluctantly gave up the packages.

"See you then," Grace said with a bright smile and closed the door. "Good night."

"Night." He stared at her door. What just happened? He was finally making some headway and all of a sudden he was right back where he started.

Matt walked across to his home, slightly dazed. He went inside and climbed the stairs, reviewing everything that had happened. Where did he go wrong? Was he pushing too hard? Not pushing hard enough?

As he took a shower, Matt considered every goal exercise. He knew he had a tendency to go for the hard, almost impossible goals, but that wasn't why he found Grace attractive. He wanted her in his bed and he was willing to take the time and effort to get her there, even if it meant slowing down and working at her speed and comfort level.

Matthew turned off the shower and wiped the moisture off of his face. Maybe that was where he was going wrong. He should stop fighting his true nature. He was driven to go higher, faster and harder. He always wondered, why stroll when you can run?

He should be the same way with Grace. Stop tiptoeing around her. Stop working for one level and then climb to the next. He should go after her and let her know it.

And watch her run in the other direction, Matt added. He dried off and wrapped the towel around his hips before going to his bedroom. He strode across the floor, doing his best to ignore the laptop computer on his bed. He headed for the window and looked out at the splattering, loud fountain.

Where was he going wrong with Grace? He should accept defeat and admit that she wasn't into him, but every once in a while he caught a glimpse. She was interested in him, but she wasn't interested in acting on it.

He had been trying the slow, steady approach. She knew him. She'd been out with him, unfortunately with a group and never alone, but it was something. How could he move to the next level without scaring her off?

Matt glanced over at her townhouse. He saw light from her upstairs hallway streaming into her bedroom. His senses took a jolt when he saw Grace getting ready for bed.

Her nightgown was an oversized T-shirt, but the way it draped against her breasts made his cock stir. It reached to the middle of her thighs. Matt couldn't believe an old T-shirt was turning him on. He must have it bad for Grace.

She walked to the bed under the windows, not stopping to lower her blinds, and lay down. Matt frowned. Why didn't she close her window or lower the blind? They might live in a gated community, but he could see right into her bedroom at this angle. The windows didn't hinder his view. He could see all of her.

The beep of his computer distracted him. Matt looked over his shoulder, resisting the call of the computer. He knew he shouldn't, but he looked back at Grace's bedroom window.

He flinched when he saw her turn to reach the bedside table. The hem of her T-shirt rose, revealing the soft, bare curve of her ass. Matt curled his fingers, scratching his palms. He imagined cupping her ass, kneading the soft flesh as he drove into her creamy—

Whoa. He was *not* going there. He was not a Peeping Tom, and if Grace couldn't remember to close her shades, he would refuse to look over there.

It was a good plan, and it might have worked if she hadn't pulled out a long, hot pink vibrator from the drawer.

Matt's eyes widened until they burned. *No way.* That vibrator had to be at least eight inches long. The girth might be close to two inches wide. Could she take it all? Matt's cock began to twitch.

He squinted when he saw her grab something that looked like a dark cloth. What was *that* for? Matt pressed his forehead against the glass, idly stroking his hardening cock. His fingers froze as he watched Grace tie the fabric around her eyes.

What the hell? The woman is *blindfolding* herself before she uses the vibrator? Why? To forget that it was a battery-operated toy? Good luck on that.

Or did Grace Russell have a deeply kinky side? He wouldn't have guessed it unless he saw it with his own eyes. The sight of her bringing the hot pink vibrator to her lips and twirling her tongue along the tip was burned on his brain.

His cock grew hard and heavy, knowing how it would feel to have her wet tongue dart along the mushroom head and make it shiny. He wanted her to lick his cock like that, but murmur with pleasure and smile wickedly.

He lifted his arm and supported his weight against the window as he stroked his cock with his other hand. Matt groaned when he saw Grace wrap her mouth around the tip.

Her mouth was on the small side. Or at least it seemed that way. But he wished it was his cock in her mouth, pumping in her mouth, feeling the hot walls squeezing his length until his balls curled into his body, ready to shoot.

He hissed with relief as she withdrew the hot pink toy from her mouth and trailed the vibrator down her chin. She arched her neck back and trailed the tip down her throat and along the valley of her large breasts.

Matt pulled the towel from his waist and wrapped his hand around his cock. He fisted the hot length and pumped as he watched Grace fumble with the switch.

With both hands she guided the toy between her legs. He watched her body quiver with tension. Matt's gaze darted to her face. The scarf covered the top half, but her mouth was open and slack. It was almost as if he could hear her moan dragging from her throat and echoing inside of him.

He fisted his cock, his heart beating, roaring in his ears as she rubbed the vibrator against herself. Her hips bucked and rolled, and his hips canted in response.

When she tossed her head from side to side, Matt longed to be there, to capture her face with his hands and plunge his tongue in her mouth.

Matt watched as her hips lifted off the matterss, her hand pulling up her T-shirt as she sought her breast.

Take it off, he silently pleaded. *Take off the shirt. Yank it off. Tear it. Let me see all of you.*

Grace showed no interest in removing the T-shirt. She rocked against the bed, shaking. He could see the shudders ripple through her, one by one, feeding off each other.

Matt pumped his cock, wanting to come fast and powerfully, pulsing like she did. He messed up his rhythm as he saw Grace widen her legs and slowly insert the hot pink vibrator in her core.

Oh sh— He couldn't see every detail, but he watched as she worked the vibrator slowly, her hips twitching and shaking. She was determined to get every inch.

Matt fisted his cock as tightly as he could, imagining Grace sheathing him with her clasping, wet sex. Grace surged up violently, her head tossing on her pillow and her hips vaulting off the bed.

Matt came hard. Dark spots danced before his eyes and his knees buckled. He gasped for air as he sank to the floor, his hand fanning against the discarded towel.

He closed his eyes and weakly rested his head on the cool glass window. He needed to get up. He wanted to see what Grace was going to do next.

No, he needed to close his shades before she saw him. If Grace knew, if she suspected that he had seen her, he would never have another chance to get close to her.

Matt dragged himself from the window and headed back to his bathroom. He was going to kick up his strategy to get into Grace's bed, or he was going to go stir-crazy.

CHAPTER TWENTY-SEVEN

Why did she agree to this? Grace wondered the next morning. She grabbed her latte and allowed the heat to seep into her hands. It was nine in the morning, but her eyes felt bleary and gritty. She hadn't slept well, and all she wanted to do was fall back into bed.

Okay, fall back into bed with *Matt*, but if she waited around for that to happen, she'd be a walking case of insomnia.

Matt was the cause of her lack of sleep. Knowing she was going to see him the next day, wishing she had the brazen attitude to do something about the overwhelming attraction. It was a wonder she fell asleep when she did.

"Hi, Grace!"

Grace glanced up and saw one of her friends standing beside her. Kathy was smiling at her, but her gaze kept drifting over to Matt. "I haven't seen you for so long. Mind if I join you?"

She gritted her back teeth. *What's one more?* So what if she regretted the impulse to invite Leah to coffee. It was amazing what she would do to have coffee with Matt.

"Leah, you know Kathy." Grace gestured to her friend, a stunning redhead. "And this is Matthew Collins. He's a life coach."

Matt's eyes narrowed at the introduction, and Grace was at a loss as to why. Because she introduced him as a life coach and not as a friend? She did think of him as a friend, but she didn't want to share him. He was more than welcome to approach Leah and Kathy as a life coach, but she had no plans to meet with Matt on that level.

Of course, she couldn't tell him that, Grace thought as she watched Kathy pull up a chair a little too close to Matt. She knew Matt had invited her to coffee to offer his services—his coaching services, that is. The last thing she wanted Matt to know was that *he* was her number-one goal!

She glanced across the table and found him watching her. Grace quickly looked at Kathy as heat bloomed in her cheeks. Which just made it worse. But there was something in the way he had looked at her. It was hot. It made her blood zing in her veins.

Grace knew she was merging fantasy with reality. It was obvious. Thinking of Matt while she played with the hot pink vibrator would do that to her. Now she thought he was checking her out. That he saw her as highly desirable.

She was cracked. Losing it. Grace shrugged and took a lick of the whipped cream in her drink. It made perfect sense. No other explanation needed.

It would probably be a good idea to stop looking in his direction. Stay away from him altogether. The idea depressed her. He made the average day fizz and sparkle like a glass of champagne.

She glanced at Matt again. Her gaze collided with his. Her heart pounded against her rib cage.

There was something about the way he was watching her. The chatter of her friends washed over them, but his attention was on her. Leaning back in his chair, he propped his elbow on one of the armrests and set his face on his hand.

He wasn't just watching her. He was *studying* her. What did he plan to find out? He wasn't going to discover anything she didn't want him to.

Grace arched an eyebrow at him. *Ooh, yeah, Grace,* she thought with self-disgust. That's calling him on it. *That* should make him stop. If not, raise the *other* eyebrow.

If anything, her reaction amused Matthew. She saw the crinkling of his eyes, the light glowing in the blue depths.

She frowned at him, getting the sense that the guy knew something. It was in his eyes. Like he had a secret about her. Grace couldn't imagine what it was. He was probably mistaking her for someone else. That happened a lot, and it should be no different with Matt.

What she wasn't used to was how he played havoc on her composure. He sat across from her with a table between them, but she felt jumpy. That made her even more determined to remain as still as possible. She set her coffee on the small table and folded her hands in her lap. Composing her face to show nothing but calm, Grace listened to Leah talk.

She was used to sitting still and not making a move. Her friends found that trait in her peaceful. She couldn't do what came naturally today. She kept her eyes firmly on her friend as she rambled about all the disappointments of her life, which Grace knew by heart. That was probably why it was so easy to watch her friend but have Matt as the center of her attention.

Her skin prickled with awareness. Her pulse throbbed. She felt warm, her skin tight. She tried to breathe normally, but couldn't. Each breath scratched at her throat. The rise and fall of her chest made her aware of the full, heavy sensation of her breasts.

She couldn't resist. Just one more peek to see if Matt was still looking. For all she knew, he could have fallen asleep, and she was getting worked up about nothing. Grace looked from the corner of her eye.

Matt winked back.

Aw, geez. He caught her checking. Grace busied herself by taking another drink of her coffee.

Why was Matt looking at her? Was there something wrong? No, she wasn't getting that vibe. She felt like she was on display for him.

Her nipples tightened as heat washed over her, gathering in her sex. Grace shifted in her seat. She wished she could give him something to look at. Flash him. Tease him.

No ideas popped into her head. Naturally.

Sure, she had no problems watching him. When he worked out every morning in his living room, she loved watching him from her window. It was like he was putting on a show just for her.

She could never respond in kind. Only in her fantasies, where she was bold and everything would go her way. In real life, she could barely hold the man's gaze. In her dreams, she would stand up and walk around the table, perching on the edge in front of him.

In her fantasies, she wouldn't wait for him to make the first move. She would be in control. She would surprise the man of her dreams by her audacity.

In her dreams, she wouldn't compete for attention with the other women. Leah and Kathy would be her handmaidens, assisting her as she undressed for Matt.

Leah would slowly, methodically unbutton her shirt. Grace would stand still, feeling the fabric give and sag, but never breaking eye contact with Matt. She would enjoy watching the desire build inside him.

Matt would try to take matters into his own hands, but she wouldn't let him. Once Leah removed her shirt, Kathy would step forward and remove her bra. She would slowly peel the lace away, revealing Grace's large breasts as if they were works of art.

He would reach for her, but with one gesture her friends would hold him back. She'd cup her breasts and watch his eyes glitter with need. She'd roll her nipples with her thumbs and forefingers, shivering freely as she pinched them. Her hips would roll as sensations crashed through her.

"Kiss me, Matt," she would order. "Kiss my mouth."

She'd brush his lips with hers before tilting her face away. Matt would want more and go for it, but her handmaidens would stop him.

"Again," she would say. She'd ignore his warning growl and play with her nipples, knowing he was watching every move she made.

He would kiss her, trying to capture her mouth. Leah and Kathy would hold him back, allowing him to be close, but not close enough.

She was in charge, and she wouldn't let him free until he was dancing on the edge of wildness.

"Give me your tongue," she would whisper against his lips. He would swipe his tongue along the bottom curve of her lip before darting it in her mouth. She'd draw him in deeper, teasing him with the flirty curl and lave of her tongue.

And when she tasted the primitive need in him, she would relax her hold. He would know the moment she passed the control to him, and his victorious growl would vibrate deep in his chest.

He would drive his tongue in her mouth, and this time nothing would hold him back. He'd cover every inch of her mouth before pulling away and smiling, obviously thinking he had kissed her into submission. He would trail his lips down her throat and chest until he latched onto a rosy, hard nipple. He would suck so hard that Grace would mewl, her toes curling as the pleasure sparkled inside her.

"Wait," she would order. Her handmaidens would be at her side and lower her down until she lay on the table, her legs dangling over the edge. They would step away as she played with her breasts, watching Matt's face tighten with impatience.

She would hear Matthew's growl as she squeezed her breasts together. They would appear heavy and plump. Her nipples would stand erect and proud. "Now you may touch me," she would say.

Matt would shuck his jeans and boxers before climbing up next to her. The table would rock as he straddled her sides, high above her waist. His cock would be thick and hard. He would pump it with his hands before driving it through the channel of her breasts.

He would grind against her, his legs pressing against her ribs. The friction of his cock sliding between her breasts would be edged with pleasure and pain. She would be distantly aware of it all as she watched the emotions flitting across his face. His hips would lurch and retreat, harder and faster as he chased his goal.

She would watch him as his eyes squeezed shut. He would ride her fast and furiously. The pleasure he would feel was something only she could give him.

And then he would come. His shout would be guttural and elemental. She wouldn't see the sticky ropes of his release, but would feel it splatter on her chest and neck.

And he would finally open his eyes and look down at her with satisfaction. As if the evidence of his pleasure on her rosy skin was a sign of his possession. A brand claiming her to be his.

"Thanks for inviting me, Grace."

Grace fell out of her daydream with a thud. She glanced up from her cold drink and saw the others standing up, ready to leave. Whoa ... she was really losing it today.

"Sure. It was great seeing you," Grace told Leah. She said good-bye to her friends before they left with promises to call and e-mail.

"Are you feeling okay?" Matthew asked as Leah and Kathy walked out of the coffeehouse.

She jumped out of her seat and grabbed her purse. "Um ... yeah. Why do you ask?" Great. He hadn't been watching her because he thought she was pretty. He had been keeping an eye on her because she was showing symptoms of being ill. Terrific.

"You kept pulling at your shirt." He reached out and flicked the collar with his fingertip. "Like it was too hot or something."

Oh, jeez. "I was?" She automatically grabbed at the top button of her shirt. It was, thankfully, closed. "Really?"

Matt nodded and his gaze traveled down her white shirt again. His attention was drawn to her breasts. Grace felt her nipples tighten and sting.

"Uh ... it's a new shirt." She pulled at the collar, which suddenly felt too tight. "Scratchy tag."

"You should have worn your scarf."

Her eyes grew big. She was wide awake and alert now. "Huh?" How does he know about the scarf? Did he send it to her? No, that wasn't right. It was sent from woman to woman. Unless . . .

"It's soft, isn't it?" His gaze held hers. "You *always* look good in that."

What is he talking about? I only wore it once. "Thanks." She barely dragged the word out of her mouth. "It was a gift."

"You look good in purple." He paused as if he wanted to say something more. "Real good."

She stared at him. She looked good in purple? She did?

"See you around."

Grace watched him walk away. She looked good in *purple?* She didn't own anything in that color. Great, another trip to the mall was required. Grace closed her eyes and whimpered.

CHAPTER TWENTY-EIGHT

Matt stepped into his home, closed the door behind him and breathed deeply. He shouldn't have done that. Mentioned the purple. He was courting trouble.

But she hadn't picked up on it. It had been a near miss, but he lucked out. There was no telling how she would have handled it.

She definitely didn't like being looked at. It rattled her. He liked having that kind of power over Grace. He saw how she straightened her spine every time she looked in his direction and found him watching. She had angled her body in the chair, almost shielding herself. Like she would keep him from seeing too much.

Little did she know that he had seen quite a lot.

The question was, what was he going to do about it?

Well, obviously not that much. Matt shook his head and climbed the steps to the top floor of his townhouse. When her friends had left, had he stuck around? No. He should have, but she seemed tired and sleepy. When he was alone with Grace, he wanted all of her attention focused on him.

Matt chuckled, his voice echoing in his hallway. He made it sound like he had control over that. If he was going to be completely honest, he should admit that he wanted Grace Russell any which way he could.

But he was afraid to act on it. He wanted her so much that the ferocity shocked him. What if he messed up? What if he scared her off? There wasn't going to be a second chance.

Matt leaned against the wall and stared at his bedroom window. It didn't make sense. How could someone so quiet and unassuming turn his world inside out?

Because he saw her blindfold herself before solo sex. The purple scarf was dark and mysterious against her pale face. It hid him from her, but it also kept him from seeing the emotions flitting through her eyes.

No, the blindfold only intrigued him. The way she rode out her orgasms—wild and untamed—made him realize that she could be charming when she wanted to be and wild when the occasion called for it. She had control over her passions.

That kind of restraint was undeniably sexy. And challenging. He always liked to conquer the impossible, but there was something different about Grace's serenity. He wanted to see if he had the power to transform that restraint into something brighter. Bolder.

Well, first you have to get her naked, he reminded himself. She wasn't going to transform long-distance. And he was going to have to kiss her before anything happened. Kiss her thoroughly. Taking her out on a date would be a good start.

She seemed the type who would make a guy jump through hoops before she'd invite him to jump into her bed. He was up for the challenge. He would achieve anything she threw his way.

But it would be worth it, Matthew mused as he crossed his bedroom floor and looked out the window. He could be patient a little while longer. He wasn't going to set a deadline to gain admittance to her bedroom.

But not too much patience.

What if he was wrong? he wondered as he opened the blinds fully. What if he was kidding himself in thinking that Grace was interested? Was he seeing what he wanted to see?

Nah. No way. Matt peered into Grace's bedroom. It looked different than how he remembered it that night. Her room was bright white and sparsely furnished. It didn't look like the shadowy, exotic room of his fantasies.

Had he been looking in the right room? Matt immediately searched for the house number next to her dark blue door. He sagged with relief when he was certain it had been Grace.

The room didn't have that sensual quality because Grace wasn't in there. It didn't matter if she was sleeping or stroking herself. Her simple presence made all the difference.

He was realizing how true that was, especially today, Matt decided as he got ready to meet with a client. The Starbucks seemed to be humming with expectancy because she was there. Her smile made the overcast day seem brighter. He hadn't noticed it until now.

Grace didn't have the personality that would make a room crackle with electricity, but she did have a glow. It turned out to be more powerful than he imagined, because it anchored him. It gave him the peace he craved.

He had to stop this and take action. Matt knew he had to come up with a way to see Grace more often or go stark raving mad. He would do anything to be with her.

But what did he have to offer? She seemed perfectly content and self-sufficient, right down to the hot pink vibrator that probably had more speed and variations than he did.

Matthew exhaled sharply, frustration welling inside him. He stalked off and got ready for his meeting. He stepped out of the room and remembered the blinds were still open. Matt crossed the room and grabbed the blind handle, automatically looking over at Grace's townhouse.

She was there. Matt stood still, his ribs pressing against his lungs, as he watched her pace around her room. He couldn't take his eyes off of her.

He had been right. The room looked different when she was there. It appeared mysterious and sensual. Magical.

Grace kept pacing and thrusting her fingers in her short hair. Matt squinted as he watched her mouth. It looked like she was muttering to herself.

She stalked over to the bedside table. Matt's gut twisted with hope. He forgot to breathe as she wrenched open the drawer and pulled out the purple scarf.

Anticipation stormed through Matt's blood. She wasn't going to blindfold herself now, was she? He turned his head just far enough to look at the other townhouses facing Grace's bedroom. Most of the windows were closed, the shades drawn. But it was still risky. Didn't Grace stop to think about that?

He turned back just in time to watch Grace tear off her shirt. She wore a white sports bra underneath.

Aw, man, like he hadn't been staring at her enough. Now that he knew the stuff she wore under the oversized clothes, he was going to have an even more difficult time not staring.

He should stop staring right now, Matt reminded himself. He stood frozen as he watched Grace remove the bra, her breasts bouncing and swaying with each move. She discarded it with a vicious swipe of her hand.

She had the most amazing breasts. He didn't know why she hid the lush curves beneath big shirts and chunky jackets. Or why she wore bras that flattened her breasts. She should flaunt them.

Correction, she should flaunt them just to him. Matt smiled at the idea, mesmerized by the way her breasts swayed. He wanted to buy her something strapless that she would only wear when they were alone. If that would ever happen.

She reached for her jeans.

Stop staring. Look away. Close the blinds.

Yeah, right... Matt didn't move. He hungrily watched her shove the jeans and panties down her legs. She reached for something in the bedside drawer, but Matt couldn't see what it was. It was probably the hot pink vibrator. Grace flopped onto the bed and grabbed the blindfold.

Matt frowned. What was with the blindfold? He still couldn't figure it out. Did it help her fantasize better? Was she in the habit of being blindfolded when she had sex?

After she tied it on tightly, she dropped her hands down her face and throat. Her fingers splayed against her collarbone before gliding down to her breasts.

She played with her nipples for so long that Matt felt like he knew exactly how they would taste and feel in his mouth. He rolled his tongue along the edge of his teeth, longing for a sample. A lick.

His cock strained against his jeans. He wished for it to lie down, but that wasn't going to happen. His pulse thudded in his ears as his blood pushed through his veins.

It felt like *everything* slowed down as Grace touched herself.

As Grace slid one hand down to her hips, Matt stepped closer to the window, his head bumping the glass. He watched, mouth open, as she parted the folds of her sex. She glided her fingers up and down her wet slit. Her hips rolled and wiggled as she caressed herself.

Matt wanted to open his window and listen to her moans and jagged breaths mingling with the sound of wet, slippery flesh. He wanted to inhale the scent of her sweat and sex. Taste every inch of her and enjoy the feel of her smooth, yielding body under his.

He saw her body pulse with pleasure. Soft, gentle ripples that probably only took the edge off when she needed something hard and brutal ramming through her until she screamed.

Grace reached for something next to her pillow. He saw her wicked smile when she grabbed it. It was as if she knew satisfaction was moments away.

He almost choked on his own spit when she withdrew a large red cone. It looked like a freaking pyramid, with pronounced ridges. That sucker was huge from the very tip to the wide base. Grace must have pressed a button when she retrieved it because it started to vibrate in her hands.

If he ever got into bed with Grace, she was going to be seriously disappointed with his equipment. He didn't have that many shapes, speeds or positions. He was going to have to make it up with a lot of creativity and attention to detail.

Grace set the cone on the bed. The red toy stood tall and proudly pointed to the ceiling. She got on her knees and crawled over the machine, feeling her way around the bed as she was still blindfolded.

She straddled the cone and Matthew felt all of his blood pooling in his cock, which swelled painfully as he watched Grace slowly lower herself on the tip of the cone.

He couldn't see everything. He growled with frustration. He wanted to watch her sex grip the toy and suck it in.

Matt glanced up at Grace's face. She was biting her lower lip. He discovered that he was biting his own lip. Was she not wet enough to guide it in and give her the maximum pleasure? Or was she trying not to make a sound?

If she was straddling him, he'd make sure she was wet and ready for every inch of him. He'd grip her by her hips and control her descent until she was begging for more.

Grace seemed to have found the hilt of the cone and started to swivel her hips. Matt groaned, watching her hips move and her breasts bounce as she rode the cone.

He wanted to cup her breasts and squeeze. Grind his pelvis against hers. He wanted her on top of him and riding with full abandon.

But would she? Would she be this open and wild for him? Or was this what she saved and savored for herself?

He watched as her body took on a dark flush, rising from her breasts to her chest, scaling up her neck and face. He felt the same fire. Matt wanted to pump his cock when he saw her mouth sag open as she mouthed a word.

Matthew . . .

Matt jerked upright, his head colliding with the window. He pressed his hand against the side of his head. He couldn't believe it.

She had just called out his name.

CHAPTER TWENTY-NINE

Grace tapped her pen against her desk and stared at her office door. Night had fallen, and she still hadn't gotten her work done. She was far behind on everything—all because she was distracted by a strip of purple silk.

She tapped the pen hard against the sharp corner. The fast, angry pings matched the tap of her foot. She had to get rid of the scarf. If she didn't send it off, she'd throw it away.

Grace cringed at the thought. She couldn't do that. The scarf was too beautiful. Who knew how old or sacred it might be? She wasn't that strong, to carelessly toss it in the garbage.

But she had to be strong enough to send it away. Far, far away. She needed that chain letter out of her house. The purple scarf was taking over her life.

Grace tossed the pen onto her desk and watched it skitter before she held her face in her hands. She was being overly dramatic. If she was going to be completely honest, it was more like her fantasies about Matt were taking over her life!

She couldn't even drink her morning coffee without thinking about having sex with him. She had wanted to crawl on the table that separated them. Her skin tingled at the idea of offering her breasts to Matt. If she wasn't careful, she'd find herself pouring half-and-half over his naked body and licking it all up!

Grace gripped her hair tightly in her fists and was tempted to give a good yank. What had gotten into her? She was *not* a sexual person.

It was the scarf's fault. It was making her act like someone she wasn't. Someone she wasn't sure she wanted to be. It was time to send the chain letter to the next victim.

She should have gotten rid of it long ago. Why hadn't she? Chain letters were nothing but hoaxes. How many did she delete a day in her in-box? But this one she didn't ignore, all because she wanted the scarf and what it promised. She actually thought the silk would give her everything she didn't think she could get on her own. How pathetic!

She had even fulfilled the rule of having sex while wearing it. Now that was a new level of desperation. Grace stood up and paced the small office as anger rolled inside her. So what if she followed the rule by having solo sex? Sex was sex.

But if she really believed that, if she knew she had completed the task, why was she still using the scarf? She was aware that she'd fulfilled the requirements the second day she had the chain letter. She should have sent it off that night. Why was she still blindfolding herself?

Well, there was the one glaring fact that the promise in the chain letter hadn't exactly been activated. She would know what living out her ultimate fantasy would feel like. She was going to have to use the damn scarf until the last possible moment to get her prize.

Grace halted in the middle of her office. Well, which was it? Was she going to send the scarf off right now, to the first woman in her address book, or was she going to keep the scarf for two more days? She couldn't have it both ways.

Her gut instinct told her to keep it. Grace shook her head in self-disgust. As much of a burden as the scarf proved to be, she hated the idea of giving it to someone else. She wanted to keep the scarf; hide it in her bedside drawer and hoard the magic.

But that was the problem. It *wasn't* magic. She gave it more power than it deserved. If it had been magic, she would have what she wished for. A lover. A perfect bed partner. Or, even better, Matthew Collins.

Grace weakly closed her eyes. *That* was why she held on to the scarf. Deep down, she really thought the purple silk would give Matt to her on a silver platter. Each time she used the scarf, each time she thought about it, she kept waiting for the magic to happen.

It wasn't going to happen. It never was going to. She was just fooling herself. Grace exhaled slowly and dipped her head in resignation.

If she was tired of being overlooked, of always wondering if her sexual allure was on the fritz, then she had to get over her own hangups and take more risks. Not stupid, dangerous risks, but the ones that made her face her fears.

One fear in particular. The one that had her standing naked and willing in front of the one man she most wanted to impress and saying, "Here I am. This is as good as it is going to get. Take me, I'm yours." And then she would have to wait and see what happened next.

She knew she needed to face that fear, but the idea made her want to curl up in a ball and hide. All this week she had secretly been hoping for some fairy dust and to have it sprinkled over Matt. Have *him* change. That would have been so much easier. Magic was always easier. Magic didn't shove her out of her comfort zone.

If she looked at the scarf right now she would see it for what it truly was—an old scrap of silk. Grace determinedly walked into her bedroom and flipped on the light. She went straight to her bedside table and opened the drawer.

She hadn't noticed it before, but the scarf lay in a place of honor, neatly folded, and nothing else crowded it. Her toys were shoved to the side. Grace glared at the silk, wondering why she placed so much importance on it. The gold threads glimmered back at her.

Grace was momentarily dazzled by the scarf. She could feel herself weaken. Why send the scarf away now? She had a couple of more days. Why not wait until the deadline?

Because she had already lost five days of her life on this damn thing, she reminded herself harshly. She had wasted time believing that her fantasies would come true. Hoping that it would happen fast. Wishing for the impossible.

Disillusionment burned in the pit of her stomach. She had never felt so unfulfilled and empty in her life. Where was the satisfaction the letter guaranteed? Where was the promise of a wondrous sensual odyssey?

She grabbed the scarf and balled it up in her hands. Why should she send this to another woman and let her get her hopes up? She should do everyone a favor and shred this scarf. Burn it. Cut it up into tiny pieces.

Grace wrapped the edges of the scarf around her hand and pulled it taut. The desire to destroy roared through her veins. She stared at the gold and purple, her muscles shaking as she kept tugging, before she abruptly lowered her arms and let the silk sag.

The sharp edge of anger began to dull, leaving her weary. Grace looked up at the ceiling, her vision blurry with tears. It wasn't the scarf's fault. It was hers for being so unrealistic.

She couldn't destroy the scarf. She didn't want to give up on the magic. She didn't want to believe that her fantasies were too out of reach. Grace just wanted two more days of hope that anything could happen.

She frowned at her train of thought. What? She already sounded like she was defeated. She had gone this far and she was going to give up? Because a chain letter didn't work?

Who said she had to surrender her fantasies? She wasn't going to give up. Not this way.

Why not face her fears the hard way, with the scarf at her side? She felt a spurt of hope. Tomorrow she would wear the scarf when she asked Matt out.

The plan made her jittery, but she wasn't going to back out. She wanted to be bold in real life, not just in her fantasies. She was going to seduce Matt and chart her own sensual odyssey without some hocus-pocus chain letter.

And she'd use the scarf until she had to send it away. Keep it for the full seven days and mail it off. Just in case. She might as well use everything she had in her power.

Grace quickly shed her clothes and lay down on the bed. This time she tossed the scarf over her face. There was no reason to fold it and carefully tie it. Tying it didn't give off more magic. It only showed how much she believed—how she wanted to believe that it would work.

With a wiggle of her hips and a slide of her shoulders, she settled onto her mattress. She really didn't feel like doing this, but her deadline was fast approaching. Grace cupped her breasts, but her nipples didn't respond. She circled her fingers around her areolae, but her nipples wouldn't tighten and pucker.

She allowed her hands to fall to the side. Oh, what was the use? Deadline or no deadline, she wasn't in the mood. She wasn't going to maximize her time with the scarf. She needed to start thinking about who to give it to next. It should be someone who had a better chance of getting the most out of it.

Someone who really didn't need it.

She knew she shouldn't credit the scarf with so much power. But she wanted to believe that she was getting some extra help. Deep down, she knew the only way she would get her fantasy life with this scarf was if she hooked it around Matthew Collins and drew him closer to her.

Grace smiled as she imagined that scenario very clearly, although it would never work. How could she walk up to him, as bold as you please, and claim him?

But she liked the idea. Grace shifted on her bed as pleasure bloomed inside her chest. She wanted to wrap the scarf around him like a lasso and hold him still.

Grace rubbed her legs together as her skin tingled. Her sex felt heavy as she thought about how she would draw him close, holding the scarf tight around his arms. But once she got him right where she wanted him, what would she *do* with him?

That was the problem. It wasn't that she couldn't come up with an idea. It was that there were too many things she wanted to do. And far more things she wanted him to do to her.

First thing on her list was always for him to strip naked. She'd like to see what was underneath those jeans and boxers. She knew there was a lot of power lurking in that body, and she wanted it all directed at her.

That was what she wanted more than anything, Grace decided as she caressed the undersides of her breasts. She wanted Matt's sole attention on her. She wanted to lavish attention on him and have it come right back at her.

She wanted to feel like she was made for loving. She wanted to break free from this bright white cocoon and feel the life scorching inside her. Grace rolled her nipple with her fingers, imagining bright, jeweled colors suffusing her body at every touch.

A warm, honeyed sensation trickled down her chest to her abdomen. It heated and flooded her pelvis. Grace reached down and slid her fingers along her wet slit.

She imagined Matthew kissing every inch of her breasts before trailing his lips down her abdomen. She would gasp as his tongue would trip down her ribs before he kissed her navel, dipping his warm, wet tongue in the shallow dips.

He would continue his journey, kissing down to the cloud of blonde, damp curls. He would find her clit and tease it with his tongue, refusing to let go as she screamed and shuddered with pleasure.

Her sex would be swollen and throbbing for his touch. Dark pink, like the rest of her, except for the tufts of blonde hair and the purple scarf.

Purple. She would have to wear the scarf for Matt. Grace's mind latched onto what Matt had said. "You always look good in that scarf." *Always.*

Grace frowned as her fingers slowed. Why had he said that? *Always.* She only wore it once out in public. That didn't make it "always."

What she did in private was different. She *always* wore the scarf when she was blindfolded—

A chill swept her body. Her stomach cramped with sickening speed. She lurched up into a sitting position, the scarf tumbling down her sensitive breasts and landing haphazardly on her lap.

She abruptly turned to the window, crossing her arms over her breasts. But it was a little too late for that. Matt stood at his bedroom window, nestled deep in the shadows.

Watching her.

CHAPTER THIRTY

Grace reacted fast. She rolled off the bed and out of sight, dragging the quilt along. It fell on top of her, but offered no warmth or comfort. Nothing could protect her now.

She squeezed her eyes shut as her body went from scorching hot to icy cold. Her stomach twisted and flipped as a wave of nausea hit. Grace held her hands flat against her stomach. She wanted to die.

Matt saw her. He had seen her naked and uninhibited. He had watched her orgasm as she played with her toys. How many times had he watched? Grace desperately tried to remember how often she had the lights on.

Too many times. She cringed. Had he seen her *every* time? Grace scooped up the quilt and whimpered into the soft folds. She wanted to die. Have the floor open up and swallow her whole.

She glanced at the window and noticed that the shades were still open. Grace crawled to the wall and peered over the windowsill. Matt was no longer there.

Her ragged breath of relief stuck in her throat when she saw him step out his front door. Grace slid to the floor with a thump. She hoped he hadn't seen her peeking. Considering how her luck was going, he probably had.

That's it. She was moving out of this house and out of town. Immediately. Hell, she might as well make it out of the country.

She'd make up some excuse. No one would think it was odd. Matt would soon forget about this whole little episode—especially since she planned never to return.

Now she understood why he had been studying her so strangely at Starbucks. Grace groaned as the embarrassment hit a new level. And all this time she had worried that he had guessed what she had been daydreaming!

Grace rocked against the bed, really, really wishing she could roll over and play dead.

The doorbell rang.

She froze, her blood pressure skyrocketing as her stomach took a sudden, horrible dive. Grace pressed her lips as her mouth went dry. A chill swept her and goose bumps prickled her skin.

It had to be Matt. What was he doing here? Couldn't he leave her in peace so she could die of shame?

He rang the doorbell again.

The insistent peal grated on her nerves. Grace pressed her hands against her ears. She had to block him out and stay put, but she had a bad feeling that he wasn't going to leave. He might even cause a scene.

She could see it now. He would wake up the other neighbors. They'd wonder why he was bothering her and he'd say something like that he saw her in her bedroom. It looked like she was having a seizure, so he came to check up on her.

And his excuse would work, because he was Matthew Collins.

And she would have to face grumpy neighbors who would want to know why she didn't pull her shades down. Because that was how her life worked.

He rang the bell again. It sounded like he was leaning on it.

She breathed in, filling her lungs until they burned. The move didn't calm her a bit. Enough stalling. She was going to have to face Matt.

There were a few ways she could survive the next couple of minutes. She could act stupid. That maneuver was a classic, but Matt might see right through it. She could also act like nothing out of the ordinary had occurred. That was a little more difficult to pull off, but she would have the surprise element working in her favor. Or she could brazen it out.

If there was ever a time to be brazen, this was it. Grace shook her head in defeat. She would have preferred a different baptism of fire, but now wasn't the time to be choosy.

Grace slowly stood up. Her knees felt weak and wobbly. She reached for her clothes, but knew it would take too long for her to get re-dressed. Instead, she wrapped the quilt around her trembling body.

She reluctantly stepped out of her bedroom, hitting the hallway lights with the tip of her fingers. The doorbell abruptly stopped ringing.

Grace hesitated and then slowly made her way down the steps. She walked down the last flight of steps staring at the door. For once, she wished there was a window. She needed to know how to handle Matt before she saw him.

What was Matt thinking? Was he disgusted? Was he going to tease her mercilessly? Tell her she was doing it all wrong?

She unbolted the lock and felt tension zoom in the air. Her hands shook and slipped on the doorknob. Grace wiped her sweaty palms on a quilt pane before she slowly opened the door a crack.

Matt stood in front of her, his eyes blazing with lust.

Lust? Out of all the scenarios swirling in her head, she hadn't ex-pected that. "Yes?" she asked hoarsely, doing her best to get this over and done with.

Matt lifted his hand and slapped it on the door, slowly pushing it open. Grace stepped back, her feet catching on the quilt. Matt fol-lowed her, stepping inside and shutting the door behind him.

Ooh . . . boy. Grace nervously licked her lips. Matt's gaze focused on her mouth. She stared at the man in front of her. The intense look on his face, the darkening of his eyes, made her realize the truth. Matt was hers for the taking.

He always had been.

She needed only the courage to reach out and take him.

A sense of power bloomed inside her chest. But still she didn't take action. She was afraid she would reach for the opportunity and watch it disappear in a wisp of smoke. Grace stood silent and watched as Matt took another step and another. Closer and closer, crowding her, surrounding her.

Her chest rose and fell. She gripped the quilt tighter. What was she waiting for? She wanted to live out her fantasy. But would reality live up to her dreams?

One kiss wouldn't tell her enough. And yet, it would tell her everything. All she had to do was reach out and take what she wanted.

She wasn't very bold. Not in real life, and not in her fantasies. Did she have the courage to pursue those dreams, or was she going to push them aside and act like they didn't exist?

She watched as Matt lowered his head. She felt the heat of him and inhaled his scent. A low, pulsing ache nestled deep in her belly.

A part of her wanted him to take the decision out of her hands. The other part wished it wasn't so hard to be bold and wild. Her breath hitched in her throat when he stopped at the last possible moment.

It was her choice. Either she invited him in or she sent him away. He would stay like that all night until she took a course of action.

Grace tilted her head up and brushed her lips against his.

She hadn't expected his mouth to feel warm and firm. She had never dreamed about the taste of his kisses. She leaned into him, placing her hands tentatively on his chest. The pounding of his fierce heartbeat startled her.

Matt shuddered under her touch before he curled his arm around her. Her gasp of surprise was muffled as he swept her up against him. Her breasts collided with his hard chest as her pelvis bumped with his. The man was solid muscle.

He lifted her and she felt the quilt slide. She didn't pull it back up. Instead she wrapped her arms around Matt's shoulders as he carried her up the stairs. Grace found his tenderness and strength a heady combination. The knowledge gave her an extra buzz of excitement.

She didn't say anything as he carried her to her room. She didn't know what to talk about. Nothing seductive or sophisticated came to mind. By the time Matt lowered her down in the center of her bedroom, Grace's throat was tight and raw with nerves.

He stroked her cheek with his hand and turned away. The break of connection confused Grace. She reached out for him, but dropped her arms when she saw he was going to the window.

Matt closed the shades with one sharp move. She jumped when the blinds slammed against the sill. Grace noticed that he didn't explain his actions. He didn't have to. She knew that what was about to happen was for the two of them. Matt didn't want an audience, and all she wanted was his sole attention.

As he returned to her, Matt paused and scooped up the purple scarf that had fallen on the floor. The silk looked fragile against his hand. She was rooted to the spot as she watched him roll the scarf around in his hands.

"Wear the blindfold," he requested. His tone was quiet, but she heard the urgency lurking underneath.

Grace hesitated. How could she explain that she really wasn't into getting blindfolded? After watching her this week, Matt wouldn't believe her, and she wouldn't blame him.

"Why?" she asked, stalling. She wanted Matt. Her body shook with need, but she wanted him just as vulnerable and naked. She wanted to watch the pleasure twist him inside out and know that she did that to him.

"I don't know," he said softly. Matt looked at the scarf in his hands. "I've never blindfolded anyone before."

It would be a new experience for him as well. She liked that, but she wasn't thrilled at the idea of being blindfolded while he wasn't. Grace wasn't nervous about what he would do, but she wanted to watch his face. His eyes wouldn't hide what he really felt.

But how bold and carefree could she be if she was constantly gauging his reaction? Waiting for his approval before she made the next move? That she didn't want, and maybe the blindfold would be a blessing. "Okay," she finally agreed.

Passion flared in Matt's eyes, and the dark excitement curled inside her chest. As he covered her eyes with the silk, the sudden darkness alarmed her. It was a struggle not to step away or reach for the fabric. She pressed her arms closer to her body, gathering the quilt close to her breasts.

"We can get rid of this." His hands brushed against the top of her breasts. Her nipples tightened and she felt the tug of the quilt. She instinctively held it closer.

Matt gave a sharp yank and pulled the quilt from her. The tugging caused her slowly to spin around. Turning and turning, the quilt unraveled from her body and fell away.

She felt dizzy. She couldn't tell which way she was facing. She couldn't find Matt. He hadn't made a sound.

"Matt?" she whispered.

Grace jumped when she felt his mouth on her shoulder. The tender touch warmed her until she realized that he wasn't behind her anymore. He stood in front of her.

She automatically covered her breasts with her hands. Grace flinched when she felt Matt encircle his fingers around her wrists. He silently pulled her arms away.

Grace's nipples puckered until they stung. Her skin felt tight and hot. She stood before Matt, completely naked, arms outstretched. What was he doing? Where was he looking? Did he like what he saw?

The silence scraped at her. She wished she could smile provocatively and hide her fears, but instead her lips trembled. Was he changing his mind?

Matt roughly pulled her forward and gathered her hard against his body. He cupped her face with his hands and drove his tongue past her parted lips. She felt the tremors in his hand, knowing he fought to contain the wild energy that whipped through him.

The wildness that *she* sparked inside him. Grace was stunned. She never knew she had this kind of power. She wanted to test it out and see how far she could go.

Grace pulled at Matt's clothes, her lack of sight causing her to fumble with the zipper and buttons. Grace pulled off his clothes in between hungry, wet kisses. She finally stripped him bare.

She reached for Matt, wanting to explore what she had uncovered, and suddenly she was falling. Grace called out, gripping his strong arms. She gave a sigh of relief when her spine hit the mattress.

Matt explored her with his hands and mouth, each touch unpredictable and daring. Grace's excitement popped and fizzed in her veins, rushing and gaining momentum. It felt like wild, colorful ribbons of fire were streaking through her body. She grabbed for him to bring him down for another kiss, and he dodged her hands.

"Matt," she pleaded, but he ignored her. His mouth slid across her collarbone, nipped her breasts, and she almost caught him before his mouth latched onto her nipple.

She arched back as he drew her into his mouth. It felt like the fierce tug of his lips went straight to her clit. Grace bucked her hips, but her pelvis didn't collide with his. Where was he? She desperately wanted to see all of him.

Grace reached for the scarf, but Matt stopped her, placing his hand over hers. "No," he said in a husky tone. "Not yet."

Matt cupped her sex and played with her clitoris. With his other hand, he stroked her slit before sliding his finger in. Grace licked her lips and stretched as pleasure flooded her. She swayed her hips as he teased her with his fingers.

She glided her hands along her hips and stomach before she caressed her breasts. She pinched and rolled her nipples, murmuring and growling as she felt the bite and sting.

Grace splayed her legs wider, slowly stretching and arching, letting the sensations course through her until the tips of her fingers and toes tingled. She loved the freedom of flaunting her body at Matt. She twisted and rocked against his hands. Sparkles showered in her mind as he dipped another finger into her core.

Her eyes rolled back with pleasure as her vaginal walls gripped him tight and drew him in deeper. She flexed her hips, the fire searing through her.

Matt settled between her legs and she greedily ran her hands over his body. She smiled when she found a ticklish spot under his ribs and was tempted to skim her fingertips over that area again. She continued to slide her hands onto his back and against his firm buttocks. He was lean, muscular and sexy. She didn't need to see to know that.

Grace's exploration paused when she felt the crown of Matt's cock nudge against her. She shivered with anticipation and tilted her hips as he teased her, rubbing the crown of his cock against her labia. Her muscles clenched, ready to grip his thick penis.

"Please, Matt," she whispered.

He entered her with one stroke. Grace's moan rang out as he drove deep. It was a snug fit and she wiggled her hips to find relief, but found a pulsing, addictive heat instead. The fire radiated with each move. Her skin prickled as the thick warmth seeped into her.

She wished she could see him. She wanted to watch his face as he struggled to make it last. Grace needed to see the triumph flash in his eyes at the moment of his release.

Matt's thrusts grew rough and wild, the bed underneath them squeaking in protest. Grace knew he was about to come. She felt the quiver of tension, and one final, savage thrust that triggered her climax. It was like a glittery swirl bursting and roaring into a white-hot blaze.

She was shaking, gasping for breath as Matt fell on top of her. Grace slid her hand against the scarf and shoved it up over her sweat-slicked hair.

She couldn't believe it. Grace glanced down at Matt, his face nestled against her neck. She had gotten what she wanted.

But now she had to send the chain letter to another woman. She was afraid of the consequences if she kept the purple silk, but would she lose all this the moment she gave the scarf away?

CHAPTER THIRTY-ONE

G race hesitated in front of the drop box at the post office. Her fingers shook against the cold morning air. She looked at the tan, padded envelope in her hand. Did she really want to do this?

Kali's letter and the scarf were safely tucked inside. She knew she had to do this if she wanted a chance for a lifelong sensual odyssey, but wasn't quite ready to let go.

After all, the chain letter had given her Matt. If she gave up the scarf, would Matt disappear as well? Was she willing to take the risk?

Grace mulled it over as she nibbled her bottom lip. She hated to admit it, but holding on to Matt hadn't been her wish. She wanted him. She had never asked to keep him. The scarf wasn't going to have that kind of power.

She smirked at her train of thought. She was giving this scarf way too much credit. The chain letter wasn't magic. It didn't make everything happen. It simply gave her a nudge and made her open her eyes.

Grace held her breath and let go. Her eyes widened as she watched the package slide into the bin. Her heart lurched when it disappeared.

There. She snatched her hand back and let the door close with a bang. It was gone. Out of her life like she had wanted yesterday. Nothing she could do about it now.

Grace grabbed the handle, her fingers squeezing the metal bar, as she opened the door again. She needed to get the scarf back!

Stop being a scaredy-cat. You already have Matt. Grace reluctantly let go of the drop box. It was true. She did have him. Right now, in her bed. Naked. What was she hanging around a post office for?

Grace pivoted on her heel and hurried down the sidewalk. She wanted to get back home before he left. She wanted to know if he was still interested in her once the scarf was out of her possession.

As she quietly entered the house and crept upstairs, Grace noticed that it was silent. Empty. Had he already left? Her stomach cramped with disappointment.

Okay, don't worry about it. Grace pressed her hand against her abdomen. If he left, she would go after him. She would let him know what she wanted and not be shy about it. She'd learned her lesson.

Grace hurried into her room and halted when she saw the bed. Matt was still there, asleep. He hadn't disappeared once she mailed off the scarf.

Now she felt silly for considering the possibility.

Matt lay sprawled, taking over most of the bed. His tanned body contrasted sharply with the white, wrinkled sheets. Grace stared at his sculpted muscles and lean angles, sharp desire tugging at her.

She kicked off her shoes, determined to crawl back into bed. She grimaced as one shoe hit the bed. Her eyes widened when she saw Matt stir awake.

Grace froze while removing her sock. Matt opened his eyes and ensnared her. She felt a lick of excitement curl down her spine. She felt like, no matter what move she made, he was going to catch her.

"Are you going somewhere?" His voice was gravelly from sleep.

"Coming back to bed, actually." She meant to sound casual, but the crack in her voice ruined the effect.

He rubbed his hand over his face and she heard the rough stubble on his chin graze his palm. "Where were you?"

She yanked at the sock, but it wouldn't budge. She bent her leg at an awkward angle and pulled harder. "I had to send off the scarf."

Matt propped himself up on his elbow. "What is up with that scarf?"

"It's part of a chain letter." She hopped on one foot and finally tugged off the sock. "You use it when having sex, and then you send it to the next woman."

The corners of his mouth twitched as he suppressed a smile. "You're kidding me, right?"

Okay, no matter how matter-of-factly she tried to present it, the chain letter did sound silly. Still, she hadn't wanted to believe it, but she did.

Matt tilted his head as he tried to comprehend. "The chain letter told you to blindfold yourself?"

"Not exactly." Hmm ... why did she decide to blindfold herself? She couldn't explain. "It's a long story."

"Then save it and come back to bed." He flipped back the covers. Desire spiked in her blood as she saw his hard, thick cock.

Let him know what you want. So what if she was shy about undressing in front of him? So what if she didn't have a plan on having her way with him? Grace knew two things: She wanted Matt, and she wanted him now.

Grace grabbed the hem of her sweatshirt. Now she wished she had put on a shirt with lots of buttons so she could tease him with hints and glimpses of skin. Unfortunately, there was no elegant way to take off what she was wearing now. She hadn't planned to do a striptease first thing in the morning!

Grace slowly shimmied out of her sweatshirt. Her mind played sis-boom-bah with the drums, which wasn't helping. Gypsy Rose she wasn't.

She tossed the shirt onto the floor and felt chilly. She dared a glance at Matt's face. Her heart gave a twist when she saw that his eyes had darkened with pleasure. Grace felt her nipples poke against the cotton bra in response.

A spurt of confidence warmed her and she reached for the snap in her jeans. She slowly dragged the zipper down, loving how Matt seemed spellbound. His attention was riveted on every move she made.

A hot excitement built inside her. She felt like she was melting inside. Grace shucked the denim from her legs. She had meant for it to be a leisurely move, but her baggy jeans fell to her feet in one swoop. She stepped out and pushed her jeans to the side with a nudge of her foot.

Grace reached for her sports bra and felt a pang of regret. Now she wished she had bought something breathtaking from the lingerie shop. She quickly discarded her bra and panties, hoping Matt didn't notice that they weren't pretty or sexy.

She stood nude before Matt. Her skin prickled, and she found it difficult to take deep breaths. She did her best not to hide, which would have been pointless, but she couldn't quite get herself to pose provocatively. Her arms and legs refused to move. She couldn't jut out her hip if her life depended on it.

Grace finally gave up. Posing wasn't her, and she wasn't going to pretend otherwise. But there was *one* thing she wanted to try.

She strode toward the foot of the bed and bracketed her hands around Matt's feet. Grace slowly crawled onto the bed, letting her shoulders and hips dip with each step. She felt her breasts sway.

Matt slowly lay down on his back, watching Grace's approach with a wicked gleam in his eyes. He swallowed roughly and opened his mouth, but no words came.

Grace kind of liked being the aggressive one. It was scary, but liberating at the same time. She couldn't wait for the day when being this brazen would come naturally.

She gently lay on top of Matt, feeling every muscle and hard angle. She kissed his mouth, tasting him as if she had all the time in the world. Grace poured every emotion she was feeling into that kiss, leaving nothing to the imagination.

The moment she felt Matt was going to take over the kiss, Grace sat up and straddled his waist. His cock proudly rested against her sex. She grasped his cock and stroked it, enjoying the feel of containing him in her hands.

He bunched his pillow with his hands as he restrained himself. Matt's cock swelled under her touch and she couldn't wait to sink on top of him. She raised herself to her knees and guided the shiny wet crown of his cock against her slick entrance.

As she slowly sheathed him to the root, heat streaked through her body. She remained still as her vagina gripped him hard. She tried to fight off the white-hot pleasure rippling from her core, wanting this to last.

Matt couldn't let her take charge anymore. He clamped his hands on her hips and guided her in a fierce rhythm. Grace relinquished her control and watched the expressions chasing across his face. She enjoyed seeing the muscle tic in his clenched jaw and the primitive hunger in his eye.

She made him this way. *She* drove him over the edge. Satisfaction bloomed in her chest. She had just as much power over him as he did over her.

Grace leaned forward and braced her hands on the mattress. The movement caused Matt to groan. He stopped, his fingers digging in her hips, before he launched into a ferocious pace.

The harsh thrusts triggered her violent climax. She cried out as it consumed her. Matt gave a hoarse shout, his hips bucking one final time as he came.

Grace slumped against Matt. She was breathing hard and her heart pounded against her chest and in her ears. She felt overheated, her skin sticky with sweat.

She rolled off of Matt and lay next to him, their bodies barely touching. She brushed off the damp hair from her forehead and looked at him. Matt hadn't said anything since she stripped in front of him. She hadn't noticed until just now.

"You know," she said as casually as she could while she struggled for her next breath, "the blindfold wasn't bad, but I like being able to watch you."

"I don't know. I kind of liked knowing you couldn't see me." Matt offered a lazy smile and turned on his side. She felt like he could see right through her, his eyes missing nothing. "Who'd you send the chain letter to?"

She gave a shrug. "A woman who I think would like it."

"So there's no chance of borrowing it?"

Grace's heart pinched, but she kept her smile up. "Oh, you want it back?"

"Not really, but it has sentimental value." He leaned forward and placed a soft kiss on her parted lips.

Grace closed her eyes and slowly exhaled. "Don't worry," she said against his mouth. "The scarf hasn't gone far."

He lifted his head. "What do you mean?"

"I sent it to Tiffany Martin. You know, the hairdresser a couple of houses down."

"Why her?"

"She's definitely the type who would enjoy a fantasy chain letter." Grace reached for Matt, still finding it hard to believe her fantasy had come true. "Mark my words, Tiffany will thank me for it."